JIMMY COATES
SURVIVAL

When Jimmy Coates
goes rogue, only one
thing can ensure his
survival. Destruction.

Also by Joe Craig

TEAM UP WITH

JIMMY COATES ON MYSPACE!

WWW.MYSPACE.COM/JIMMYCOATES

JOE CRAIG

HarperCollins *Children's Books*

First published in Great Britain by
HarperCollins *Children's Books* 2008
HarperCollins *Children's Books* is a
division of HarperCollins *Publishers* Ltd
77-85 Fulham Palace Road,
Hammersmith, London, W6 8JB

www.harpercollinschildrensbooks.co.uk

1

Copyright © Joseph Craig 2008
Map by Tim Stevens

ISBN 13: 978 0 00 727099 6
ISBN 10: 0 00 727099 2

Joseph Craig asserts the moral right to
be identified as the author of the work.

Printed and bound in Great Britain by
Clays Ltd, St Ives plc

Mixed Sources
Product group from well-managed
forests and other controlled sources
www.fsc.org Cert no. SW-COC-1806
© 1996 Forest Stewardship Council

FSC is a non-profit international organisation established to promote the
responsible management of the world's forests. Products carrying the FSC
label are independently certified to assure consumers that they come
from forests that are managed to meet the social, economic and
ecological needs of present and future generations.

Find out more about HarperCollins and the environment at
www.harpercollins.co.uk/green

To Mary-Ann Ochota, bessway.

Thank you to Sarah Manson, Ann Tobias,
Nicola Solomon, Sophie Birshan,
Miriam Craig, Oli Rockberger and
everyone at HarperCollins, particularly
Stella Paskins, Geraldine Stroud,
Emma Bradshaw, Catherine Holmes
and Gillie Russell.

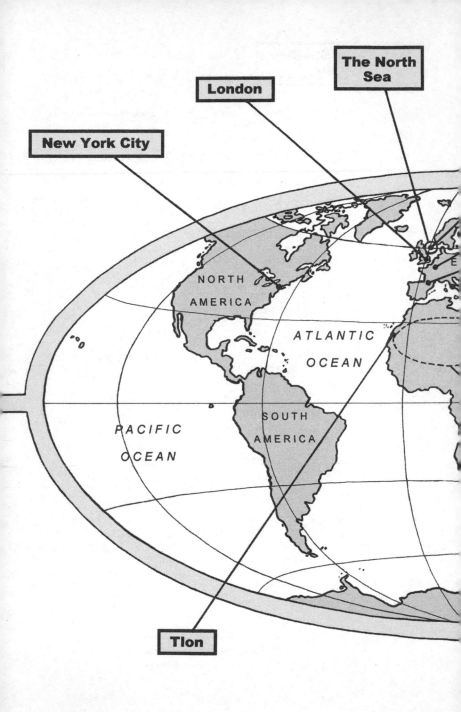

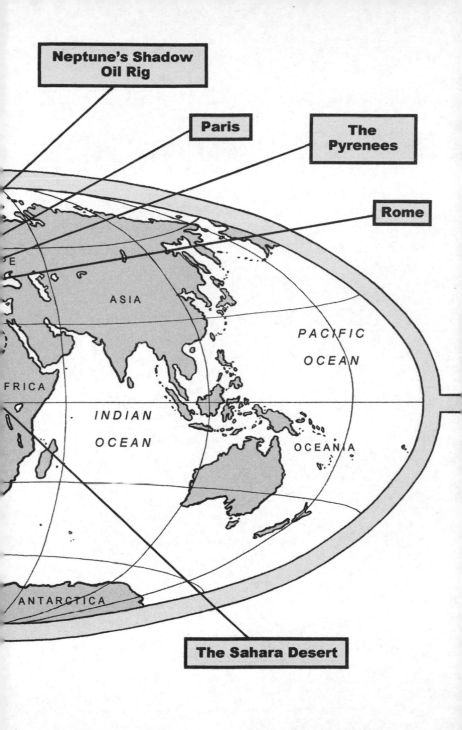

**Neptune's Shadow
Oil Rig**

Paris

**The
Pyrenees**

Rome

ASIA

PACIFIC

OCEAN

FRICA

INDIAN

OCEAN

OCEANIA

ANTARCTICA

The Sahara Desert

THE BIG BANG

One minute it was a man-made wonder of the world: Neptune's Shadow, the second largest oil rig in the world. Its lights glowed in the black fog of the North Sea, like an alien space ship. Towers craned out in all directions, metal arms trying to grab a piece of the night, while the pistons and pumps worked ceaselessly, dragging up the liquor from the belly of the world.

The next minute, it was a raging mountain of fire that lit up the whole of the night, a beacon visible as far away as Denmark. The noise of the blast shook birds from their nests in Northern Scotland. The source of billions of pounds for the British Government erupted with more rage than Mount Vesuvius.

In the morning it blew up again a million times, flashing across TV screens in digital reconstructions and vivid newspaper reports, each one exaggerating the size of the explosion a little more, and on the

Internet, where people discussed why and how it had happened – and what the Prime Minister was going to do about it.

And it exploded over and over again in the mind of the one person who had survived actually being there – Jimmy Coates.

01 SLIPSTREAM

First it was a light on the dashboard, then a clunk in the engine. Jimmy had been expecting this for the last three hours. *I could ditch the plane in the water*, he thought. At that moment he was somewhere over the middle of the Atlantic Ocean and a part of his brain was already working out the best angle for the Falcon 20 to hit the waves. He could even feel the muscles in his shoulders warming, preparing for the longest swim of his life.

He gritted his teeth and stared straight ahead out of the cockpit. He knew ditching wasn't an option. He had to reach Europe. Then came the answer.

The plane rocked slightly. A roar drowned out the sound of the Falcon's engines. Jimmy peered upwards, squinting at the brightness of the sky. There it was – the shadow of a commercial jet looming above him.

"Time to catch a ride," Jimmy whispered under his breath. He glanced one more time at the fuel gauges. They were deep in the red zone. He powered the Falcon higher, his fingers gliding over the plane's controls. Blood covered his palms – black, coagulated blood that left sticky marks on every switch and button. But they were healing already. He could feel it. The pain was far away, buried by his senses. He stared at his hands, but saw past the shredded streaks of red and black skin to the dull grey layer underneath.

Next to the Airbus A490, Jimmy's Falcon was like a fly around the back end of a hippopotamus. Jimmy was stunned at the enormousness of the plane. He guessed it must have been nearly a hundred metres long, with an even larger wingspan. Its deep rumble vibrated in Jimmy's chest.

Sooner than he expected, Jimmy was flying just a few metres beneath it. *Please work*, Jimmy begged, searching inside himself. He knew it was the force inside him that had put this plan into action. Jimmy could never have dreamed up anything so outrageous without it.

He let the world fall into a blur, focusing all his energy on a point deep inside, somewhere between his stomach and the base of his spine. His inner power was coming. It had to be. It was destined to take over.

Then came the familiar buzz. His muscles flooded with energy. His neck fizzed and his brain throbbed. Jimmy was full of hatred and exhilaration simultaneously. This would save him, but there was a tiny voice inside that knew this power would also eventually destroy him.

Jimmy jerked on the sidestick controller and the nose of his plane hurtled towards the airbus. Just as he thought he was going to burn to death in a mid-air collision, the Falcon was lifted back and upwards, wafted away on a cushion of air – the slipstream from the airbus engine.

At that moment, Jimmy cut the power to the Falcon's engines. The dull whine disappeared and Jimmy was deafened by the thundering of the airbus and the roar of the air blasting past. Violent turbulence rocked him in his seat. He gripped the flightstick more tightly, desperate to control the shifting of the plane's weight. He was surfing on air.

"Hey, look at this, Pritchie," said the airbus pilot, sitting forward in his seat. A fragment of lettuce fell from his sandwich. His co-pilot had his cap down over his eyes and didn't bother to move.

"What is it?" His voice was gruff.

"Message," replied the pilot, taking another bite of his sandwich. "En-route controller. Something about a ghost on the radar."

"Ghost?" Pritchie reluctantly heaved himself into an upright position and set his cap back on his head. "That's, like, two blips where there should be one, no?"

"Well, it's not some dude in a white sheet, is it?"

They both peered at the data link system. Then they

checked their panel displays, both suddenly very alert.

"Found anything?" asked the pilot. Pritchie shook his head.

"Hey, what's this?" he said. "Another message."

Together they studied the communications system again. The pilot shrugged.

"Huh," he started. "Funny. Must have been a glitch."

"A glitch?"

"Well, we've found nothing and now they're saying things are back to normal."

"Guess that's why they call them ghosts."

They looked at each other for a second, each trying to work out if the other was going to make a big deal out of this or just get on with the flight. Eventually Pritchie broke into a smile.

"Let's hope it wasn't a flock of birds heading for an engine," he said with a rough laugh, reclining in his seat and putting his cap back over his eyes.

"No worries," the pilot snorted. "I don't smell any roast chicken."

Jimmy was riding the slipstream expertly. The slightest twitch of his muscles made tiny adjustments in the balance of the plane. Gradually he manoeuvred down and to the centre, where the airflow was strongest. If he was going to get away with this, he knew he needed to stay as close as possible to the airbus so the air-traffic control radar system would read the two planes as a single entity.

Now all he had to do was stay there until they reached Europe. Then he'd have to work out a way to land. He just hoped he wasn't too late.

02 WILLIAM LEE

"Shall we get started then?" Miss Bennett announced brightly.

Eva Doren felt like a schoolgirl. But unlike most thirteen-year-olds, she wasn't at school. She was at an operations room deep under the streets of Central London, in the bunkers of NJ7, the most technologically advanced and well-funded Secret Service organisation in the world.

She didn't think there were many girls who came to work every day at a place like this: three breeze block walls, bare grey except for the multicoloured horizontal stripes of the electrical circuitry, and a fourth, newly installed glass partition which allowed extra light in from the corridor.

The doorway was an empty arch – there were hardly any doors at NJ7 Headquarters. The place was designed so that if it was ever evacuated it could be completely flooded by the Thames within two minutes, to protect all of the secrets it held.

"I thought we were waiting for someone?" said Eva.

"We are," replied Miss Bennett. "But he's late. So we'll start without him."

Eva pulled her ponytail tighter to stop her reddish-brown hair falling about her neck, and brought out a notepad and pencil from the top pocket of her shirt. She was sitting at a glass conference table big enough for twelve, but for now there were only three.

Miss Bennett was to her immediate right, sitting totally upright. Her hair was also pulled back in a tight ponytail, but it was longer than Eva's and, Eva thought, glossier. At times Eva almost wondered whether Miss Bennett became more beautiful with every cruel act.

Miss Bennett sifted through a pile of folders, all of them plain brown apart from the NJ7 emblem on the front – a short, vertical green stripe. Then she produced a tiny digital recorder and placed it at the centre of the table. She pressed a button, cleared her throat and began, in a business-like tone:

"Present is NJ7 Field Agent Mitchell Glenthorne and Support Staff Eva Doren..."

She continued with some of the details of the meeting, while Eva watched Mitchell, sitting directly opposite her. His eyes were downcast, as they often were, but his shoulders seemed to grow broader, pumped with pride at hearing himself described as a 'field agent'.

"Oh, and also present is myself, of course," Miss Bennett added. "Miss Bennett, Director of NJ7."

As she finished, a shadow fell across the table. Standing in the doorway was an incredibly tall man. Eva thought he was the tallest man she had ever seen, but he didn't look strong or muscly. He was so thin Eva wondered whether someone had stretched him out when he was a teenager. He had to stoop to enter the room.

"Ah," Miss Bennett said, leaning back and giving a dry smile. "It looks like our guest has decided to join us."

The tall man didn't respond, but took the seat directly opposite Miss Bennett. His features looked vaguely Indian, with a nose that was the same shape as the rest of him – long and thin. His hair was dark black and shaved on the sides of his head, which made him look even taller.

"Do we have to have a kid at every meeting?" the man asked, even before he had pushed his legs under the table. He stared at Eva. She felt her heart pounding, but didn't flinch. She'd learned to hide her emotions. "I can understand the need for Mitchell to be here, but, erm..."

"Eva," said Eva. She felt the urge to stand up, but resisted. It would only have made her feel even more tiny opposite this giant. Instead she dropped her eyes to her notepad and started scribbling.

"Eva plays a vital part in the running of NJ7," Miss Bennett explained, "and in particular my office."

"Isn't it time we sent her home?" the man protested. "From what I understand her parents think she's dead." Only now did Eva look up. *Look homesick*, she told herself. She was surprised at how easily the fake emotion came to her. Was it fake? *Play the part. Be the loyal little girl.* She could almost feel Mitchell's examining gaze, but kept her own fixed on this new man's face.

"How long are you going to maintain that... situation?" he asked.

"Indefinitely," Miss Bennett snapped back. "Someone of your background must know how useful it is for the world to think you're dead. By the way, what is your background?"

Eva relaxed a little. Miss Bennett was an expert at manipulating the conversation. It was a thrill to have someone so powerful on her side. The man had no answer. He just gave a reluctant smile, lips pressed together.

It was Mitchell who filled the silence.

"Without Eva," he explained, "we would never have been able to kill Jimmy Coates in New York."

Now Eva's heart rate leapt again, but this time with elation. Mitchell was still watching her. She made sure that her face revealed nothing. *You serve your country*, she repeated in her head, telling herself lies to fool her body. *Jimmy was a traitor.* At the same time every sinew buzzed with joy that her friend had escaped New York in secret – and alive.

At last the man gave a small shrug and pulled out his files.

"This is William Lee," Miss Bennett announced to Eva and Mitchell. "The new Director of Special Security. He replaces Paduk."

The tall man offered his hand to them with an over-the-top grin, revealing a shiny regiment of teeth. Eva shook his hand, but Mitchell refused it. They had no choice about the grin.

"You've been appointed already?" Mitchell asked, confused. "Paduk's body is still warm. Probably. Wherever it is."

"It's highly unlikely that his body is still warm," Lee replied calmly, "now that he's scattered in tiny pieces around ten square kilometres of the North Sea. Not to mention all of the bits of him that were probably consumed by fish..."

"Thanks for the graphic sketch," Miss Bennett interrupted. "I think we get the picture."

"Which picture is that exactly?" asked Lee sarcastically. "The one in which our largest oil rig explodes? The one where my predecessor bumbles into a rescue job and gets himself blown up? Or the one where our economy and energy infrastructure will struggle to recover?"

There was silence and they all avoided each other's eyeline.

"That's one of the things we need to discuss, isn't it?" Miss Bennett muttered, gesturing at her files.

"Go ahead," said Lee.

Miss Bennett pulled out several sheets of paper and spread them around the table. Eva leaned forward to have a look, but she'd seen them already. Some were photographs of the remains of the oil rig, but most were closely-typed pages – the report from the SAS. They all bore the same bold green stripe.

"According to my forensic team," Miss Bennett began, "all the evidence suggests it was a botched sabotage job carried out by a single agent."

"One agent?" Lee confirmed. "An agent who didn't intend to blow himself up as well as the rig, yes?"

"It was a girl," Mitchell cut in. Everybody turned to him.

"Mitchell was there," Miss Bennett explained. "Part of the SAS team."

"I see," mumbled Lee. "And you saw the agent?"

Mitchell nodded.

"She was masked and covered in oil, but from her size and capabilities, it was definitely Zafi."

"Zafi is..." William Lee took a moment to consult one of the pages in his own files. "...the French child assassin, correct? Mitchell's counterpart? Another genetically modified humanoid assassin?" He grunted a dry laugh.

"Humanoid?" Mitchell exclaimed in horror. "What do you—"

"Yes." Miss Bennett cut him off sharply. "Zafi is the French child assassin."

"*Was*," Mitchell corrected. "She was blown up with the rig, remember?"

"Do we have her body?" Lee asked brightly.

"I said she was blown up. You know – *kaboom*!" Mitchell gestured an explosion with his hands. "As in 'scattered in tiny pieces around ten square kilometres of the North Sea'. Do you want me to hunt down all those fish you were talking about and make them give excrement samples?"

"OK, fine. So the French blew up the oil rig, but now at least their operative is dead. The question is, how do we strike back?"

"The PM has my dossier on that," said Miss Bennett.

"The PM has read your dossier. But I'm afraid he's been unwell. Everything goes through me for the time being."

"You?" Miss Bennett was taken aback, but quickly hid it. Lee perused his files, then carried on as if Miss Bennett weren't even there.

"Mutam-ul-it," he announced. The strange word seemed to linger on his tongue and in the air. "I have a strong suspicion we'll be going with that option. Have everybody on standby."

He got up to leave and Eva was shocked at his height all over again. It was almost as if he'd grown during the meeting.

While he gathered his papers a thought struck him.

"By the way, did you see the memo about my predecessor's memorial service tomorrow?"

"I see every memo," Miss Bennett hissed.

"It's at the Mercantile Marine Memorial," he continued. "The PM is expecting everybody to be there. Paduk was his friend."

"Of course we'll be there," said Mitchell. "Paduk was our friend too."

"And one more thing," Lee added, ignoring Mitchell's annoyance. "What about this Jimmy Coates? Anything to worry about there?"

"The file is closed." Miss Bennett pulled a slim brown folder from the middle of her pile and threw it across the table. One page slid out. In the top right corner was a grainy image of Jimmy's face, next to yet another green stripe. Large red letters were stamped across his forehead. They read 'TERMINATED'. Under that was typed 'New York, USA'.

"I know all of this," Lee snarled, looking down his nose at the file. "But do we have a body yet?"

"Another tasty meal for the fish," Mitchell cut in with a smirk.

"There are no fish in the East River," Lee said, reading the details more closely. "Too much pollution." There was a moment's pause, then he tossed the file back on to the table and shot an expectant look at the others. "Well?"

"We had divers trawl the river," Miss Bennett explained with a sigh.

"No bodies?" asked Lee.

"Too many bodies actually."

"Children?" Lee was shocked.

"This is New York we're talking about." Miss Bennett shrugged. "We're not the only organisation to use children as operatives. There's the Mafia, the Triads, the Capita..."

The thought made Eva's skin crawl. Could there really be that many people in the world prepared to kill children, and to use children as killers?

"In any case, Jimmy could breathe underwater," Mitchell put in. "He could have drifted miles before finally dying."

Miss Bennett agreed. "The search area is far too big for us to cover," she said with another shrug. "And without jurisdiction..."

"But we're sure he's dead," Lee asked, stooping to lean one hand on the table. He and Miss Bennett stared at each other. She slowly nodded.

"That many bullets in him? We're sure."

Lee absorbed the information, nodded, then marched out without another word. Miss Bennett waved Mitchell out of the room as well. He gave her an awkward salute before he left and dropped a nervous glance at Eva.

Before Eva could follow the others, Miss Bennett held up a hand. She leaned to the centre of the table and tapped the stop button on the digital recorder. Concentration furrowed her brow.

"Find out about that man," she whispered, without looking up.

"William Lee?" Eva frowned. "Find out what?"

"Everything. Where he's come from, who he is and what he wants."

"What he wants? What do you mean?"

"Everybody wants something." Miss Bennett slowly tapped her finger on the table and raised her eyes to Eva. "If you find out what it is, you find their weakness."

03 A WING AND A PRAYER

Jimmy Coates had been chased, kicked, shot at and throttled. He'd been blown up, nearly drowned in oil and set on fire. But it was the lies that had done the damage.

He shivered violently. Several hours at 10,000 metres was taking its toll. Without the climate control systems of a commercial jet, it was almost as cold as the Arctic. The Falcon wasn't designed for it and Jimmy certainly wasn't dressed for it. His jeans were ragged and torn, and his hoodie was too thin to provide any real insulation.

Keeping control of the plane was even more difficult now. He had to shift the flightstick with the weight of his shoulders because he couldn't rely on the delicate touch of his fingers any more – he couldn't even feel his fingers. Not only that, but soon his chest was straining for every breath. It felt as if each rib was barbed wire.

Despite the pain, all Jimmy could think about were the lies that had brought him here. First, the head of the CIA had tricked him into blowing up a British oil rig. He knew the British were blaming the French and were ready to strike back. Any second a war could start between France and Britain. *It's partly my fault*, Jimmy thought. His stomach lurched and it wasn't because of the turbulence.

His whole life had become a network of lies and secrets. Secrets like the fact that he was even alive. The British Secret Service thought they'd killed Jimmy in New York, but he'd tricked them and survived.

Lies like the ones his so-called father had told for twelve years, before revealing that Jimmy wasn't really his son. Then Ian Coates had taken over as Prime Minister and issued the order to have Jimmy hunted down and killed.

Lies suit him, thought Jimmy. *He's a professional at it now.*

Even I'm a lie, he thought.

38 per cent human. He could remember with cruel clarity the exact moment when he'd first heard those words. The intense dread rushed back to him. He'd discovered he was genetically designed by the Secret Service to grow as a seemingly normal child, but to develop the skills of the perfect assassin by the time he turned eighteen. He was to remain unnoticed by the rest of the world, while his true nature was kept secret even from himself.

But instead of waiting for Jimmy to grow up, the Government had sent him on a mission early. *They didn't even care that I'm a child, but they wanted me to kill.* He couldn't help imagining the terror he would have experienced if he'd gone through with the mission, instead of rejecting it at the last moment. That's when NJ7 had turned on him.

Ever since, Jimmy's assassin skills had been growing and causing nothing but distress. *Now they might cause a war*, he thought with horror.

Jimmy had been searching desperately for ways to prevent it. The simplest way seemed to be for him to reveal that *he* had blown up the oil rig – not the French. But to turn up in Britain now, alive, would bring all the heat from the Secret Service back on to him. *I can take that*, he thought. *If it stops a war it must be worth it.*

But he knew it wasn't that simple. His mother, his sister and his best friend were in London. British agents watched over them every second. As soon as Jimmy revealed that he was still alive, the people he loved would be under threat again. At best they would be taken into custody. At worst... Jimmy didn't dare imagine what nightmares NJ7 would put them through to extract information.

He shuddered and tried to focus all his energy on balancing the plane. But still his dilemma tore at him. It was simple: either he prevented a war, but left his family at the mercy of the Secret Service, or he could stay in hiding, protecting his family, but potentially destroying the fragile peace in Europe.

By now, Jimmy knew he was somewhere near the

French-Spanish border, over the mountains. He had tuned the Falcon's radio into the airbus's communication system. On the seat next to him and across the floor of the cockpit, he had spread out all of the aeronautical charts he could find. Every signal to the airbus came with an automated verbal repetition – standard safety set-up on commercial flights. So Jimmy had picked up enough clues to work out the flight path. It was almost like Jimmy was listening to the plane's thoughts.

And in his own head came the beginnings of an idea. *France*, he thought. *Maybe that's the answer...* Could there be a way to keep his family safe *and* prevent war? *Keep going*, he told himself. The voice in his head was insistent, but his thoughts were muffled by the oxygen deprivation.

Jimmy was slowly suffocating. He realised he had to reduce his altitude, regardless of where he was. He flicked his eyes between the charts next to him and the nose of his plane, always watching and feeling for the constant adjustments in the airflow that was keeping him in the sky.

Time to dive, he told himself, and thrust the flightstick to the side.

It was like tumbling off the back of a rodeo bull. The huge body of the airbus ploughed onwards, while Jimmy watched the distance between them growing. Soon the commercial flight was a smudged shadow soaring far above him.

Jimmy was in freefall. With hands blue from the cold, he punched two buttons and flicked two switches. The Falcon's engines sputtered into life.

I'll make it to France, he thought, triumphant, as his head began to clear. *I'll warn them about a British attack and I'll ask to see Uno Stovorsky.* He remembered Uno Stovorsky from his last trip to France – the agent of the French Secret Service. The man had been gruff, but he had helped Jimmy and his family. Jimmy was sure he would help again.

Then the engines died.

Jimmy felt a violent explosion of panic in his chest. It was immediately dampened by a huge inner wave of strength. Jimmy tried the ignition switches again. Nothing happened. Again and again he tried restarting the Falcon's engines, but they wouldn't even splutter. He watched his hands moving calmly around the controls, while inside he was frantic.

No fuel. No engines. He heard the words repeating like a drumbeat in his head.

Jimmy's genetic programming had already changed tactics. It felt like someone else was routing messages through his brain, but so quickly he couldn't understand what was being said. Then the knowledge came to him fully formed, as if he had always known it.

He manoeuvred the flaps on the wing and the ailerons until the plane was gliding through the air, not plunging downwards. The design of the Falcon was on his side here

– in case of engine failure it wasn't meant to just fall out of the sky. But Jimmy knew it couldn't stay up forever either.

He looked around for a parachute and the ejector mechanism. Then he remembered: every passenger and member of the crew had taken their parachute with them when Jimmy had taken over the plane in mid-air. He'd made sure of it – he didn't want to be throwing anybody to his death. Jimmy knew that decision might now condemn him. He was gliding in a tiny plane, several thousand metres up, without any power and without a parachute.

Suddenly the left side of the plane dipped. *This is it*, thought Jimmy. A vertical draft sucked the aircraft downwards. Jimmy felt his whole body reeling. He plunged through the clouds and saw the stark, white snowscape below. The plane was nose-diving towards the side of a mountain somewhere in the Pyrenees.

Every one of Jimmy's muscles tensed. The scream of the air rushing past the plane seemed to pierce straight to the centre of his brain, doubling his terror. But he didn't freeze. In fact he moved so fast he could hardly keep track of where he was.

He rolled out of his seat and climbed up, towards the back of the plane, digging his nails into the carpet. The friction forced some feeling back into his fingers. When he reached the cabin he grabbed hold of the passenger seatbelts and heaved his legs at the emergency exit. It flew open with such force that the door snapped off its hinges and hurtled into the sky. The wind blasted into Jimmy, knocking him back against the seats.

He crunched his stomach muscles to swing his entire body out of the door. He tensed his arms to rip the seatbelts from the seats. He slammed against the wing of the plane and slid along it, the back of his head knocking against the metal.

Jimmy's body strained against the wind and the G-force while his hands worked to save his life. He wasn't even sure what he was trying to do and after a second he could hardly see because water was streaming from his eyes. He just had to trust that something inside him knew how to survive. He had to force his programming to take over from the terror.

He swung the two seatbelts over the lip of the wing, catching it with the buckles, then shifted into a crouching position, facing directly downwards, holding himself in place by gripping the straps at his sides. The wind in his face was so strong he thought the lining of his cheeks was going to tear.

Then he flexed his knees, rocking the wing. Over the roar of the wind in his ears, Jimmy heard a definite creak. The joint where the wing met the body of the plane was weakening. With the friction from the fall it wouldn't take much more to snap the wing off completely. Jimmy rocked harder. He bounced on his haunches, listening to the creak growing louder. Then there was a massive splintering noise, like gunfire, then another. Jimmy kept rocking.

The ground charged towards him. He was close enough now to pick out the rocks and bare patches in the snow. He drove all his energy to his legs, frantically pushing against the end of the wing. Then, at last:

CRACK!

The wing lurched away from the rest of the plane. Jimmy was almost thrown off, but he squeezed hold of the straps and kept his footing. Then he threw his head and shoulders backwards, forcing his heels into the metal. The shift of his bodyweight pushed the wing underneath him. Now he was standing on a horizontal platform – and using the wind resistance of the wing to slow his fall.

All the time he felt the wing swaying violently beneath his feet. It wanted to flip on to its side again, but Jimmy wouldn't let it. Now Jimmy was surfing again. But this time there was no slipstream to help him – just a vertical drop.

The side of the mountain loomed towards him. Then the rest of the plane crashed into the rocks. What little fuel was left in the tanks sent up a huge black and orange cloud. Jimmy felt the heat of it before he heard it. But he knew instantly that heat could save him.

The rush of hot air was like a cushion under Jimmy's wing, but the updraft threw him off-balance. His feet slipped from under him and he pitched on to his front, smacking his chin against the front edge of the wing.

Then it was over. The wing slammed on to the snow

with a cruel bounce. Jimmy clung to it as it raced down the slope. It was so steep Jimmy felt like he was still falling, but he could hear the fierce *swoosh* of solid snow and ice under him.

His surfboard had become a snowboard. Jimmy crunched his elbows straight, throwing his body upright again. He couldn't see anything but a huge fountain of slush thrown up all around him. He shifted his weight from foot to foot, reading the undulations in the mountainside.

The wingtip cut through the ice, firing chips of it into Jimmy's face and chest. But he didn't care. He could feel himself gradually slowing down.

Then he hit a rock. The wing leapt into the air, catapulting Jimmy with it. He was thrown up with such force that he thought his bones would be ripped free from their joints. He heard his own voice crying out, distant and unfamiliar. The cold bit at his skin and all he could see was intense whiteness.

Then: *THUD*!

He hit something – and the total white turned to total black.

04 SEND THE ENFORCER

Eva watched the shadows shift across the turrets of the Tower of London to distract herself from the stifling air inside the car and the awkward silence. She and Mitchell had been parked there for at least half an hour, she guessed, with specific instructions not to get out. In that time, they had barely spoken. She was quite happy to keep it that way, but eventually Mitchell broke the silence.

"So your parents think you're dead?" he blurted.

Nice conversation starter, thought Eva. She shrugged and turned to look out of the other window, across Trinity Square, to the sombre crowd around the Mercantile Marine Memorial. She couldn't see anything that was going on, just a neat row of people's backs about twenty metres away. She noted how unusual it was for so many people at a memorial service to be wearing bright colours. That was because a lot of them were military personnel in finest dress uniform. The civil servants and journalists were all in black though, making the overall effect like a mingling of peacocks and ravens.

"Don't you mind that they think you're dead?" Mitchell pressed. "They might, like, miss you or something."

Eva sighed. "We didn't get on that well, OK?" she explained. "My brothers know I'm fine. That's all I care about."

"You're lucky you even know your parents," Mitchell mumbled.

For a second, Eva felt a pang of sympathy. Mitchell never spoke about his own family. She felt the urge to explain that she knew all about what had happened to him: that his parents were killed in a car crash when he was a baby... that he'd escaped from his foster home... that his brother had beaten him... But she also knew what lay at the root of it all: Mitchell was the first child to have been genetically programmed to grow into the perfect Government assassin.

Eva shuddered and deliberately pushed away her sympathy. The boy next to her was the enemy. She had to remember that. Already he'd been sent several times to kill Jimmy Coates. The thought of it made her catch her breath. Jimmy's sister was her best friend. It was for Jimmy and Georgie Coates that she risked her life every day, undercover at NJ7.

She reached forwards to the driver's seat and turned the ignition one click so she could open her window.

"Hey," Mitchell objected. "The windows are tinted for a reason, you know."

Instinctively he tried to lean across her for the button. When he realised how close that brought them to each other, he froze. Eva glared.

"It's just a couple of centimetres, OK?" she protested softly.

Mitchell pulled back.

"If anyone finds out the British Secret Service is employing two thirteen-year-olds Miss Bennett will go mental."

"Who's going to find out?" Eva asked. "Even if the press see us they can't print anything about it, can they? Everything has to be approved by the Government press office."

"I dunno. Miss Bennett said to stay out of sight. That's all. Otherwise we'd be standing over there, wouldn't we?" He nodded his head towards the throng of people. "And I should be out there. You know, paying respects, or whatever. I went on a mission with Paduk. I was partly trained by him."

"You train yourself," Eva snapped. "You went for runs with him, that's all."

Mitchell didn't answer. He knew she was right. She was always meticulous about detail and Mitchell wasn't in the mood to challenge her. He also wasn't keen to dwell on the sort of training that went on in his body: his muscles developing as he slept, his programming sending thousands of signals through his synapses every second to give him new skills that he'd never guessed could be his. The skills of an assassin.

They were both glad to be distracted by the Prime Minister's voice floating through the window on a waft of cooler air.

"Paduk died in the service of his country, trying to defend one of our most precious assets from foreign sabotage…"

They had to listen hard. Every time a car drove past it drowned out the words.

"…response will be diplomacy… for a peaceful resolution… but if pressed we are ready…"

Eva didn't want to hear it. Whatever the man said, she knew he would probably be lying. But it wasn't the words that upset her. It was the voice – that calm, reassuring, authoritative voice. To her it wasn't just the voice of the Prime Minister, it was the voice of her best friend's dad, Ian Coates.

A few minutes later he was marching back in the direction of Mitchell and Eva, flanked on either side by Secret Service agents in plain black suits. The sun glinted off their dark glasses and picked out the green stripes on their lapels. They were big men, but Ian Coates wasn't much smaller. Eva remembered that all the time she'd thought he was an ordinary businessman, he'd in fact been an NJ7 agent, along with Georgie's mother, Helen. Since becoming Prime Minister, he'd clearly gone back to a strict regime of physical training. The shoulders of his suit were bulging.

Eva watched him striding towards them, his jaw jutting

out in grim determination. But the closer he came, the more she noticed something was wrong. His swagger was slightly off-centre and his face was pale, with patches under his eyes that were almost yellow.

He forcefully raised a hand to wave to the press, before they were escorted away as a pack by more Secret Service staff. No time to pay private tributes to the fallen hero they'd all come to commemorate. Not that they seemed bothered, Eva noticed.

Eva and Mitchell's car was one of a row of five. Their driver appeared out of nowhere and opened the rear door, motioning Mitchell to shift over to make room, ready for Miss Bennett. As he shuffled towards Eva, the backs of his arms stuck to the leather, making a soft squeak. The Prime Minister's car was the one directly in front of theirs. He paused with one foot in and one foot out, and raised his head back in the direction of the memorial.

Eva followed the direction of his stare and saw Miss Bennett approaching across the grass. She moved gracefully and with a slight sway in her hips. Eva was amazed she could walk so effortlessly fast in high heels. One side of her mouth was curled upwards in a half-smile and as she came closer a flash of sunshine caught the subtle green stripe in the weave of her pencil skirt.

As she reached the Prime Minister's car, they started talking – quickly and without waiting for each other to finish their sentences. Eva couldn't quite make out their words, but it was obvious they didn't agree about something. She opened her window a little further to catch their conversation.

Mitchell tried to object. "What are you...?"

"Shh!" Eva hissed. "Can't you use some special skill to tell me what they're saying?"

Mitchell snorted a sarcastic laugh, but before he could reply, a loud click cut him off. The back door on the other side of the Prime Minister's car opened. Eva and Mitchell both sat to attention and leaned forward. Out of the car stepped William Lee.

His presence stopped Miss Bennett's conversation dead. Ian Coates looked from Lee to Miss Bennett and back again. For a second, nobody said anything. Then the Prime Minister seemed to glance up at the sky before issuing an order that Eva could hear perfectly, though it meant nothing to her.

"Mutam-ul-it. Make it ours."

Lee's response cut through all the background noise.

"I'll send the *Enforcer*."

Eva turned to Mitchell and read in his expression that he was as mystified as she was. Within seconds, Miss Bennett was sliding in next to them.

"What's Mutam-ul-it?" Eva asked, not caring now that Miss Bennett would know she'd been eavesdropping. "And who's the enforcer – what did he mean?"

"He means we've got work to do," Miss Bennett replied calmly. Then a darker expression came over her face. "He means we're attacking the French."

05 NASU MISO

Felix Muzbeke's fingers trembled on the glass of the door. Usually he had no doubts about walking into a restaurant, but tonight he hesitated. His arm seemed frozen. He stared at his reflection: large brown eyes a little too far apart and a chaos of black frizz on his head. But in his mind he was seeing something else.

He was remembering another glass door just like this one, nearly five thousand kilometres away in Chinatown, New York. And he could see the scene that he'd replayed in his imagination so many times. Hiding in the darkness when that long black car pulled up. The two huge men in black suits who'd calmly stepped out, grabbed his parents and forced them to the ground. His mother looking up from the pavement, signalling to him to escape.

"It's OK," came a whisper from behind him, startling him out of his memories. "It's not like Chinatown." It was Georgie.

Although he was a couple of years younger, these days

Felix felt almost as close to Georgie Coates as he always had to her brother, Jimmy. And behind Georgie stood her mother, Helen. Both offered the same reassuring smile, lips pressed together, concern in their eyes.

So Felix opened the door and entered one of the few remaining sushi restaurants in Soho, in Central London. There was a time when the place had been packed with them, when there would have been hundreds of people around to eat in them as well – tourists, locals, shop workers. But Felix and Georgie had never seen it in those days and tonight Brewer Street was deserted. The buildings twisted above them, Victorian and Georgian styles butting edges like brickwork pick 'n' mix.

Before Georgie and Helen followed Felix in, they both instinctively glanced up and down the street. They all knew they were watched every moment by NJ7, either on camera or by field agents. Checking over her shoulder was an old habit for Helen and had become a new one for Georgie. A habit it was safer not to break.

Just as Georgie stepped over the threshold of the restaurant, a man swept along the street so fast he was already past them. But Georgie heard the echo of his whisper:

"Nasu Miso."

Nasu Miso? Georgie repeated the words in her head. Was it some kind of message, or just a foreigner saying "excuse me"? She watched the man's silhouette marching away along the street. His body and head were both round – like a satsuma balanced on a melon.

Her mother hurried her into the restaurant.

It was only a small room, with a low bar and about thirty stools, all of them empty. A conveyor belt snaked its way through the place, carrying dozens of small dishes, each loaded with different morsels. Japanese waiters with crisp white coats and stern expressions hovered about, their arms behind their backs.

"Three green teas, please," announced Felix nervously, perching on the nearest stool.

They all knew they weren't there to have a meal. They just had to look like they were, for the sake of the NJ7 surveillance. Georgie knew they were all thinking about the same thing: whether the man they would be meeting could find Felix's parents. He was from a French charity that specialised in tracking down people who had been made to disappear by the British Government. It all made Georgie feel sick, not hungry.

She'd hardly sat down when her mother announced, "OK, let's go."

"Wait," Felix blurted. "Aren't we..." He looked around at the waiters. They were all watching. Felix knew he couldn't say anything, but his face was a picture of anxiety.

"He's just late," Felix whispered. "We should wait. This could be the only way to—"

Helen hushed him with a smile. She'd taken a single dish from the conveyor belt: chunks of aubergine in a gloopy-looking sauce, their purple skins glistening in the low lighting.

Georgie glanced at the menu and scanned the pictures. There it was. "Nasu Miso," she mumbled under her breath.

"So let's go," Helen repeated softly. She slipped her fingers under the dish and pulled out the three cinema tickets that had been concealed there. "We don't want to miss the trailers."

As Helen, Georgie and Felix took their seats in the centre row of the cinema, the opening credits were already finishing. A black and white title card announced that the film was called *The Lady From Shanghai*, then the actors started talking in American accents.

"What sort of cinema is this?" Felix whispered. "How come they're allowed to show American movies?"

"Old films are OK," Helen whispered back. "This was made in the 1940s."

Felix scrunched up his face, as if the images on the screen were giving off a bad smell.

"They expect people to sit through a movie that's older than me, not coloured in and about some Chinese woman? No wonder the place is empty." He slumped down and started fiddling with the tattered velvet seat cover.

In fact there were a few other people there – a solitary bald head in the front row that reflected the flickering light from the film and two girls a few years older than Georgie. Felix thought they were probably students and wondered whether they had boyfriends. He was so desperate to think about anything except the reason they were there that he forced himself to pay attention to the movie.

Then came a sharp whisper from the row behind.

"Don't look round."

It was a man with a French accent. Felix and Georgie froze in their seats, but Felix couldn't help very slowly trying to glance over his shoulder.

"Enjoying the film?" snapped the man behind them. He leaned all the way forward, until Felix could smell the popcorn on his breath. Felix quickly turned back, before he'd caught a proper glimpse of the man. Helen didn't turn round at all, even when she started speaking.

"I assume you got my message?" Helen began.

Felix felt his blood fizzing with excitement. Maybe the man already knew where his parents were. But his hopes died almost immediately.

"A lot of people have disappeared since this Government came to power," the man said. "My organisation is overstretched already. Every day we get new messages begging for help to find family members, friends, teachers. Thousands of them. Anybody with any views this Government doesn't approve of. Anybody who shows any kind of support for Christopher Viggo. They all disappear. What makes you think your case is so special?"

"If there's nothing special about our case why did you agree to meet us? Why take the risk?" countered Helen.

"In your message you said you thought NJ7 might use your friends for some political purpose. That's unusual. What did you mean? These people weren't politicians. Were they public figures? Scientists perhaps?"

"No."

"Then don't waste my time."

Felix heard the man heave himself to his feet. He wanted to reach back and grab him, or shout out – anything to get the man to stay and help them. Then, to his shock, Helen Coates spun round and stated loudly: "I used to work for them."

The man slowly walked back to them. The bald man at the front of the cinema turned round and gave a loud "Shh!".

"For this boy's parents you mean?" asked the French man, crouching again behind Helen's seat.

"No – for NJ7." There was a pause, filled only by the voices from the film. "Many years ago. I was NJ7, but I left when..." She stopped, suddenly wary of her surroundings.

"It's OK," the man reassured her. "This building still has walls lined with lead. It makes it difficult for them to listen in or to watch without having an agent inside."

"Well, that's all." Helen added no more details.

"I see." The man pondered for a moment and shovelled in a fistful of popcorn. "It makes sense now. Your method of communication, you demanding this meeting..."

While the man considered everything, Felix couldn't help peering round. He didn't want to miss a single word. Now for the first time he got a proper look at their contact's face: podgy and sullen, with a neat, blond moustache.

Suddenly the moustache twitched. "Neil and Olivia Muzbeke could be more significant than I first thought," the man announced.

Felix shuddered slightly at the mention of his parents' names. *They are significant*, he insisted in his head. "You're going to help us?" he exclaimed, with a surge of energy. He could barely keep his voice to a whisper.

The French man ignored him and spoke directly into Helen's ear.

"You said in your message they were taken in New York, so they could be at any one of dozens of British detention centres all over the world. But from what you've told me I don't think they'll be dead. Yet."

Felix felt a lump lurching up in his throat. He fought back tears.

"If I need to contact you again?" asked Helen.

"You'll never see me again," replied the French man. "But somebody will contact you."

He left them with instructions to stay until the end of the film and go straight home afterwards. Felix sat in the darkness thinking of nothing but his parents and how wonderful it must be to be French.

06 WHITEOUT

Jimmy opened his eyes. He was surrounded by a whiteness so intense that at first it hurt the backs of his eyes. He tried to look down at his body, but moving his head was awkward, as if it was being held in place by a surgical clamp. Every bit of his skin was prickling from the cold. It grew more acute the more awake he became, until it was the pain of a thousand stabs.

The pounding of his heart and the flow of blood through his ears were the only sounds. Beyond that was unwavering silence. His slightest movement caused a low creak that was like a hurricane in comparison. *What is that?* he asked himself. Then he realised it was the noise of densely packed snow shifting.

Only now did Jimmy remember the details of his crash and that he must be suspended in a snowdrift in the Pyrenees. Every sensation became less disturbing because he could explain it. But then he was attacked by another memory – the reason he was here in the first place. *Britain is going to attack France. How long have I been unconscious? I have to warn the French.* For all he knew he could be too late.

Jimmy tried to raise his right hand to wipe his face, but the weight of snow packed in around him held it down. He jerked it free, sending a stab of agony through his ribcage.

He struggled to think clearly. He didn't even know which way was up. He spat out a globule of saliva. His mouth was so dry it took some effort. The spit dribbled up his cheek, then froze just below his eye.

Great, he thought. *I'm upside-down.*

At last he loosened enough of the snow around him and tumbled backwards, just managing to avoid landing on his head. It was only a short fall, but the impact doubled every pain in his body. He gripped the right side of his ribcage and let out a cry of agony that rang off the cliff faces and echoed back to him.

The world was still almost completely white. Plumes of mist swirled around him, only parting for fleeting seconds to reveal glimpses of the mountain peaks. Massive rock formations, hundreds of times the size of Jimmy, poked their heads out of the whiteness to peer down at him, then disappeared again as if they'd seen enough.

Apart from these flashes of clarity, Jimmy's visibility was less than a couple of metres. His body had developed the ability to see in the dark far better than any normal person and he had used it to escape some nasty situations in the past. But this wasn't darkness – it was the opposite. His night-vision wasn't going to help him here.

He glanced back and just made out the hole where he'd been stuck. Buried about half a metre into a wall of snow and ice was a cavity roughly the shape of Jimmy's inverted body, with extra holes where he'd wriggled free.

He struggled to his feet, still clutching his ribs. Without realising he was doing it, his palms were prodding around the bones. When he came to the origin of the worst pain he winced and let out another cry. *Two cracked*, he heard himself thinking. He knew his programming was evaluating his condition and keeping him alive. Without it he would certainly have frozen to death hours ago.

He pulled the hood of his sweatshirt over his head and tried to calm down. He took several deep breaths, but every gulp of air chilled his gullet. Now he was out of the shelter of his snow hole, the wind brought the temperature plunging down. And Jimmy felt it threatening him. His shivering was brutal and uncontrollable. Then he looked down at his hands and knew that two cracked ribs were going to be the least of his problems. The ends of his fingers had turned yellow and white.

Immediately Jimmy found himself marching away from his snow hole. Every step sent a severe stab of agony from his feet. He assumed they were turning the same colour as his fingers, but he didn't have any choice but to keep going. He deliberately planted every pace more firmly, almost revelling in the torture, challenging his programming to lessen the anguish. It was the only way he could make himself carry on walking.

Soon he developed a rhythm, then at last his programming swelled inside him. It felt as if he was growing an extra protective layer against the cold – almost like a fleece just underneath his skin. But still the wind bit into him, attacking every pore.

The further he walked, the more the snow around him revealed blackened corners of debris, like spots on a Dalmatian. A few paces on he saw the wreckage. It was a mess of ashen detritus and twisted metal, hardly recognisable as a plane. It might have been invisible in the snow except for fragments of metal shimmering under the thin layer of frost and blackened, burnt-out corners flapping in the wind.

Jimmy rushed forwards as fast as his body would allow. He crouched among the wreckage, desperate for some shelter, and dug around the ash and snow looking for anything that could help him. He tucked his hoodie into his trousers and scooped up armful after armful of ash from inside the body of the plane, stuffing it down his top for added insulation. Some he forced down his trouser legs too, until he felt like he was wearing a fat suit.

His hands were virtually useless now. He had no sensation in them except throbbing agony and couldn't flex his fingers. Nevertheless he forced them into the snow and shovelled.

The only recognisable piece of debris he pulled from the wreckage was a half burned, blackened, in-flight washbag. The cloth cover had protected its contents surprisingly well. Jimmy pulled out an eye-mask, a mini-toothbrush, a tiny tube of toothpaste and a shoehorn.

With a rush in his veins, he snapped the shoehorn in two and used the elastic from the eye-mask to strap the pieces to the soles of his shoes. The upside-down curved shape would dig into the ice and give him vital extra grip.

Then he snatched up the travel-size tube of toothpaste, squeezed it in his fist and forced the contents down his throat.

Take all the energy you can get, he told himself. *You've got some walking to do.*

The waves attacked the shoreline with such ferocity, it was as if the water was angry that it couldn't reach any further. For all its might, it couldn't change the fact that just a few metres away was the edge of the largest desert on Earth. This was the battle line where thousands of miles of water met thousands of miles of sand – the West Coast of Africa.

On a mound overlooking the beach stood a single figure, lean and supple. She seemed to bend with the wind, not letting it bother her, and held a Zeiss-Ikon rangefinder steady at her eyes. Behind her trailed a stream of hair as black as her skin. Against the sand, her limbs stood out like charcoal twigs on snow.

Suddenly her whole body stiffened at what she saw in her scopes.

Through the thunder of the waves approached a ship so powerful and furious it looked like a salivating beast on its way to fight the whole of Africa single-handed. A Type 48 destroyer; 7500 tonnes of warship. She recognised the curious straight edges of the bridge section and the slim, arrow-like construction of the bow. From the centre rose a huge mast, which was more like an Egyptian monument. Radar balloons stuck out on either side and when the sun hit them they glinted like scowling eyes.

The destroyer was charging through the swell of the ocean towards the shore. She estimated the rate at over 30 knots. And at the sharp point in the front of the ship flew a bright Union Jack flag.

The British are coming, the girl thought, fear creeping into her joints.

She looked to her left, down the coastline, and adjusted the triangulation of the rangefinder. From here she had the perfect view of the only buildings for several kilometres. A couple of heavily marked tracks scarred the sands to the south and led to parallel lines of high fences. Within that was a complex of low buildings, connected to a dozen vast warehouses that backed on to the water. And there were two concrete towers supporting crude look-out stations, both topped by sun-bleached flags of red, white and blue – the French Tricolore.

Despite the distance, the girl could also make out human figures around the outer fence. Were they running? Yes. That's when she knew for sure.

Mutam-ul-it was preparing for an attack.

So should we, she thought, steeling herself. *Time to raise the alarm.*

07 FEAR, PAIN AND A RED BEARD

Jimmy had been on the move for hours. The terrain was rugged and the air was thin. He could hear his brain assessing the surroundings. He had to be over 3000 metres up, he guessed. Above the snowline. That put him somewhere on one of the highest peaks, in the centre of the mountain range. But however difficult it was, he had to keep moving if he was going to stay alive. And there was the constant fear at the back of his mind, driving him on – the British attack on France. He had to stop it.

By now the agony that shot through his body with every step had mutated in his mind into some kind of reassurance. It told him he was still alive. That he was still moving. His legs felt so heavy that his feet dragged along the ground as he walked.

He travelled in a dead straight line, but the going was getting steeper. At least the fog had cleared a little so he could see his route further ahead. In the crash he'd slid a long way down the slope and he was paying for that now, always having to march against the gradient. Every few minutes he came to what looked like an impassable rock face, but his body seemed to relish the challenge. Despite the onset of frostbite and the cracked ribs, Jimmy free-climbed as if he'd been born a mountaineer. The hooks of shoehorn he'd fixed to his soles served as makeshift crampons.

With his eyes squinting against the elements and his body straining to keep his basic systems going, Jimmy fought on. But the real torment was in his mind. The whiteness that surrounded him seemed to reach into his brain to plant fear and worry, but most of all anger.

As he heaved himself up the cliff face, he thought back to the very first night that NJ7 had come for him. From that moment, almost everybody he trusted had betrayed him. He had believed Miss Bennett to be his form teacher and he'd even gone to her for protection. She had turned out to be the one woman who most wanted Jimmy dead. He felt a bitter laugh scratch at his throat.

But it had happened again and again. Eva's parents had pretended to protect him, then betrayed him to NJ7. Colonel Keays had fooled Jimmy with the promise of CIA refuge. Jimmy's stomach turned over when he thought of his own gullibility. How had he trusted any of these people? He had even convinced himself to use his assassin skills to work for Keays.

Never again, Jimmy thought. He told himself that if

he made it across the Pyrenees to see Uno Stovorsky – or any other agent of the French Secret Service – he would beware every word that was said.

Trust your instinct, he urged himself. But in his heart he knew that even his instinct was untrustworthy. Sometimes it was the human part of him acting out of fear, or loyalty, or emotion. Sometimes it was the assassin in him, spurring him on towards self-defence, survival and violence. Perhaps even murder.

How could he know which instincts to trust and which to resist?

Around him, the light was fading. When darkness fell Jimmy knew the temperature would plummet even further. But there was no time to dig shelter for the night and rest. He had to keep going. There was a battle coming.

The largest destroyer in the British Navy dropped anchor 16 kilometres off the coast of Western Sahara. The waves pounded against the iron, but to the commanders and crew of *HMS Enforcer* the conditions were irrelevant. Two hundred and fifty men and women in pristine white or navy uniforms moved through the vessel with such precision and efficiency they were like parts of a single machine.

In no time the Tomahawk Land Attack Missiles were primed. The targets were locked into the guidance system. Everything was perfect. Nobody needed to say a word.

Except one.

The front section of the central mast contained the command centre – a triangular room with a low ceiling and a door at each corner. This was the brain of the ship. The longest wall, the base of the triangle, was a huge window that looked out over the front of the vessel. All along it, at hip level, was the control desk. From here, the senior officers and their staff made all their decisions and issued their orders.

But one man was completely out of place. He was wearing a suit and a life-jacket and was at least 50 centimetres shorter than everybody else. Compared to their naval steel, he was made of pie pastry.

"Remember," he said, his voice quivering, "we can't—"

He was cut off by a glance from Lieutenant-Commander Luke Love. Love's expression was harder than the iron of the ship's hull. The sunlight coming through the glass picked out the proud gold braid on the upper part of his sleeve – two stripes with a single loop.

"A single misplaced explosion..." the other man whispered, so intimidated by Lt Cdr Love's glare that he could hardly speak. "It's such a delicate environment, that's all. And we don't really know what safety systems Mutam-ul-it has in place. You know, for the..."

"Don't worry, Dr Giesel," Love replied calmly. "We know enough." His voice was strangely cheerful, but deep and serious at the same time. Like an experienced headmaster. "Your report told us which specific buildings to hit and which to avoid," he explained. "The place will remain fully operational and almost all in one piece, ready for your team to take over."

The muscles round the officer's mouth creased into a grim smile. Then he lay his hand on the number pad of the control desk in front of him and punched in an eight-digit code.

"Right," he declared under his breath. "Time to nationalise this hellhole."

Even the walls of the town of Tlon showed the troubled history of the state of Western Sahara. Almost a century of graffiti was layered on top of itself. The oldest protested against the rule of the Spanish, from the time when they had colonised the country. It was no longer visible under the blurred mess, but since then there had been plenty of other people to complain about: the Moroccans (Western Sahara's neighbours to the north), the Americans (first for them being there, then for them leaving), a dozen different football teams (from the time when the politics were so complicated even the locals didn't know who to protest about) and, most recently, the French.

Every building bore the marks of unrest and instability. Cracks ran through the stone walls and holes in the roofs had been covered with ragged, sun-bleached tarpaulin to keep the heat out. These days the cracks and holes couldn't be fixed, even though they let the rats in, because they were conduits for the cables of the rudimentary electricity and telephone systems. They were also used for signalling.

A series of flashes reflected the sunlight from the low roof of a house. Nobody would have noticed the dark figure hidden under the tarpaulin. Five hundred metres away the signal was acknowledged with another flash, then repeated at a new angle. It was acknowledged again, a little further away this time, towards the centre of town.

The rooftops of Tlon glittered with rapid flashes. There were sounds too, on top of the normal bustle in the labyrinth of narrow streets. Across the town, telephones rang once, stopped, then rang again before being picked up. But no words were spoken – there were only sequences of taps and breaths.

In the small central market there was a sudden eruption of squawking. A boy ducked under one of the stalls, disturbing a small chicken coop on his way through. He sprinted across the street, hidden in the cloud of dust he kicked up. He slipped past a market stall selling bootleg DVDs and burst into the building opposite – three storeys, almost completely masked by a huge Coca-Cola billboard.

Inside was a bare room, dark except for the horizontal stripes of light cutting through the shutters, making the floorboards look like a zebra-skin rug. There was another door at the back, partially concealed by a stained red curtain.

In front of it stood a young guard with a machine gun across his chest and a silver rod where his left leg should have been. In the darkness that was almost all that was visible, until he recognised the boy and smiled, revealing three rounded, pearly teeth.

The boy didn't smile back.

"Mutam-ul-it," he gasped, trying to catch his breath.

The guard's smile vanished. He nodded and knocked on the door behind him. It flew open immediately. In the doorway stood a broad man, silhouetted against the harsh light of the bare bulb inside his room.

A European observer might have noticed this man's wild red beard, deep-set blue eyes and the explosion of orange hair on his head. But to everybody in this town he could be identified simply as 'the white man'. Certainly nobody paid any attention to the thin black tie worn loosely around his neck, or to his slender-lapelled suit – black, dusty and worn at the elbows. Who here would even notice that on one lapel was a short, green stripe?

When this man spoke it was in grammatically perfect Hassaniya Arabic, but with a strong northern English accent.

"I told you this would happen," he announced, waving the boy away. He turned to his guard. "Go get the trucks. Now."

08 BIRDS IN FLIGHT

At last Jimmy could feel the temperature creeping up a couple of degrees. The sun was rising – not that he could see it with the fog still so thick. He'd made it through the night. But the white world around him seemed to close in. Then it started spinning.

If I stop I'll die, he told himself. But the voice was faint, as if something inside him was still shouting, but he had lost the ability to hear it. *Keep walking*, it continued, so feebly it was quieter than a thought. Then came echoes of the phrases he had repeated to himself over and over thousands of times since he started his trek: *Find Uno Stovorsky. Warn France.* But they were confused and lost beneath the wind.

Then even that noise stopped. Jimmy no longer knew where he was or where he was going. For a second it even felt like his thoughts were completely detached from his body. All the pain floated from his limbs...

No, he heard. *Find Stovorsky... France...* But the words didn't mean anything any more.

A light pierced his eyes. Something silver and glimmering. It seemed to pull Jimmy towards it. He was overwhelmed by the sensation that this was the most wonderful thing he had ever seen. The surrounding whiteness flickered from grey to blue to black. *Is it night again?* Jimmy wondered.

It was his last thought before his head hit the snow.

"Birds in flight, sir," came a voice through Lt Cdr Love's intercom. *"The launch was clean."*

Dr Giesel ran his hands nervously up and down the front of his life-jacket, then straightened his tie.

"They're definitely on target?" he whispered. "Because if they're even slightly off—"

"This is the British Navy," Love cut in. "We don't *do* 'slightly off'." He kept his gaze straight ahead at the clutch of buildings on the horizon. The Tomahawk missiles twinkled above them. There was a glint of pride in his eye. But when he caught sight of the other man's concern his expression softened. "The missiles are guided by GPS," he explained, "and the targets can't move. They're buildings. Not people."

Dr Giesel was satisfied for a second, until fear crept into his face again.

"What's up?" Love asked. "Worried about killing a few Frenchmen?"

Dr Giesel's mouth fell open in horror. How could

this man be so flippant? Didn't he realise he was effectively starting a war?

"Don't worry," chuckled Love. "Much as I would have loved to blow up some Frenchmen, we've got a live satellite feed that shows us they started evacuating as soon as they spotted us on the horizon. Our missiles will take about ninety seconds to reach them. That's more than enough time for whoever's left in there to clear out. Then the place is ours." He winked and turned back to wait for the explosions. "It's almost too easy, isn't it?"

The intercom crackled into life again. "*The last French truck has left the site, sir. The place is deserted.*"

Love turned to Dr Giesel and gestured as if to say, 'I told you.'

"Send the satellite feed up to my monitor," he ordered, into the intercom.

A second later, one of the screens on Love's control desk switched from a graphical display to a pin-sharp satellite image of the coast 16 kilometres ahead. The sand was a beautiful reddish-orange, but it was blemished by groups of square white buildings and criss-crossed by tracks. Then there were six much larger rectangular buildings lined up next to the water. They would have been overwhelming on the ground, but here they were reduced to knots of pixels. And racing away towards the edges of the screen were dozens of small black squares.

For a few seconds everybody on the bridge stood in silence, while French jeeps and trucks fled the compound. It was like watching germs squirming under a microscope. Some of them twisted and turned as if they didn't know where to go. This was no orderly retreat, thought Dr Giesel.

In contrast, the atmosphere on the *Enforcer* was totally calm.

"Only a few people in the world have ever seen these images," said Love softly. "You won't find this place on Google, that's for sure. And only a handful know what really goes on here." He looked round at Dr Giesel. "Soon you'll be the one in charge."

Suddenly the screen went white. Dr Giesel's eyes jumped from the monitor on the control desk to the horizon. Two towers of black smoke erupted into the sky. After a split-second they were lit up with orange flames. Then came the sound – two deep booms that shook the floor. Dr Giesel placed a hand on the control desk to steady himself, but noticed that he was the only person affected.

"Better prepare your team," Love announced, so casually it was as if he had asked what was for dinner. "Mutam-ul-it will be under your control in no time."

Dr Giesel was terrified to see what damage had been done, but at the same time he couldn't look away. The smoke finally cleared enough for the ground to be visible again on the satellite feed. In the exact spots where there had been two white squares there were now two black patches, each surrounded by a ring of fire in the footprint of the destroyed buildings. The precision was incredible. But then the doctor noticed something at the edge of the screen.

"What's that?" He nervously leaned forwards and laid a finger on the monitor. The black dots that had been rushing away from the compound were now rushing in every possible direction. Some had stopped completely, but after a few seconds they turned around and went back the way they came.

Lt Cdr Love peered at the screen. "What's going on?" he barked into the intercom. "Don't the French know how to evacuate? What are they doing heading back in?"

There was a pause, then a crackle. "*It doesn't appear to be the French, sir.*"

"What?"

"*It's another force.*"

"Another force?" There was confusion from everybody on the bridge.

"*That's right,*" confirmed the voice on the intercom. "*They appear to be taking over the French vehicles and...*"

"I can see what they appear to be doing!" raged Love. "Why are they doing it? And how are we going to stop them?" He spun round to each of his officers in turn. Every one wore a blank stare.

"Well?" he bellowed. "Who the hell are these people?"

*　*　*

One second Mutam-ul-it was there; the next it had vanished in a plume of black smoke. Hot ash rained down around the girl, then hailstones formed out of the sand that had been melted together by the explosion.

The girl buried her face in the sand and covered the back of her head. But she didn't have time to hesitate. She had waited as long as she could remember for this and she knew that the dozens of people waiting around her were going through exactly the same rush of disbelief, joy and dread. Some were much older than her, a few were even younger, but they were all looking to her for leadership.

For a moment she felt a surge of pride. Her father would never have believed that any woman could be in charge, let alone a sixteen-year-old girl – even his own daughter. Impossible. But no one in her parents' generation had trained as hard or studied strategy as widely as she had.

Then her pride was overwhelmed by sadness. So few of her parents' generation had survived. She forced away that thought. It was time to move. It was time to prove why the others were glad to be led by her.

She raised her head and checked that the fighters immediately around her were watching. Then she lifted her arm and signalled, indicating which teams were to head for which vehicles, exactly as she'd been trained. Time to run.

The signal was passed down the line and they acted on her command. As a single unit, they rose from behind the mound and charged towards the chaos. They were a silent force among the panic. Everywhere were French shouts, engines roaring and the din of the fires raging at Mutam-ul-it. But the unit ran in silence.

And none was faster than her. Her black hair flew behind her like a rebel flag. Before she had time to be afraid, she tumbled deliberately into the path of an open-top French jeep.

It swerved to avoid her, but came so close she reached up and caught the bumper. Sand mixed with exhaust fumes seemed to get inside her skin. She strained her arms to keep hold of the jeep. Though she was slim, her biceps bulged. It was as if every fibre of her body was muscle and passion. *Just like training*, she told herself, trying to ignore the darts of terror in her heart. She clawed her way up the back of the vehicle until she could reach the tread next to the rear wheels.

Inside were two huge soldiers in desert camouflage. But she took them by surprise. She punched the base of her palm into the nose of the passenger. Blood exploded all over the cab. Now she had a firm footing on the running board and she grabbed the blood-spattered man by the shoulders. He was unconscious, which made him all the more useful as a battering ram.

She forced the soldier's head into the face of the driver. He scrabbled for a sidearm, but the girl stabbed her elbow into his shoulder with perfect aim. She struck the sternoclavicular ligament with such power she heard the bone beneath it shatter. The man cried out in pain and the gun dropped from his hand, while the jeep veered across the sand, out of control.

She was desperate to grab the wheel, but first she had to reach for the door handle and push the soldiers out of the jeep one by one. She couldn't believe the adrenaline inside her. Her hands were shaking.

At last she took control of the jeep. She could feel tears itching to come out, but she swallowed the fright and steered the vehicle round to point straight back at Mutam-ul-it.

Through the thick smog she could make out everything she needed to know. Her teams had sent a shockwave through the French retreat. Their soldiers were reduced to escaping on foot. Some lay down, defeated; others tried to sprint away, flailing and staggering over the sands. Their jeeps were now hers. And every one of them was hurtling back towards Mutam-ul-it.

With a smile, she slammed her foot down on the accelerator.

HMS Enforcer was suddenly frantic. Crew scurried in and out of the command centre, handing print-outs to each other, poring over charts and conducting muttered conversations. Dr Giesel couldn't keep track of what was going on. His breath was suddenly short and he had to sit down.

"*We think it's the local rebel force, sir,*" came the voice through the intercom, much less assured that it had been only minutes before.

"You *think*?" Lieutenant-Commander Love's face had turned red with fury. He strode up and down in front of the window. "Who trained them?" he bellowed. "How can they do this?"

He removed his cap to reveal a head of brown hair shaved aggressively short. He furiously massaged his scalp, then ordered, "Arm two more missiles."

Dr Giesel sprang up from his seat at the back of the command centre and rushed towards the Lieutenant-Commander.

"Sir," he panted, "we can't do that." Love spun round and glared with the look of the devil. Despite that, Dr Giesel insisted, "We don't have another safe target."

"We can't have these people going in and occupying the place," Love replied, his voice resounding about the command centre. Giesel's response was less decisive, but immediate.

"We don't know which other buildings—"

"So we'll hit the same places again."

"But the heat from the explosions..." The two men faced off against each other, but Dr Giesel knew his subject. He wasn't going to be shouted down. "It's already risky. Another blast could—"

"What is this – a negotiation?"

Love slammed his cap back on his head and rushed back to his control desk. He jammed his thumb into the keypad with such anger it threatened to split the plastic cover.

"No!" Giesel shouted. Love ignored him. Giesel took a deep breath and threw himself at the control desk. Love swatted him away without even looking up and pressed the final digit.

Giesel heaved himself to his feet and stared out of the control centre window, aghast. A second later, two missiles soared into the air.

"Right," announced Lt Cdr Love, mopping his face with a handkerchief. "Get your team on board the chopper. We're sending you in."

"We can't."

"What?" Love scowled as if he was trying to shoot lasers out of his eyes straight into Dr Giesel's forehead.

"I tried to warn you," Giesel said quietly. "Sir." He deliberately emphasised the word. "My report recommended that Mutam-ul-it would remain stable if you hit those two specific targets."

"We did hit those targets!" roared Love. "And we'll hit them again!"

"But my calculations were based on a single strike. The heat from two explosions will throw everything off."

Love froze. Giesel waited for his message to sink in, but it didn't look like the man was listening any more.

"Do you understand now?" Giesel asked, as gently as he could. "After those missiles hit, the whole place could be unstable. There's no way we can go in."

Lt Cdr Love turned away and rested his hands on the control desk. His head hung between his shoulders, hiding his face. Then he coughed and scratched at his collar.

"Signal Command," he whispered to nobody in particular. "Tell them we have a problem."

09 FRENCH WELCOME

Opening his eyes felt like lifting up a building. Every part of Jimmy's body was either totally numb or in excruciating pain.

Pain means I'm alive, he told himself again, but it wasn't reassuring. Then he felt a sudden heat in his chest. Within seconds it washed through his body, melting to a soft warmth. It was like diving into a pool of warm honey. It didn't soothe his pain completely, but it made it bearable.

Slowly Jimmy became aware of his surroundings. The first thing he saw was soft beige light all around him and a huge ceiling fan whipping round above his head. His nostrils tingled with a bitter smell. It made him think of school on the first day of term. Then he remembered the same smell when he'd lightened his hair as a disguise. *Bleach*. Jimmy thought. *I'm in a hospital.*

There was something soft behind his head which he assumed was a pillow, but when he tried to feel around to check whether he was in bed, he found that he had no sensation in his hands.

Then he heard the squeak of soft shoes on lino and a shadow fell across his face. Jimmy felt the kick of a strong force inside his gut. His programming wasn't only working to dull the pain. It was on full alert. *Have they examined me?* Jimmy wondered. *What have they found?* Maybe whoever had examined him had simply followed the usual procedure for victims of extreme cold and not noticed any unusual results yet.

"Uno Stovorsky?" came a high-pitched male voice.

"Yes," Jimmy tried to cry out, but his throat felt like it had been slashed from the inside. He didn't care. Somehow whoever was looking after him had found out that he needed to see Uno Stovorsky.

"Hello, Uno," the man said in a thick French accent. "You are English?"

Jimmy's heart crumpled. Why would anyone think he was Uno Stovorsky? He strained his neck to get a better look at the doctor. He was a short, middle-aged man with scars on his cheeks and a tidy goatee beard. A line of biros stood to attention in the top pocket of his immaculate white coat.

"I'm not Uno," Jimmy said. His voice came out deeper than he was expecting and with a rough tone. He repeated himself, but this time relaxed his lips and tongue, letting his programming take control. His words came out in perfect French. "*Je ne suis pas Uno Stovorsky.*"

The doctor apologised, obviously shocked that his patient spoke the language like a native. He continued in French. "It's the name you were muttering when they brought you in. You said it over and over. You have no identification on you, so we assumed it was your own name. Tell me—"

"When who brought me?" Jimmy didn't have time to make a fuss about introductions and he certainly didn't want to explain what he was doing in the Pyrenees in the first place.

"You set off the alarm when you touched the border fence." The doctor's face turned sour at Jimmy's interruption. "That is only about five kilometres from here. We don't get many who have survived a journey over the mountains. And children travelling alone..." He tailed off as if he expected Jimmy to give an explanation.

It didn't happen. The man shrugged. "The patrol picked you up immediately."

In the past, the French-Spanish border had been left virtually unmanned, with travellers free to cross one way or the other as they pleased. But that wasn't the case any more. Despite the relatively civil relations between the two countries, there were still security concerns. Now the border was clearly marked out by fences, patrols and checkpoints.

Jimmy remembered the silver glimmer he'd seen before he collapsed. It gave him a thrill of achievement. He'd made it to the border.

"Uno Stovorsky is an agent of the DGSE," Jimmy explained. "Your Secret Service. Can you contact him for me? It's urgent."

Very slowly he flexed his elbows to force his upper body off the bed.

"You can't get up," the doctor protested. He tried to push Jimmy down, kindly but firmly. "It might not seem like it because you're on powerful painkillers, but you're very ill."

"I'll be fine," Jimmy insisted. "I take vitamin tablets."

He shook his chest to get the doctor off him, which sent a harsh stabbing pain through his ribs. Jimmy winced, but kept moving. In a second he was sitting upright. The ward housed five other beds, but they were all empty.

"You don't understand," said the doctor. "Even if you can get up, you can't leave."

Jimmy stared the doctor down, trying to read what he really meant. Then the details of his surroundings flashed up in his brain – details he didn't even realise he'd noticed.

"Bars on the windows," Jimmy muttered. "Doors of double thickness with reinforced glass. What sort of hospital is this?"

The doctor didn't say anything, but glanced over his shoulder towards the thick double doors. Meanwhile, Jimmy rolled his shoulders, without knowing why. Then he realised. His programming was testing his mobility.

He had to know which movements were impossible and which were just painful.

He raised his hands to look at what damage the cold had done and for the first time saw that they were completely wrapped in bandages. He looked down. So were his feet. The balls of bandaging looked like four large portions of candyfloss, one stuck on the end of each limb. Now Jimmy also noticed the tube inserted into his arm, attached to a saline drip next to his bed.

"I don't need this," Jimmy announced, surprised at his own confidence. It increased as his programming fuelled his strength. Jimmy was feeling the effects of several weeks' recovery condensed into a few minutes. It was thrilling. He hooked one bandaged hand under the tube and yanked it out of his skin. "Thanks for your help, doctor. I'm leaving."

"Stay where you are," the doctor ordered. "This isn't a hospital. It's the medical wing of a border control detention centre."

"Detention centre?" said Jimmy, testing how far he could flex his knees.

"It's where we keep people who try to cross the border illegally until they can be identified and—"

"Are you going to help me or not?"

"We *are* helping you. That's why I can't let you—"

Before he could finish, Jimmy swivelled in the bed and stuck a leg out. He hooked his bandaged foot round the bottom of the metal stand his drip was hanging on and flicked it upwards. The base of it smacked the doctor in the knee. The man stumbled forwards.

Jimmy grabbed the pole between his forearms and stamped down on the wheel lock on one leg of his bed. Then he kicked against the wall to send himself rolling across the lino on the bed.

The doctor scrabbled for a whistle that was round his neck and gave it a huge blast. The echo had barely died when the double doors burst open. Two armed security guards charged towards Jimmy, one reaching for the baton on his belt, the other going for his gun. Jimmy kept rolling, using the metal pole as a paddle.

He crouched low on the bed and waited until the very last second. His programming was thrusting power into every corner of his being, as if it was grateful to be let off the leash at last. At the same time it gripped Jimmy's mind, controlling his actions.

Just as the guards descended on him, Jimmy steered himself round in a sharp twist. He twirled the pole over his arm and smacked it into one guard's face. The momentum spun the bed all the way round so Jimmy was facing the wrong way. Jimmy brought the pole under control and jabbed it backwards, under his arm. The foot of the stand connected with the other guard's chest, then Jimmy snapped it upwards into his face.

When both guards hit the floor they stayed down.

But two more were hurtling towards the ward. Jimmy stayed calm. He rubbed his feet together to loosen the bandaging, then twisted his right hand into it and pulled. Within seconds it had unravelled, exposing his blackened and twisted left foot. Jimmy stared, relieved that the power of his programming combined with the painkillers meant he could hardly feel it.

The new guards were through the ward doors. Using his wrists and forearms, Jimmy wrapped the length of loose bandage round the metal pole. Then he kicked the pole directly upwards. The foot of it caught on a strut of the ceiling fan above Jimmy's head.

Jimmy twisted his arms into the other end of the bandage and swung into the air, leaning back to control his direction. He slammed his knees into the guards' faces and they toppled like skittles.

By now the first two guards were rolling over, trying to get up, but they were too late. Jimmy was through the doors. He hurtled down the corridor, half running and half sliding, with one foot still cocooned in bandage.

A quick glance at the emergency evacuation notice told him the layout of the building. As he ran, he tore at his bandages with his teeth, desperate to free his hands. He turned a corner, heading for the nearest fire exit.

Another guard sat in front of the exit reading a newspaper. When Jimmy tore into view, the guard leapt to his feet and held up a hand to signal "Halt!".

Does that ever work? Jimmy wondered. He picked

up speed, while the guard scrabbled for his walkie-talkie, then his gun. By then Jimmy was on him. He crashed his shoulder into the man's midriff and the pair of them tumbled to the floor. Jimmy dived for the exit in a flurry of newspaper pages. He clattered through and an alarm erupted throughout the building.

Jimmy felt the ice-cold air hit his skin. It brought back the terror of his mountain trek. He looked around to find himself in a fenced courtyard, with a watch tower looming overhead. The guard's newspaper was fluttering all over the courtyard.

"Stop immediately," came a stilted voice, speaking in English, but with a French accent. "Otherwise you will be shot."

Jimmy buzzed with the strangest feeling of delight. His programming hummed through him, relishing the battle. His brain whirred with a thousand calculations – the angle of the shot, the velocity of the bullet, the distance between Jimmy and the fence...

To his shock, a smile twitched in the corners of his mouth. He felt his muscles bracing for the sprint and was actually enjoying it. But then his eyes fixed on a single sheet of newspaper and the delight froze in his heart. Jimmy suddenly knew that there was no point trying to outrun the French shooter. He stopped dead still and raised his hands.

The newspaper's front page swooped along the concrete. It was dominated by one image: the skeleton of a burnt-out building, with a huge grey battleship looming on the horizon. The ship was flying the Union Jack.

Suddenly four guards pounced on Jimmy, pushed him to the ground and cuffed him. He didn't resist. He knew it was too late for that now.

10 LIES WORK

Mitchell jumped out of the shower and grabbed his towel. The red light above the sink had just come on. It reflected around the black tiles and gave the steam an eerie, hellish glow.

He rushed through to his bedroom, randomly drying bits of his body as he went. Drips ran down his nose and bounced off his brawny chin before hitting the carpet. He leaned over his laptop, careful not to drip on it, and found what he knew would be waiting for him. The red light only came on when there was an email from Miss Bennett.

He clicked it open and pulled his desk chair closer with his foot. Before his shower, he'd been absorbed in one of the SAS combat simulators. It was intended as part of the training for recruits, but to Mitchell it was just the best console game he'd ever played. The handset was discarded on the floor next to a packet of crisps and the image of a mangled enemy corpse was still paused on his TV.

His room was quite small, but it had everything he needed. In fact it had everything he had ever wanted: TV, HD-DVD player, and imported luxuries like a Bose sounddock. Even the shower responded to voice commands.

But he knew there was a price for living in such luxury. Looking around the room, with its smart black and red design, there was one obvious reminder of his situation: the lack of windows. The British Secret Service had taken over his life so much that these days he lived underground, in one of the few residential apartments at the NJ7 network.

Miss Bennett's email had no message in it, but a video popped up instead. Mitchell settled back to watch.

The image was jerky, as if it had been filmed on a hand-held device, like a mobile phone, and at first it was too dark to see anything. Mitchell turned up the contrast on his screen.

The video appeared to have been filmed in a snooker hall. There was the noise of balls being hit and in the corner Mitchell made out a sliver of green baize. But everything was obscured by the shoulders of people around the camera. The place was packed. Then Mitchell finally realised what the focus of the filming was.

At the front of the crowd was a tall figure addressing the others. His manner was relaxed, but powerful. Mitchell turned up the volume. He could just make out snippets of the man's speech above the cracking of the snooker balls and the murmurs of the crowd.

"The British Government has become a dictatorship," the man declared. "They invented this system of Neo-democracy to give them power to do whatever they wanted."

The murmurs from the crowd grew louder, but it was clear they were all starting to listen to the man. The rest of the background noise fell away.

"Some of you might like the fact that you don't need to vote any more," the man went on. "But now the Government commits horrendous acts without us having any say in the matter."

Mitchell peered closer. There was something about this man that he recognised, but the image was too dark and grainy to be sure.

"You won't find it in any British media," the speech continued, "because it's controlled by Ian Coates and his Secret Service donkeys. But in France this is public knowledge: a British destroyer has attacked a French facility in Western Sahara."

The packed hall was completely rapt. Everybody was listening to him now, mesmerised by his charisma. After a minute Mitchell was hardly taking in the speech; he was examining the picture and analysing the voice.

"Are you going to let them start an unjustified, illegal war?" the man asked, with passion shaking his words. There was a roar from the crowd.

"Are you going to let them act in your name, without serving your interests?"

Another roar, louder this time.

"Or are you going to join me in tearing down…"

The end of his sentence was lost in the cheering of the crowd. The man raised his arms and strode to the front of his platform, soaking up the applause and encouraging more. Mitchell only realised now that the man had actually been standing on one of the snooker tables to make his speech. The overhead light reflected off the green felt and caught the man's face from below. Mitchell broke into a smile. Of course he knew who this was.

Christopher Viggo: the man who represented the only realistic opposition to the Government. The man NJ7 had already tried to kill. But they'd sent Jimmy Coates to do it. That's what had started all of the trouble – Jimmy had overcome his instinct to kill Viggo and instead joined the man's cause. Mitchell had heard all about that. He remembered how careful Miss Bennett had been to make sure he hadn't challenged his own programming in the same way.

And now Jimmy Coates was dead. Mitchell's head spun as he thought about it. It was nothing new, but it still felt strange. If Jimmy hadn't joined Viggo, would he and Mitchell have fought side by side for NJ7, instead of attacking each other? Could they even have been friends? After all, they had more in common than most other people.

We were half-brothers, Mitchell reminded himself. He shook off the thought with a shudder. It was the last thing he wanted to think about. For all he knew, it could be a lie anyway.

The video came to an end and straight away the phone on Mitchell's desk rang. It made him jump. He picked it up, but before he could say anything, Miss Bennett's voice came through the receiver.

"Seen enough?"

Mitchell hauled his concentration back to the video. He ran his finger across the screen, tracing the framed pictures on the wall behind Viggo's head. They were too blurred to make out, but he knew NJ7's data team would have been able to enhance the image.

"Where was this filmed?" he asked.

"A snooker hall in Camden." Miss Bennett sounded calm, but Mitchell had spent enough time with her to know there was something extra in her voice today. Fear, he wondered? No. More like excitement.

"He's less than six kilometres from where you're sitting," she said. "And he dares to make a speech like that."

"Did we track him?" Mitchell asked. "Whoever took this film—"

"Lost him. It wasn't an agent, just a loyal member of the public. Out of nowhere, Viggo pops up at a snooker hall, makes that speech, then disappears. Who knows where else he's been doing it and how many times? It can't happen again."

"Who's he working with? He'd need help to disappear like that."

"No he wouldn't," Miss Bennett scoffed. "He's ex-NJ7. He could be alone or he could have built up his own private army. But either way..."

Mitchell's stomach turned over. It was a mixture of the assassin power inside him stirring and his human psyche making him sick with fear. Mitchell wallowed in the sickness until it turned into strength. His voice came out sounding more confident than ever.

"So you want me to—"

"I want you to send him an invitation to your fourteenth birthday party."

There was an awkward silence. Mitchell knew Miss Bennett must be joking, but couldn't work out why she didn't laugh.

"Do I have to spell this out?" she snapped. "Find him. Kill him."

The line went dead.

Jimmy's hands and feet were back in bandages, but this time his right wrist was cuffed to the bed. He hadn't been able to convince the doctors that the bandages were unnecessary and cuffs were useless. If he wanted to break free he knew he could. But now there didn't seem much point.

Some sheets from the newspaper lay open on his

lap. One of the guards was so scared he'd agreed to do almost anything Jimmy asked. Salvaging the newspaper from the courtyard was a simple place to start and Jimmy was beginning to get the hang of moving the pages around with the ball of bandage.

He stared at the picture on the front. Nothing in the newspaper's text added much; the picture said it all. Jimmy's mind went round and round in circles, retracing the same thoughts, throwing up the same furious frustrations. Britain had struck, and in a way that was obviously meant to be direct retaliation for the French blowing up the British oil rig. Except the French hadn't blow up the oil rig. Jimmy had.

As far as Jimmy could work out, a British destroyer had blown up a French facility in West Africa known as Mutam-ul-it. The paper was a bit sketchy on what actually went on there, but there was plenty of indignant discussion about how tragic it was for France to have an evil dictatorship for a neighbour. *Try living there*, Jimmy thought to himself.

"For a dead boy, you're making a good recovery."

Jimmy was startled out of his thoughts. The voice was deep and flat and the English was perfect except for a slight French accent. Jimmy looked up. In the door of the ward was a short man with only a sprinkling of hair on his head and a face like misery. His shoulders hunched up as if he was trying to keep his earlobes warm, and the tails of his long grey overcoat brushed on the floor.

"Uno Stovorsky," Jimmy gasped. He switched effortlessly into French without even realising. "You came. How did you know...?"

"Anyone trying to escape an immigration processing centre—"

"You mean a detention centre?"

"I know what I'm saying," Stovorsky countered, raising an eyebrow. "This is *my* first language, not yours, remember?"

He walked slowly towards Jimmy and stood rigid at the foot of the bed. He picked up the clipboard there and while he spoke he pretended to examine the paperwork.

"Anybody trying to escape from... from this sort of place gets flagged up and sent to the DGSE for analysis. When the person escaping is eleven and manages to knock out half a dozen guards on his way, the case gets a little more attention that usual."

"I'm twelve."

Stovorsky looked up, perhaps surprised at Jimmy's sharp tone. "Well, look at you," he cooed with mock pride. "All grown up." Jimmy forced himself to stay calm.

"Anyway," Stovorsky went on, "I heard that somebody was asking for me by name, so I had to look into it. You see, most of the people who know my name are dead."

"Including me."

"Exactly."

The pair of them stared blankly at each other.

"Nice of you to come," said Jimmy bitterly. "But it's a bit late."

He scooped his hand under the newspaper and thrust it towards Stovorsky, who grabbed it and scrunched it into a tiny ball without looking at it.

"Jimmy, you're a nice boy," he said, his fist so tight it was almost throbbing. "But I didn't come to chat and check on your health. Do you think I would have turned up if it was too late?"

Jimmy didn't respond, so Stovorsky carried on.

"Tell me if I've got this right," he said softly. "You blew up that oil rig. You found out that the British thought Zafi had done it and you knew they would strike back at France somehow. You wanted to stop them. How am I doing so far?"

Jimmy nodded reluctantly. He hated hearing the doubts and fears that had been tormenting him spoken out loud.

"But you had a little problem," Stovorsky continued, clearly beginning to enjoy Jimmy's attention. "You couldn't tell the British you'd blown up the rig because they think you're dead. And if you reveal you're alive, you'll be back to square one."

"Worse than square one actually," Jimmy cut in.

"Of course – your family."

"NJ7's watching them. Any sign that they lied about me being dead and..."

Stovorsky held up a hand to stop him. "Enough," he whispered.

There was a long silence. Stovorsky circled Jimmy's bed. *What's he thinking?* Jimmy wondered. *Why's he come?*

"Will France strike back?" Jimmy asked at last.

"Probably," Stovorsky replied with a shrug. "That's not my department."

"And will Britain attack again?"

"This isn't chess, Jimmy. You don't take turns. Anything could happen."

"But I can stop it," Jimmy insisted. He sat up straighter, rattling his cuff against the bed frame. "I can show them they've made a mistake and there's no need to go to war."

"They don't *need* to," Stovorsky growled. "They *want* to." His glare was full of fire. "You think that just by turning up and telling the British Government they've made a mistake, you'll convince them to call off their war? They're not fighting because of the oil rig, because of politics, or even because of you, Jimmy. They're fighting because it suits them to fight. And soon they'll tell the public they're at war, just to keep them afraid. Showing Miss Bennett you're still alive will only put you in danger. If she wants a war, you can't stop it."

"But if I show people the reason for the war is a lie, they'll have to stop."

A half-hearted laugh escaped Stovorsky's throat. "Lies work, Jimmy. They hurt and they can kill, but they work – especially lies to nations. Millions of people might discover the lie, but somehow they still ignore it."

"They won't ignore me," Jimmy snarled. The words rose on a sudden swelling of aggression inside him. He hadn't expected to say it, but he liked the sound of it. "Everybody in Britain will—"

Stovorsky cut him off with a real laugh. "That's the spirit, Jimmy! Send everybody in Britain a postcard. I'll buy you the stamps."

Jimmy tried to protest, but Stovorsky was enjoying himself too much.

"Tell you what," he announced, "I'll get you a slot on French TV. Or even better – you don't need me. Go rob a bank, wave to the security cameras and you'll get yourself on the news. Then everybody will know that little Jimmy Coates is still alive."

"Nobody in Britain would see it!" Jimmy shouted, desperate to be heard. "You know that. They control what's on TV and what British people can find on the Internet. All that would happen is..." Jimmy found it harder to form his words. "My family. They're being watched by NJ7. I told you. My mum. My sister. Felix too. As soon as they know I'm alive, they'll..."

"Ah," Stovorsky sighed, deliberately over-the-top. "Now we hear the real problem. You want to save the world, but you don't want anybody to hurt your precious family." Stovorsky injected every word with scorn and each syllable wrenched Jimmy's gut. He needed help, not ridicule. Stovorsky went on before Jimmy knew what to say. "Would you rather see two countries at war?"

"Than what? Than know I put my family in danger?"

"Pretty selfish, aren't you?"

Jimmy felt sick. Uno was twisting his words, making them sound worthless. Then his sickness shifted to despair. He felt his face creasing into a deep frown.

"And you came to see me," Stovorsky said quietly, "because you thought I could get your family to safety. Is that right?"

Jimmy shrugged. "Can you do it?" he asked meekly.

"What makes you think I even know where they are?"

Suddenly Jimmy's meekness exploded into anger. "You can find them, can't you?" he yelled.

"I can try to help you, Jimmy," said Stovorsky softly, coming closer. He slowly opened his fist and unscrunched the front page of the newspaper. He flattened it firmly on the bed to push out some of the creases in the picture of Mutam-ul-it.

"But I came here," he whispered, "because I need you to help me."

11 CHEMISTRY KILLS

"Mutam-ul-it," Stovorsky announced, swivelling his laptop round to face Jimmy and pushing it across the table. "On the coast of Western Sahara. It's the largest uranium mine in the world."

Jimmy ignored the laptop to concentrate on his burger. He demolished it in seconds and leaned back in his chair, satisfied for the first time in ages. They'd driven out to a nearby service station for something to eat.

It had been dark for ages, but Jimmy had lost track of the time. All he knew was that until a few seconds ago he'd been starving. The only people around now were the attendants at the food outlets and a cleaner, winding through the plastic landscape with his mop.

"It's always been under French control," Stovorsky explained, pushing the laptop closer to get Jimmy to look at it. "Until now. We think the British meant for it to remain operable so they could go in and take over. But they messed up."

"They wanted the uranium?" Jimmy clicked through dozens of windows as they talked, soaking up images, charts, maps and diagrams. In seconds he was familiar with the layout of the mine, its position on the coast, the buildings in the dock it was attached to. Then there was the street map of the nearest town, Tlon, 12 kilometres up the coast to the north.

All the information distracted from the pain in his hands and feet. His fingers were a greyish yellow, but some of the feeling had returned. At least that meant he could control them well enough to eat a burger and use a laptop.

"No," Stovorsky replied. "Actinium. Within the uranium ore, in minuscule amounts, is 90 per cent of the Earth's actinium."

Jimmy had never heard of it. He tried to think back – had he heard about actinium at school? He'd never paid much attention in science.

"I've missed a few chemistry lessons," he said. "This 'actinium' – it's valuable? Dangerous? What?"

"Both," said Stovorsky. "It's highly radioactive and incredibly rare. All of the naturally occurring actinium in the world would make a lump not much bigger than your burger was. Without this mine, the French Government would have to manufacture it using neutron irradiation."

"What's that?"

"It's like making a cake, but with more lasers."

"That's not funny."

"Well, how do I know what it is?" Stovorsky shrugged and looked away. "But apparently it would cost billions."

"Billions?"

"Put it this way," said Stovorsky. "I'd give you twenty oil rigs for a handful of actinium."

Jimmy examined the man to make sure he was being serious. Stovorsky looked like he had never told a joke in his life.

"What's this actinium stuff for then?" Jimmy asked.

"Does it matter?" Stovorsky snapped back. "Trust me," he insisted, leaning forwards. "If it were just the uranium, Mutam-ul-it would hardly be worth fighting for."

Jimmy hesitated. *Never trust a man who says "trust me"*. "So send in the army," he declared. "You don't need me." He pushed himself up from the table and turned away, heading for the exit. He didn't know where he was going, but he didn't care.

"Wait," Stovorsky called out.

Jimmy spun round. "If this actinium means so much to the Government," he whispered furiously, "send the army to storm the mine. Post one unit at Tlon, another to the south and—"

"The army can't go near it."

"You're lying."

"The blasts from the British missiles have ionised the uranium and the actinium – maybe. We don't know. If it has it's highly unstable and nobody can go near it until it's properly insulated."

"It's not properly insulated anyway?"

"Not the uranium. It's not that dangerous under normal conditions, so they store it in aluminium. They never thought anybody would be stupid enough to do anything to destabilise it. Now if it has been ionised, any human going into the mine will get a massive dose of radiation poisoning. So we need you—" Stovorsky stopped himself suddenly.

Jimmy's face was white.

"Because I'm not... human?" His voice came out as a raw hiss. His words echoed round the food court and seemed to linger long after they should have died. Jimmy wiped his face and stared down at the plastic table-top. "How do you know it's safe for me if it isn't safe for a... for the army."

"We know all about you, remember? We've studied..." Stovorsky dropped his voice and shifted in his seat. "We've studied Zafi and she's also... like you."

Jimmy didn't know how to respond. Stovorsky's words were hardly going in. He rocked forwards and had to support himself with a hand on the table. "Why not send Zafi?" he asked.

"Doesn't it make sense for her to stay in Britain and extract your family while you carry out the mission?"

"Zafi's in Britain?"

Stovorsky gave a small nod. "I meant what I promised, Jimmy," he said softly. "If you do this for me, in return I'll get your mother, your sister and Felix out to a safehouse. All you have to do," he went on, "is this: go into the mine, take some readings from the computers to assess the state of the radioactive material in the mine. That's the uranium and the actinium. Communicate that information to me. If the area is unstable I'll have a clean-up team talk you through the containment process, then come in to take the actinium away and get the mine working again. I need you to do this, Jimmy."

Stovorsky sounded more agitated now. "The British are still waiting off the coast in their destroyer. A *destroyer*, Jimmy."

He emphasised the word, but Jimmy stood motionless, his face blank. His mind was tearing itself apart. *I am human*, he wanted to scream. But his programming wouldn't let him. It was rolling through every sinew: *38 per cent*, it seemed to whisper. *Only 38 per cent human.*

"They call them destroyers for a reason," Stovorsky continued. "Not just 'big ships'. When the Brits work out there's no way of them taking over the mine, they'll destroy it." He clasped his head in frustration and let out a grunt. "It's so simple!" he cried. "I could train a monkey to do it if I had time."

"But instead of a monkey," Jimmy murmured, "you found me." He felt like a black wave was overpowering his senses. He fought his way back to the surface. "So this is the way it works," he muttered.

"What's that?"

"You lie to me to get me to go on some mission that has nothing to do with me except that you think I'm the only person who can do it."

For a moment Stovorsky was taken aback. "You've changed," he said.

"I used to be easier to fool." Jimmy was barely holding back his temper. "I told you I need to get back to Britain and you want to send me to Africa."

He saw a smile creep on to Stovorsky's face. It creased up the man's cheeks and made his eyes as small as pinholes. "You're better at geography than you are at chemistry," he announced. "I don't blame you for not trusting me."

"Why?" Jimmy barked. "Because you're lying?"

"No." Stovorsky's smile vanished. "Because I have no reason to tell you the truth."

Jimmy was thrown. His wanted to trust the man, but he remembered how wrong he'd been about Colonel Keays. Was Stovorsky any different? He certainly seemed more desperate for help.

Forget what you think, Jimmy told himself. Instead he closed his eyes and delved for guidance from inside. At first all he could feel was his burger.

I don't have to do this, he thought. *Walk away. Stay dead.* He felt a kick through all of his muscles. His programming was blaring out a warning, like a buzzer in his ears. *I can't trust him*, Jimmy thought, forcing away the noise.

That second the fear for his family connected with that massive drive inside him – the urge for control. He knew that if he wanted his family out of reach of NJ7, the best way to do it was to exploit the DGSE resources at Stovorsky's disposal. Then he could do whatever he wanted – disappear, return to Britain to try to prevent the war... *or destroy NJ7*. Jimmy shuddered violently. Where had that thought come from?

He made a decision. *It doesn't matter if he's lying. Let him think he's using you. Use him.*

His eyes burst open. He stared at Stovorsky. Suddenly the bright lights of the service station seemed to pierce Jimmy's skin and ignite his veins. He sat down and his hands grabbed for the laptop. He pulled it close to disguise the fact that he was trembling. Still, his brain was throbbing. Words screamed through his head: *no more mistakes*. They came with a fizz that thrilled every part of him. If it was safer not to trust Stovorsky, he wouldn't. *My rules this time*, he thought. *My mission.*

When he looked up Stovorsky was grinning. "Thank you, Jimmy." Jimmy ignored him. "We're on the same side now," Stovorsky went on. "So don't worry. I'm going to help you."

"I know," Jimmy replied. *Because I'm going to force you to.*

12 THE HALF-LIFE OF DEAD RABBITS

Jimmy held himself stiff in the back of the off-roader. To the right was the ocean, while to the left was the desert. It was as if each one was trying to stretch out further than the other. But Jimmy didn't feel like taking in the scenery.

He breathed deeply, hoping the ocean wind would settle his nausea, but the air was so hot and dry it felt like it was going to burn through his sinuses into his brain. It just made him feel more sick and he clutched his stomach.

The Panhard PVP 360 hurtled south along the coast of Western Sahara, bouncing as if it was trying to take off. The driver showed no inclination to ease his foot off the accelerator. Unusually the top was down. That was so the integrated armoured steel hull didn't interfere with the satellite signal to Uno Stovorsky's laptop.

Another clump of wet sand smeared across Jimmy's cheek. He wiped the back of his sleeve across his face.

The material of his camo suit was rough and it smelled as if it hadn't been washed since the last time it had been worn, but at least it fitted him, which was better than the clothes he'd been wearing for a while.

Jimmy noticed that Stovorsky hadn't changed out of his suit and raincoat. *This is the desert*, he thought. *Don't you even want to loosen your tie?*

"Fortunately actinium has a very short half-life," Stovorsky shouted over the noise of the truck and the wind. He was leaning back in the seat next to Jimmy. One arm was dangled over the side of the PVP while the other tapped away at the laptop balanced on his knee. "It will still be a year before we can safely operate the mine, but without you doing this for us it might be a hundred years – or more."

Jimmy didn't understand a word Stovorsky was saying and he didn't care. He just wished the man would be quiet so he could concentrate on not throwing up. *Actually*, Jimmy thought, *maybe I should throw up. At least that might shut him up.*

"There's just one more thing you need to know," Stovorsky went on. Jimmy's patience ran out.

"Only one thing?" he snapped. *One thing you haven't mentioned in the last six hours of endless talking?* "That's great news."

"I don't mind your sarcasm, Jimmy," replied Stovorsky, still in that loud monotone, still not looking up from his laptop. "By the time you're eighteen the assassin in you will have forced it out of your system. If you survive that long."

Jimmy felt a surge of anger, but he had no reply. Stovorsky's words were terrifying because they were probably true.

"You might find some bodies in the mine complex," said Stovorsky, ignoring Jimmy's furious glare.

"I thought you said the French team all managed to evacuate."

"They did. But on their way out they crossed paths with some lunatics who were fighting their way in."

Jimmy drew in another deep breath and half closed his eyes, trying to shut out the bumps and lurches of the journey to concentrate on information that might be important for his survival.

"That's why I can't just send a hazmat team," Stovorsky went on. "If anybody's left alive in there, they might be dangerous."

This gets better all the time, Jimmy thought to himself.

"And you're sure I won't need a protective suit or something?" he called out.

"I told you," Stovorsky replied. "You don't need one. And a hazardous-materials suit seriously restricts your movements. You'll need to be ready to defend yourself if necessary."

Jimmy shot him an uneasy look.

"For years," Stovorsky explained, "there's been local resistance. The natives had a problem with the French running the mine. They thought they should have been allowed to do it themselves. They put together some kind of nationalist force. Mostly they weren't very effective, but lately they'd seemed a bit more organised." He shrugged. "Nothing to worry about now. The Brits blew most of them up. That was the blast we're worried about – the one that might have ionised the actinium."

Jimmy couldn't believe the casual way that Stovorsky was talking. People had been blown up. Jimmy wondered how many. He was going to ask, but then a horrible shiver came over him. He realised that soon he might see for himself.

"We should be thankful to them, I suppose," Stovorsky continued. "They're probably the reason why the British messed it up in the first place. Otherwise there'd be a Union Jack flying there right now."

Stovorsky flicked a finger in the direction they were travelling, but he still didn't look up. For a second Jimmy didn't know what he meant. Then, in the corner of his eye, he caught a glimpse of something on the horizon. He turned his head, squinting against the sand and dust in the wind.

The beach stretched out ahead of them for miles and miles. It shimmered in the heat, blurring the horizon so that the blue of the sky melted into the sand and the sea. But somewhere in that haze was a short slab of black. Even from here, Jimmy could recognise the outlines of Mutam-ul-it's vast machine halls and the trace of smoke still rising from them.

"Here's your radio, Jimmy," said Stovorsky, turning to

look at Jimmy at last. He tossed a large white handset into Jimmy's lap. It landed with a thump. "The signal's encrypted and you've got lithium batteries in there with twenty-four hours' charge, so you can leave it on in case we need to contact you before you contact us. And we're watching too, to check you're OK." He tapped the screen of his laptop. *To check I'm OK*, thought Jimmy, *or to check I'm doing what you want me to do?*

Stovorsky reached forwards and gave the driver a jab in the shoulder. "This is about as close as we can go, Jimmy," he announced. The driver slammed on the brakes and the PVP skidded across the sands. "It's up to you now."

Jimmy clipped the radio to his utility belt and stared out in the direction of the mine. He knew he still had a choice. He could still refuse to go. Inside him was a cloud as dark as the smoke rising from the mine, and hotter.

The line between his programming and his own mind was more blurred than ever. He didn't know who was making decisions any more – Jimmy Coates the boy, or Jimmy Coates the assassin. *Does it matter?* he wondered, crushing the trepidation in his stomach with huge mental effort. *I know what I want.* He glared at Stovorsky. *You're going to give it to me.*

Without hesitating another second, he pushed open the door and set off across the sand.

* * *

Zafi Sauvage dipped the end of her little finger into the froth on her hot chocolate and tried to draw a smiley face. *Looks more like a dead rabbit*, she thought to herself with a smile. She sucked her finger and went back to staring out of the window of the coffee shop. Rivulets of rain zigzagged down the glass. With that, and the cap pulled down low over her face, she knew there was no way Mitchell Glenthorne would notice her.

He's meant to have the skills of a top assassin, she thought, wanting to snigger, but controlling herself. She knew that luck was on her side for now – it was only this easy to shadow him because he was preoccupied with shadowing somebody else.

At the moment her subject was leaning back on a bench across from the coffee shop, pretending to read a film magazine. It occurred to Zafi that whoever he was following might even be sitting in that same coffee shop where she was. She didn't care. She had her target; she just needed to find her moment.

Just then she was distracted by a soft vibration in her hip pocket. She pulled out her phone and discreetly checked the message. It was encrypted of course. Whoever had sent it would have used a Secret Service computer, or a mobile phone that bounced everything through a DGSE server. But Zafi didn't need any software to decipher the text. She had found out very young that she had the ability to retain incredibly long strings of letters and numbers in her head. Complex algorithms were reduced to simple codes, as if she was seeing the symbols in three dimensions, with space between the shapes for their meanings.

The message was from Uno Stovorsky.

Zafi let out a sigh of disappointment at what it said. She downed her hot chocolate in one massive gulp, then dashed out into the rain of North London. Her target would have to wait. She had confidence she'd be able to find him again fairly easily.

Her new assignment was a strange one: track down the mother and sister of Jimmy Coates. Make contact. But she wasn't to do anything else until she'd received another message – not kill them, nor protect them. Just find where NJ7 was housing them and make contact without the British Secret Service noticing her.

There was an unfamiliar churning in her gut as she jogged down the escalator into Camden Town station. Did it mean something, or was it the effect of British hot chocolate? It slowly worked its way from her stomach to her mind. Could it be confusion that she hadn't been ordered to kill these new subjects. Or was it fear that she still might have to?

13 MUTAM-UL-IT

The closer Jimmy came to Mutam-ul-it, the darker his feelings grew. The place was deserted. Even the French press helicopters had to keep their distance because of the smoke. There was no way they would have been able to see Jimmy, which was just as well. If the crew of the British destroyer found out that he was there, Jimmy was sure the mine would suffer a few more missiles.

He could almost feel their presence, just off the coast, waiting. They were probably at that moment planning their own strategy to make the mine safe, so they could take it over just as they'd planned. Perhaps they'd also realised they could send in a genetically modified assassin and Mitchell was on his way. *Or here already*, Jimmy thought.

He tensed up, his programming prickling at his skin from the inside. What if British long-range surveillance *could* see him? He tried to force away his doubt by marching faster. *All the more reason to make sure*

Stovorsky gets Mum, Georgie and Felix to safety, he told himself with false confidence. While he was inside the mine, the French would have to do exactly as he said. And they couldn't touch him.

The gates loomed over him, twisted and charred, as if they were bowing to the tower of black smoke. Jimmy broke into a jog and entered the compound. Suddenly nothing was as simple as it had seemed on Stovorsky's laptop. The smoke was low and thick now. And it wasn't so obvious which buildings were which. None of the signs had survived the blasts. Jimmy had to think back to the plans he'd seen, but whenever he thought he knew where he was, a clearing in the smoke showed him a glimpse of something out of place. Where was the central maintenance system that would tell him the true extent of the damage? And where was the actinium stored?

Jimmy choked in the smog and shielded his face with the back of his arm. As he moved through the complex, the smoke became so thick he couldn't see where he was going. There was a nasty smell too – simultaneously bitter in the back of his throat and sickly sweet in his lungs.

Every step he took was carpeted with blood. Then he realised that the stench was roasting human flesh. He breathed in short gasps to stop himself puking. *How did I get into this nightmare?* he wondered.

In horror, he picked his way through a dense forest of body parts. He felt his disgust grow into a seething anger. Didn't the British or the French Governments care that they had caused so many people to get ripped apart? How could they justify this slaughter, no matter how much money was at stake?

Jimmy felt violence throbbing inside him. Was he the only person in existence who cared about what was right and what was wrong? The whole of the rest of the world had turned rotten. Maybe he should let Britain and France destroy each other in a stupid war, he thought. They were as bad as each other.

But then he realised that in the carnage around him were real people, not governments. And there were at least three other people in the world that he knew who weren't evil. Three people he cared about in London who would be trapped in the middle of it all if there was a war. He tried to calm himself down by focusing on them, but only fuelled his anger with fear. They were so far away and yet it was up to him to keep them safe.

Suddenly there was a noise. Jimmy jumped. It was only faint and it was immediately blown away in the wind, but it was new and out of place. It sounded like an engine starting. Had Stovorsky and the driver somehow followed him? He looked around, trying to work out which direction the noise had come from. Then he picked out a black rectangle surging towards him out of the smoke. The front grill of a jeep.

Jimmy's first instinct was to jump out of the way, but his limbs wouldn't move. Yet it wasn't fear that rooted him to the spot. His muscles weren't tense. They melted in a wash of calm. His programming instantly took control. For the first time, Jimmy felt a gush of joy with it. The danger might be extreme, but the thrill of combat was even greater.

He waited until the jeep was close enough for him to pick out the detail of the grime around the headlights, then he ducked his left side and jumped at the vehicle. His shoulder crashed into the bonnet, denting the metal. To Jimmy it felt like no more than a pat on the back. He bounced all over the jeep, rolling in the air, and landed softly in the sand.

The jeep disappeared into the blackness, but Jimmy's ears were locked on to the sound of its engine. He could feel his mind using the information like a number in a simple calculation. He could pinpoint the jeep's position and velocity. It was coming back.

Jimmy had no time to think about who might be in the driver's seat. He could either start asking questions or stay alive. He crouched low and dug his fingers deep into the sand. As soon as he saw the outline of the returning truck, his hands shovelled madly, throwing up a curtain of sand and ash. Mixing with the smoke, it made Jimmy almost invisible. But still he didn't try to run.

The jeep swerved about, out of control, brakes squealing. A slim figure dived out of the driver's seat. In a single instant, two thoughts flashed through Jimmy's head. *Run*, said one. The other was, *Destroy*. He flicked away the first with ease and listened to the second, not knowing which had come from his human anger and which from his assassin's genes. He didn't care. He was already hurtling across the sand towards the figure.

Jimmy was certain: attack was the right decision. Whether this was the British coming to take over the mine, or a trap set for him by the French – it didn't matter. *Both sides deserve destruction.*

While the driver stumbled and slipped on the sand, Jimmy burst onwards, faster and faster. He was wearing heavy desert boots, but his toes still dug in to give him extra spring. The figure ahead of him was only visible for flashes at a time. Jimmy saw the desert camouflage just like his own and the limbs pumping in desperation. But did he also see long black hair?

Jimmy was about to dive to catch the person's ankles, but stopped just in time. His target side-stepped and disappeared into a dark hole in a building where there had once been a door. Jimmy followed without hesitation.

The darkness was instant and Jimmy's eyes were slow to catch up. He stumbled forwards a few steps. By the time his eyes prickled and his night-vision buzzed, he was falling – and not just to the floor. If this building had ever had a floor it had been destroyed in the blast. Jimmy fell for long enough to realise that at a mine, buildings can have very deep basements indeed.

14 KNOWING THE DRILL

Jimmy braced himself for the landing. He ducked his head and protected it with folded arms. He gulped in as much air as he could to cushion his ribs and locked his ankles together. He hit the bottom feet first, as painlessly as was possible. His legs gave way, but even before he was still he could tell that nothing was broken. There was just a sharp bite from the two ribs he'd already fractured in the mountains.

Then: *BAM!*

Something cracked into his cheek with the power of a wrecking ball. Jimmy rolled with the impact and a shower of saliva exploded from his mouth. His skull seemed to vibrate like a church bell. It was several seconds before he was able to jump up, ready to fend off another attack.

He could see now that he had fallen into a large circular pit. It was about fifty metres across and Jimmy was crouched at one edge. A faint pillar of light filtered down from where he had fallen. It was bolstered by the blue haze of his night-vision. Jimmy felt lucky when he saw that he hadn't fallen too far – only about fifteen metres.

It looked like this pit hadn't been caused by any explosion, but was part of the mining operation. The floor was rough clay and the wall was one huge circle of concrete breeze blocks, broken by gaping holes the size of buses. That told him this was just the first layer of whatever underground exploration was going on. Each hole was an entry point into the network of tunnels.

In the centre of the pit was a column of chains leading right up to the roof of the building, and on every side was a battery of huge drills. The only thing Jimmy had ever seen like them before were forklift trucks, except these had giant drills instead of forks. They looked like a small herd of metal elephants on wheels. Their trunks pointed in all directions – some aimed into the tunnel entrances, some poking out of them. Others had swivelled into awkward angles, as if they were sleeping.

Each of the drill bits was coated in clay as well as ash from the fires. Jimmy reckoned that in clear light they would have been orange and black, but with his night-vision they were blueish. At the base of each, where it joined its vehicle, was a large silver drill plate – a circle the driver would just be able to peek over. Only the very points of the drills gleamed silver in the half-light. It was like they were waiting for a giant dentist to come along and give Earth a set of teeth.

Then above them, Jimmy caught sight of a silhouette

clambering higher on the chains. He dashed across the clay to catch up, ducking between the machines, but as soon as the figure reached the scaffolding above the pit, the chains retracted swiftly towards the surface. Jimmy leapt forwards, his arm outstretched. The end of the longest chain slipped between his thumb and fingertips. He hit the ground with a bump and a face full of clay.

Immediately there was the noise of a motor. The grating sound sent a shiver through Jimmy as if his vertebrae themselves were scraping against each other. He knew exactly what it had to be, but refused to believe it. He rolled on to his back to see it: the drill on one of the machines was spinning furiously. It flung clay into two huge arcs, which fell on either side like sparks from a Catherine wheel. But Jimmy couldn't take his eyes off the tip of the drill. Centimetre by centimetre, it adjusted until it was pointing directly at the centre of Jimmy's forehead.

Then that noise multiplied. One by one, every drill started whizzing round and they all turned on their wheels to face Jimmy. Jimmy clambered to his feet and spun full circle. He was surrounded. He dashed for the only opening he could see in the line of drills. But before he'd taken two steps, the machines repositioned to close the gap. How could they be so well co-ordinated without drivers?

Jimmy skidded to a halt and doubled back. On the other side of the circle he saw another chance to break out. He dived for it, but the machines weren't just big, they were highly manoeuvrable. Two of them twisted inwards, mirror images of each other, dipping their drill points to precisely the spot that Jimmy was aiming for. He slid across the clay on his back, unable to stop himself. At last he slammed his elbows into the ground to push himself upright, just in time. Then he kicked with his heels to throw himself over the top of the spinning metal.

He thought he was out of the circle, but two more machines quickly looped round to cover their team-mates. Jimmy silently cursed the shadow above him. He knew that was the person controlling these things, trying to drill him into a slice of cheese. But why? Who was it?

Jimmy ducked and dived between the drills. They swung over his head and beneath his jumps with such rapidity that the swishing of the air sounded like the propellers of a small plane. They stabbed at his head and his body with the speed and force of automated battering rams. Whenever Jimmy had the chance he ran for an opening, but another machine was always there to cut him off.

It felt almost as if the machines themselves had minds. They were a team of murderous bullies. Their motors started to sound like laughs. Leaping and dodging for his life, Jimmy wondered whether a tiny part of the drills' programming was human. Then, with panic, he realised that if these machines *could* think, they'd probably wonder whether any part of *his* programming was human.

The breath was gone from his chest. His limbs were pumping with reserves of strength he didn't know he could call on. He wished the machines would stay still for a moment to give him a chance to dash for the walls of the pit and climb out. That gave him an idea.

Jimmy fell to the ground and hesitated there for a fraction of a second. He saw two drills spinning towards him like vultures descending on a carcass. The first stabbed at his head. Jimmy twisted his neck at the last instant. The drill plunged into the clay. As it kept spinning, it pulled itself deeper and deeper. Its own power was working against it now. Jimmy knew the only way it could pull out was if the person controlling it reversed the direction of the spin. And that would take a moment of extra care. Why bother when there were so many other drills still circling around the target?

Jimmy waited right next to the submerged drill bit. Clay slammed into his cheek and he could hear the rotations of the drill like an animal's scream. To his delight, the next machine took the bait. It charged at him. Jimmy waited as long as he dared, then dodged.

The second drill missed Jimmy's head by a hair, but connected perfectly with the first machine. With both drill bits spinning at maximum rpm, there was a piercing screech and a pounding *CLACK-CLACK-CLACK-CLACK*. A fountain of clay erupted all the way up to the surface.

Both machines were hurled upwards. They flew in opposite directions and smashed against opposite walls of the pit. For a moment, the other drills stopped. Jimmy took his chance while the drill operator was distracted. He sprinted for the edge, ready to climb. He didn't have much of a head start, but he was convinced he could make it.

Then he heard the dreadful sound of ten massive drilling machines starting up again. They were chasing him down. How could they move so fast? Jimmy couldn't understand his bad luck. Surely no drills in the world were designed to move at 50 kilometres an hour?

The wall was so close now. Jimmy could leap for it, but he knew that even then he didn't have time to climb out of reach of the machines. He would be drilled right through and pinned to the concrete. Instead he cut away at the final moment, diving into the protection of one of the tunnels.

He pushed himself up against the side of the tunnel, desperate not to be seen. From the scaffolding above, it would take a few seconds to work out where Jimmy had disappeared to. And at least one of the drills probably had its nose stuck in the wall by now.

If only he could slip out of his hiding place and stay unseen. He could already feel the tips of his fingers tingling, still fighting the remnants of frostbite, preparing to dig into the wall as hard and as fast as they ever could. He listened for the movements of the drills outside his tunnel. What were they doing? Why were they so quiet?

Then suddenly the opening of the tunnel went black.

Jimmy didn't even wait to see what had cut off the light. He could hear it. He ran down the tunnel at full speed, hoping frantically that the rougher terrain would slow down the drilling machine behind him. He glanced over his shoulder. His night-vision surged up a notch to show him as much as possible, but the detail didn't matter. All Jimmy cared about was the blurred tip of the massive drill looming towards him and the shadowy figure that had now appeared on top of the machine to drive it down the tunnel manually.

There'd better be another way out of here, thought Jimmy.

15 CHASE YOUR SHADOW

A floodlight on the front of the drill burst on. The white light was intense and urged Jimmy's body to respond with pure speed. He hurtled down the tunnel, his boots pounding the clay. He could hear the drill catching up on him. As they chased deeper, the walls of the tunnel closed. He could see his own shadow ahead of him, stretching out several metres deeper into the tunnel. It leapt and darted as he did, and gave him something to chase.

Jimmy's mind was whizzing as fast as the drill bit behind his head. Who was this person so desperate to kill him? The question was pushed out of his mind when he sprinted round the next bend. Suddenly he was face to face with a drill that made the one behind him look like an electric toothbrush.

Its central prong was as thick as a pillar box and around it were hundreds of smaller blades. It filled the entire tunnel and whirled like a tornado. And it moved towards Jimmy. He was trapped.

How had the person behind him managed to activate this huge borer and turn it around to attack him? Or had they done it as soon as they saw which tunnel he was trying to hide down? It didn't matter. Jimmy had no choice. He slid to a stop just in time and pushed off again to head back up the tunnel – but the smaller drill had already reached him.

Jimmy was trapped. He squeezed himself up against the wall of the tunnel, the cold of the clay chilling his spine. The drill from the smaller machine hit its larger brother with a screech that nearly burst Jimmy's eardrums. Massive sparks spat out from the connection. Some landed on Jimmy's face and hands, scorching his skin. Still the two drills edged closer to each other.

In seconds Jimmy would be mangled by two colliding blocks of sharp, spinning steel. But Jimmy's programming was spinning too, and his determination was made of steel just as strong. He frantically clawed at the clay behind his back, scraping with his heels at the same time. Just a small indent would be enough.

Jimmy felt his whole body trembling with terror, but his actions seemed controlled by a thick layer of assurance. It was like being hot and cold at the same time. Jimmy realised that his body wasn't quaking with terror. It was wriggling with all its force to carve out a hollow for him in the side of the tunnel. He had become his own drilling machine.

If he could create enough space fast enough, the two metal slabs could meet each other without making a minced Jimmy sandwich. He pushed all his strength into the clay. The drill bit of the smaller machine was crumpling now under the immense pressure of the larger device. The steel glowed orange, then red. The heat blasted into Jimmy. *I'll be cooked before I'm crushed*, he thought.

Then suddenly the drill bit snapped free from its holding. The two machines clapped together like lethal cymbals. Jimmy's reflexes were faster than an electric current. He jerked backwards, pushing all the air from his lungs and stretching his spine to flatten himself against the side wall as much as was physically possible. The steel edge of the drill plate rushed past his face and scraped the skin from the end of his nose.

Jimmy twisted himself free from his clay tomb. He wriggled past the body of the smaller drilling machine and forced himself out, back into the upper section of the tunnel. As soon as he was free, he ran. He felt the heat on his back growing. The noise was incredible – a screeching and whining like a pack of wolves going up in flames.

Jimmy glanced behind him, still running at full pelt. The two machines were a molten mess of sparks and shards of steel. And diving from the chaos was that silhouette – the slim figure with the streak of long black hair. The figure landed with a graceful roll and at last Jimmy caught sight of a face, highlighted by the sparks further down the tunnel.

A girl. Young, but older than Jimmy. Just as determined.

She raced away from the drills. With the intense flickering light behind her, Jimmy could just make out the strong line of her cheek and the deep black of her skin. He kept running, but couldn't help checking over his shoulder to watch how she moved and what decisions she made. Any little thing was a clue to her identity and her motivation.

Then Jimmy saw her trip. As it grew hotter, the clay around them became less stable. The footing wasn't secure and the girl had faltered. Now she was face down in the dirt.

Then: *BOOM!*

Jimmy thought the noise might crack open his skull. The heat of the drills, the sparks and the fuel driving them together – it was a highly volatile combination. A black globe ballooned up the tunnel towards them. The heat travelled even faster, nearly knocking Jimmy off his feet. But the girl was already down.

In that instant, a million connections seemed to burn in Jimmy's head. Each one came with an explosion of contradictory emotions. This young girl had gone to extreme lengths to kill him – and she'd done extraordinary things. Zafi's face flashed into his mind. Then Mitchell's. The other assassins. Was it possible that this girl...?

Suddenly Jimmy didn't care who she worked for. He didn't care that seconds before she had been trying to rip him to pieces. If she was like him...

Jimmy's muscles jerked to change direction. He leapt back down the tunnel, head first, and reached out. He snatched the girl by the hair and snapped his arm up, pulling her to him.

Locked together, they rolled to the edge of the tunnel. A metal spike half a metre long stabbed into the ground at the point where the girl's neck had been and stuck there like a flagpole. For a second, Jimmy could see nothing but the girl's eyes. They stared back at him, reflecting the orange and red of the explosion in deep brown. Then together they scrambled to their feet and sprinted for the surface. A ball of flame chased at their backs and clay rained down on their heels. The tunnel was collapsing behind them.

Jimmy made it back to the pit first. He threw himself on the ground, panting hard, and held his face in his hands. The girl burst out of the tunnel after him and collapsed against the side of the pit, her hands on her knees.

After they had taken just three breaths, they turned to each other and, in perfect synchrony, shouted, "Who are you?"

16 MARLA RAKUBIAN

Jimmy's voice and the girl's echoed off the concrete walls of the pit. They backed away from each other to opposite sides of the circle, both totally alert for an attack. Jimmy considered making a run for it – he could climb out and easily get away, but he didn't want to. Not yet. He had to know why this girl was trying to kill him.

"If you drill holes in strangers, I'd hate to see your enemies," he said. His throat was so dry that his voice felt like a dagger. When the girl answered she surprised Jimmy with the deep sweetness of her voice and the round accent on her vowels – every "oo" sounded like an "ow".

"I did believe you to be from the French army, or British, or German, or..."

"What?" Jimmy blasted. "Does it look like I'm in the army?" He dabbed blood from the end of his nose and went through the rest of his body in his head to work out which bits were seriously damaged and which just hurt like hell.

"Actually, yes," replied the girl. "Examine yourself."

Jimmy didn't need to. He could feel the army boots bruising his feet and he hadn't forgotten that underneath the layer of clay he was in desert camouflage. The coating of blood and sweat all over his body completed the picture.

"But I'm twelve," Jimmy insisted.

"So what?" shrugged the girl. She was obviously in at least as much pain as Jimmy, but was trying to hide it. "I am sixteen and I have been fighting for as long as I can remember. It is what I do."

"It's what I do too," Jimmy mumbled. Then louder, "But not in the army." His voice trembled with doubt. The whole situation was so strange he couldn't be sure of anything. If this girl had been fighting for so long, which Secret Service organisation had trained her? *Or designed her*, he thought nervously. The questions in his head felt so important they even distracted from the pain that throbbed all the way through him.

"Why not in the army?" asked the girl.

Jimmy was fascinated by the way she spoke and tried to watch how she moved, for clues. She was about a head taller than Jimmy, and slim; her long black hair reached her waist. Her combat trousers and thin shirt hugged her figure. Jimmy could see she was made of nothing but perfectly lean muscle. Was she 100 per cent human, or something else?

He remembered that appearances can be misleading:

anybody looking at him would probably think that he was a normal human.

"Age means nothing if you have something to fight for," the girl continued. "All over the world there are young soldiers. Some fight for a cause; some are forced to fight. And some fight with me here. I mean..." She tailed off and froze for a second, with her arm half raised towards the bloodshed outside.

Jimmy wanted to say something, but what could he say? And in a way she was right – Jimmy had never signed up to be in any army, but he'd been created by British military intelligence and now he was here acting on instructions from French military intelligence. *One tattoo and I'd be a soldier*, he realised.

There was still a rumbling from the tunnel they'd escaped from, as the earth settled into place, but soon it died and there was a long silence. Jimmy and the girl threw glances across the pit, each checking that the other wasn't going to attack. Both were fully aware that Jimmy had just saved the girl's life. Both were trying to work out exactly why.

From the little the girl had told him, Jimmy was beginning to suspect that she was probably fully human after all. The chance of her being another assassin was just too small. And yet her strength, skills and speed had been incredible...

"How did you know how to use these drills?" Jimmy asked eventually.

"I have been studying this place all my life. This is my country. Which means these should be our resources – not French. My community is…" She stopped herself again and all the life in her eyes seemed to die.

Jimmy couldn't see any way of talking to her without bringing back all the horror of what must have happened. He could see something about her – perhaps it was the way her shoulders slumped forwards, or the down-turned corners of her mouth. It told him that she had lost people she cared about.

"How did you survive the missile blasts?" Jimmy asked, before he realised it was another tactless question.

"I have not survived," she replied.

"What?" Jimmy tried to laugh, but it came out more like he was choking.

"I am dead."

Jimmy wasn't in the mood for jokes, but the expression on the girl's face told him she wasn't trying to be funny. Perhaps the confusion was because of her strange English.

"The blast did not kill me," she explained, "because I was lucky. But the radiation will. I may as well already be dead." Suddenly panic seemed to attack her. "You should get out now!" she yelled. "There is actinium here. The second missile…"

"I know," Jimmy reassured her. "The heat might have ionised it. But—"

"It did – I have seen the readings in the control

centre," she gabbled. "But you perhaps might still survive. You are not here as long as me and we are far from the depository. You are perhaps lucky, I—"

"So a minute ago you wanted to drill through my skull, but now you're trying to save my life?"

The girl shrugged. "You saved mine," she said softly. "In the tunnel. It means you are not French or British."

Jimmy felt a laugh coming, but the pain in his ribs killed it.

"I am sorry," said the girl. "I was wrong to attack you." She looked around, everywhere but at Jimmy. Where had all that self-confidence gone? "I am Marla Rakubian," she said, pulling herself up to stand tall again.

"Marla," replied Jimmy, "I'm Jimmy and I need you to take me to the actinium."

"What?" Her eyes expanded into huge circles.

"It's complicated. But can you take me there?"

"No," Marla insisted. "You are already too exposed. You will definitely get ill, but you might still survive. If I take you closer the damage will be worse. You will die. It is too late for me, but you can still survive if you leave now."

Jimmy didn't listen to what Marla was saying. He was already climbing out of the pit. He saw for the first time that the pit was the centrepiece of a large warehouse. The space at ground level was filled with more drills, more machinery, scaffolding and stacks of equipment that reached to the ceiling, high above him.

One thing in particular caught his eye: the control deck

Marla had used to send the drills to attack him. It set off a chain of thought in his head that ran with the force of an express train. He pictured the drills hurtling down the tunnels, all at the same time. He imagined the heat and the sparks, and the fuel in their engines. He heard the rumble of the shock waves through the ground below.

I could collapse the whole tunnel complex, he thought, without realising he was even thinking it. *Dozens of small explosions. A chain reaction. Destroy everything...*

He clutched his head in his hands. "No!" he screamed. His heart was pounding. *Do this properly*, he ordered himself. *Don't waste this chance.* "Make them listen!" he shouted.

Marla had been talking all this time, but she stopped at Jimmy's outburst. Jimmy was motionless except for the heaving of his chest. Then slowly he lifted his head and looked at Marla. She stared back.

"Take me to the actinium," Jimmy insisted. There was a long pause. Thousands of thoughts were fighting each other in his head. Finally he drew himself to his full height and sighed. "I suppose I should explain a couple of things about myself..."

Helen, Georgie and Felix were being housed by NJ7 in a council estate in Chalk Farm, North London. And they were being watched. The place was perfect from a surveillance point of view – a ground-floor flat with no back door. And there was a raised walkway separating the front door from the road, so nobody could run straight into a car without being seen first – and shot if necessary.

Zafi kept her head down, with her hair tucked up inside her cap, but her eyes took in everything as she swept along the street. The more she saw, the more she was impressed by NJ7. They'd chosen the perfect spot: the corner of a busy junction, with no tall buildings or trees to interrupt the views along the four roads that converged here. Hardly realising she was doing it, Zafi counted the buses and noted how often they pulled up at the bus stop in front of the building.

Directly opposite the estate was the perfect surveillance base – the Gregor's Elbow pub. The paint-work was chipped and faded, and the pavement all around it was carpeted with pigeon droppings. But more importantly, it wasn't too busy and wasn't too deserted. Nobody would notice the extra coming and going. Nobody but Zafi, that is.

She glanced up at the flats above the pub. There were boards on the windows, but a chink of light crept through on the second floor. Were there NJ7 agents inside, huddled over video equipment? There wasn't any need for them to be on site – it was quite simple to have all the surveillance data transmitted to NJ7 Headquarters, in real time. *They want agents here*, Zafi realised. *In case Viggo comes. Or even Jimmy.*

She hurried past the block and along Malden Road,

one of the adjacent streets. She couldn't help smiling. Thanks to Jimmy blowing up the oil rig – and wearing a mask while he did it – NJ7 thought she was dead too. It made her task much easier.

But she immediately tensed up again. She couldn't let herself be seen, or have her face caught on camera. And now she started to spot agents everywhere. They weren't just relying on their cameras and microphones. Zafi picked out a plasterer in one of the houses. He was wearing jeans that fitted him too well. There was also a parking attendant who wasn't issuing any tickets. To Zafi, they couldn't have been more obviously NJ7 agents if they'd had green stripes stamped on their foreheads.

Then finally Zafi saw something that NJ7 hadn't been able to control. Rolling towards her in a straggling bunch were half a dozen boys. One was definitely older than her – he must have been at least sixteen. He was dragging his bike along with him. The others looked between thirteen and fifteen. But Zafi wasn't bothered about age. Her eye homed in on the shortest: a pale boy, not much taller than Zafi, swaggering across the pavement with a grim smirk on his face, barely visible beneath the huge hoodie that cloaked his whole head. *Perfect*, thought Zafi.

By the time this gang had noticed Zafi, she already knew exactly what they were going to say to each other and what they were going to do to her. Or try to do. Her ear picked up their conversation at a distance, while her instincts read their body language. Then, when most people would have done their best to get out of the way, Zafi made sure she walked straight into them.

"Hey," grunted the boy with the bike.

Zafi immediately turned to him, grimaced and puffed out her chest. "You asking for it?" she barked, perfectly imitating the London accent and the rhythm of the boy's speech.

"You what?" His face was a mixture of confusion and amusement. He looked round at his mates and gave an awkward laugh. Zafi held herself totally still, staring up at the boy, who was at least 50 centimetres taller than her.

"Get out my way," the boy ordered, his face returning to his usual sneer.

"It's *my* way," Zafi snapped back. "But I'll let you walk on it."

The boy ignored her and shoved his way past, jerking his elbow at Zafi's face. She calmly swayed backwards to avoid it and let him walk on. But the others were eyeing her, half amused, half nervous.

"Sorry, mate," Zafi called out after him. "Can't talk to you now, I've got to go and fix your mum's face."

The boy whipped round, scarlet with shock. "You wh—?"

"Calm down," Zafi cut him off. "I'll try your sister's too, but I'm a plastic surgeon, not a miracle worker."

The boy lurched at Zafi, stumbling over his bike, but Zafi darted away with ease, slipping between two houses to escape. She could hear the others yelling and chasing after her, but it didn't matter. There was no way they could catch her. *You'll see me later*, she thought, already concentrating on the next stage of her plan and heading for the nearest grocery shop.

Half an hour later she was climbing up the fire escape at the back of the Gregor's Elbow. She was so light on her feet she barely made a sound. When she reached the roof she sprinted across to the other side of the building and lay down on her front, ready to watch.

She had a perfect view of the flat where Helen, Georgie and Felix were living. She knew that soon Georgie and Felix would be coming home from school, so she waited. Meanwhile she turned her attention to the transmission equipment on the roof next to her.

NJ7 had set up a sophisticated network of receivers – black metal boxes of various sizes, wires and small dishes, all pointed straight at the flat's front door. Without touching the equipment, Zafi made a quick analysis of the structure of the system and waved her hands around the various parts, assessing which were warm and which were cold. She was relying on the fact that all the visual and aural feeds from the whole operation came to this unit, before being relayed downstairs to the flat, where the agents could watch and listen.

From her examination it looked like she was right, but she knew that almost anything she did to tamper with the unit would backfire. It was probably alarmed, and in any case, it would be immediately obvious to all of the agents in the area that somebody was on the roof disrupting their equipment.

So instead of cutting the wires, magnetising the boxes or even nudging the dishes off target, Zafi reached into her jacket pocket and pulled out a large wedge of brie. She ripped the plastic from the cheese with violent energy because the packaging was covered in Union Jacks – the corner shop she'd found had only sold British cheese. *English brie*, she thought. *Ridiculous*. Even the smell, which would usually have made her mouth water, turned her stomach.

She carefully laid the cheese at the heart of the network of electrical devices, right on top of the hottest of the metal cubes. That was all she needed to do. A few minutes later she spotted Felix and Georgie arriving home together. Shortly after that, Zafi saw the same gang of kids hanging about outside the estate. Everything was falling into place and by now the brie was melting into the receivers. *Just a little more*, Zafi thought, delighted that the stench of cheese was getting stronger.

At last the first pigeon flapped down. *Time to go*, thought Zafi. She sprinted back across the roof and down the fire escape. How long would it be before the glutinous coating of cheese disrupted the NJ7 surveillance? And when an NJ7 engineer or agent came to investigate, there'd be a flock of feasting pigeons pecking the wiring to tatters. Too bad she wasn't going to be around to see the result of her handiwork.

Keeping her head low, she charged across the road. There was no time to waste. Who knew how long it would be before NJ7 solved their surveillance blackout? Zafi headed straight for the raised walkway outside Felix's front door. The boy with the bike saw her straight away. Then his mates did too and they moved like a pack of dogs to cut her off.

Not yet, thought Zafi, counting down the seconds in her head – *ten, nine, eight...* The boys caught up with her a couple of metres from the front door of the flat. *Do nothing*, Zafi could hear in her head. *Seven, six, five...* In the corner of her eye she could see the plasterer across the road, watching. She turned and saw the parking attendant bending his head for a better look at what was going on.

BAM!

A fist slammed into the back of Zafi's head. She stumbled forwards, thinking her eyes might fall out of their sockets, but still counting: *four, three, two...* She heard the cackles of the group of boys. Then came a knee, punching into her nose. Zafi jerked her head backwards, absorbing the force of the blow, but still didn't fight back.

The seconds ran out. She glanced back towards the road. There it was – the next bus. It pulled up at the bus stop. Lightning fast, Zafi's eyes flicked in the direction of the plasterer, then the parking attendant – the bus cut off their sightlines. Zafi exploded into action.

She kicked both legs up behind her, flipping on to her

hands. Her feet connected with two of the boys, instantly flattening them. Zafi completed the flip, her heels crunching into another boy's head on the way down. The oldest boy reached for a knife in his pocket; Zafi had already read the contour of his jeans. She swivelled on the ball of her foot, snatched the bike and twisted the handlebars. The front wheel chopped into the boy's knee. He crumpled. Zafi snapped the handlebars the other way to send the back of the wheel into his groin.

That was all it took. As one, the boys staggered away from her, desperate to escape. Before they could run, Zafi grabbed the smallest by the shoulder. In one movement, she slapped his arms above his head and hauled off his hoodie. Just as the bus closed its doors, Zafi planted her cap on the boy's head, spun him round and pushed him away to follow his friends. She pulled on the hoodie the exact moment that the bus pulled away, then she went for the front door of the flat.

While three NJ7 agents were arguing with a pest control expert and an engineer on the top of the Gregor's Elbow pub about how to clean their surveillance equipment of cheese and pigeons, an undercover plasterer and a fake parking attendant saw a young boy in a hoodie waiting at the front door of the flat they were watching.

They both shook their heads in disappointment – they'd seen the gangs hanging around and now it looked like Felix and Georgie had fallen in with the wrong crowd. There was nothing worth reporting though. They even thought nothing of the massive grin on Felix's face when he answered the door.

Contact had been made.

17 STONE IN A BARREL

The PVP 360 was proving to be a poor operations centre for Uno Stovorsky. With the roof up there was limited communications access, but without that roof the desert sun was unbearable. To compromise, he'd had to instruct his driver to pull back to the nearest town, Tlon, where they were parked in the shade of a fading Coca-Cola billboard.

Then a message buzzed on his phone. It was from Zafi.

"Good news," said Stovorsky, sitting in the passenger seat, but with the door open and his feet planted on the ground. "Our London operative has made contact." Despite the sweat dripping down his neck and the flies dancing round his bald spot, he sounded relatively satisfied.

"Do you want me to radio Jimmy?" asked the driver, a young soldier. "He'll be pleased." Stovorsky huffed and shook his head. "Are you contacting Zafi then?" the younger man continued, peering over Stovorsky's shoulder, trying to get a look at the computer. "She'll wait with the subjects until you issue the extract and secure order."

Stovorsky shrugged. "It might suit us more," he explained, "if Jimmy thinks his family is still in danger, for now."

"You don't trust Jimmy?"

"Do you?" Stovorsky looked up for the first time and gave the driver an examining stare. "But that's not what matters," he said casually, returning to his laptop. "We need to keep him in the dark for now because *he* doesn't trust *me*."

"I don't get it."

Stovorsky sighed. "Jimmy thinks that by showing NJ7 he's alive he can somehow stop Britain attacking France." His fingers tapped away at the keys while he spoke. "But if he turns up NJ7 will immediately use his family against him. So as long as Jimmy thinks his family is still being looked after by NJ7, he'll stay out of sight and do this job for us." He looked up again, a business-like calm on his face. "As soon as he's secured the mine, I'll give him the good news."

Jimmy kept his head down and his eyes firmly on his feet while he stomped through the mine compound alongside Marla. It was almost as if he was trying to keep pace with the words rushing off his tongue.

At last he ran out of steam. He knew he had left out so much, but couldn't bring himself to say any more. He looked across at Marla and waited anxiously for her reaction. He couldn't remember the last time he'd had to tell anybody so much about himself. Hearing it aloud felt as foreign as the desert setting, and as frightening as the burnt-out shells of the mine buildings and the lumps in the ground where the wind was quickly covering bodies with sand.

Marla nodded slowly. "There is a man you should meet," she said.

"Is that it?" Jimmy gawped. He wasn't sure what reaction he'd been expecting, but such a calm one shocked him. "I just told you I'm 38 per cent human and that's all you can say?"

"What do you want me to do?" Marla asked. "Cry? Shout? Pretend I do not believe you?"

"Yeah, I mean, I don't know." Jimmy could hear agitation in his voice and he felt anger in his chest. *Relax*, he told himself. *She's helping*. But the thoughts came with a rush of suspicion. "How do you speak English so well?"

"English radio," she replied. "We listen to the BBC."

That explained her strange way of talking, thought Jimmy. "What do you mean, 'we'?" he asked.

Marla froze up. "You want *my* life story now?" she snapped.

Jimmy missed a step to stay level with her. "I'm sorry..." he stammered. "I just..."

"They are dead!" she screamed. "You cannot see?" She started crying, but kept her body totally controlled.

"My whole town... We are fighting for years to control this place. That is my life story. Now I am here and I am the only one left. The others I killed!"

"How could you have—?" Jimmy tried to calm her down, but she cut him off.

"We came in after the first missile," she said, her eyes glazing over. "I went straight to the block that was hit. There." She pointed behind them, where the smoke was thickest. Jimmy couldn't see anything through it.

"I led my unit into the fire," Marla went on. "We had to find out why the British had targeted that block. I thought there had to be something in there and if we were quick we could take it. Some piece of machinery, or some information at least."

"You did the right thing," Jimmy said in his most soothing voice. He held up his hands and edged closer to her. She reacted with an explosion of rage.

"It was the canteen block!" she yelled. Jimmy jumped back.

"But it wasn't the fire that killed them – it was the second British missile, wasn't it?"

"We saw it coming." Marla was trembling slightly now. "I never thought they will hit the same building twice. I ordered the others to stay where they are – to keep them safe, you know?" She looked up at Jimmy for the first time and he saw the fury in her expression, mixed with desperation.

"I ran into the open to see which building the missile

142

was heading for. I thought..." She tailed off and stood there, her heart almost visibly crumpling.

Jimmy stayed silent. He had never seen any face so vulnerable. How could he ever have doubted that this girl was anything but totally human? He wanted to tell her she'd done the right thing. She'd been trying to protect the people fighting alongside her. She'd made logical decisions, he wanted to say. Jimmy couldn't imagine how hard those decisions must be without that genetic force inside, making them for her. But he knew that didn't matter to Marla. Logic wouldn't bring back her friends.

Should he tell her how much, despite everything, he longed to know what it was like to have to make those judgements himself? As a normal, 100 per cent human?

Suddenly the nervous silence was cracked by a blast from Jimmy's radio. The words came in French, but Jimmy hardly noticed the difference in language now.

"Are you there, Jimmy?" It was Stovorsky.

Jimmy unclipped the radio from his belt and was about to speak into it when he caught sight of Marla's reaction.

Jimmy had explained everything about himself, but he'd been a little hazy about the fact that he had been sent here by the French so they could take over the mine again. Now, if Marla's face was anything to go by, it was becoming clearer. She'd obviously worked it out. To her, Jimmy was suddenly an enemy again. She was ready to kill. The muscles in her shoulders tensed and she set her legs ready to pounce.

"Stop," Jimmy told her, as calmly as he could. "It's not what you think."

"You are using me," she whispered. "I should have guessed the French would send an English boy to trick us. They must be desperate."

The radio crackled again. *"Jimmy,"* came the voice. *"Do you copy?"*

Jimmy's finger hovered over the controls, his mouth five centimetres from the device, but he didn't respond. "I'm not working for them," he insisted. "They just think I am." Marla's face didn't change. "I'm working for me. For my family. I'm going to make them do what I say."

At last he squeezed his thumb against the large white button on the side of his radio.

"I copy," he said, slipping into French without thinking about it. He kept his eyes firmly on Marla, who was still watching suspiciously. "There's nothing here but body parts. But everything is so messed up it's hard to find my way around." He glared at Marla.

Stovorsky replied, but Jimmy wasn't paying attention. He and Marla were having a tough conversation – without saying a word. Had either of them done enough to show they could trust the other? At last Marla dipped her head to one side and narrowed her eyes. Jimmy felt a sudden stab in his chest – the look reminded him of Georgie.

He smiled a flat smile and Marla's expression softened. Then she jerked her thumb at the next building, a long, low concrete bunker, and together they jogged towards the entrance.

"How are my mum and my sister?" Jimmy asked softly, into the radio.

Stovorsky replied straight away. "We're working on it."

Jimmy put his radio back on his belt and entered the bunker. It felt like a rabbit warren. He walked cautiously down the dark staircase, followed by Marla. Just when he thought the steps might carry him down to the centre of the Earth, he came to a reinforced metal door that was slightly ajar

"Actinium," Marla whispered. "Are you ready?"

Jimmy pushed the door open and went through cautiously. The light was dim, but his eyes adjusted quickly. The bunker looked like a large science lab, but it was in disarray: broken glass, chairs tipped over, laptops smashed.

"They left in a hurry," Marla explained.

"Not too much of a hurry to destroy the place first." Jimmy circled the room, inspecting the vandalism. "If they didn't want anybody using the actinium, why didn't they just take it with them?"

The middle of the room was dominated by a huge floor-to-ceiling cylinder. It was made of the fattest layer of glass Jimmy had ever seen. It must have been at least thirty centimetres thick. He moved towards it, scrutinising the bolts and steel brackets that held it in place, because inside this unique cabinet, on a small shelf, stood a single silver canister, about fifty centimetres high. The only way to reach it was through plastic glove holes hidden behind a lead screen, which was also bolted in place.

Jimmy didn't need a degree in nuclear physics to work out that the canister contained the actinium.

"They did not have time to take it with them," Marla explained. "The British deliberately took them by surprise. The actinium is most delicate. There are procedures for removing it. It takes hours. They make, um..." She struggled for the words. "...vacuum? ...de... contamination?" She pointed to a line of large silver suitcases, some of which had obviously been used to smash the computers and other instruments. "Lead-lined," Marla explained. "But to put the actinium into it needs proper equipment and many scientists. And now, without even these..."

She kicked at a pile of half-burned rags and melted plastic.

"They set light to their hazmat suits?" Jimmy muttered.

Before Marla could react, Jimmy grabbed the handle of one of the lead suitcases and slammed it into the glass cabinet. Marla jumped back with a cry of shock. Small cracks shot through the glass. Jimmy heaved the suitcase round again and smashed it into the cabinet a second time.

The suitcase should have been incredibly heavy, but Jimmy's arm muscles locked and swung it with huge momentum. His blows came harder and faster. He felt the sweat forming on his neck and grunted with the strain, but kept going.

For the first minute, Marla could only stand by in amazement. But then, to Jimmy's surprise, she heaved on the handle of a second suitcase and joined in. She couldn't match Jimmy's force or speed, but every impact counted. Together they attacked the same single point in the glass.

At last they broke through. Jimmy didn't hesitate. He brushed away the shards from the edges of the hole in the glass and pulled out the canister. It was nowhere near as heavy as he had been expecting. Was there really so little actinium in the world? He was beginning to realise just how valuable this mineral must be.

"So this is it?" he asked. "The whole mine – for this?"

"No," Marla replied, still panting. "There is another bunker for the uranium. Bigger than this one. They find more of it. Then it goes to the dock."

Jimmy planted a hand on the lid of the canister, ready to open it, but his arm muscles jerked awkwardly. His heart tripled its pace. He suddenly felt the urge to run out and as far from Mutam-ul-it as possible. Was that his assassin instinct or his human fear? The two melded together until he couldn't feel the boundary between them. *It's OK*, he reminded himself, breathing deeply to settle the doubt that swirled through his muscles.

He glanced up at Marla. The mixture of fear and

respect in her expression was obvious. It sent an unexpected shiver of pride through Jimmy. Before he could have any more second thoughts, he gave the canister lid a sharp twist. It opened with a click and Jimmy's face was lit up by a pale blue light.

Here it was: a small mound of stones at the bottom of the canister that looked like they contained tiny light bulbs. There was no smell – just the magical appearance and a waft of warmth. He felt like some kind of demon or a crazy scientist in an old horror film. Despite all of the fear, the one thought he couldn't get out of his head was: *Felix would love this.*

At last he was able to tear his eyes from the mineral, and when he smiled at Marla, he saw the wonder on her face as well.

Jimmy quickly opened the lead-lined suitcase and poured in the stones as carefully as he could. His hands were trembling. And were they also turning red? *It'll fade*, Jimmy told himself. *It can't affect me.* Then he slammed down the lid of the suitcase, shutting off the blue light. He grinned at Marla, an unnatural confidence surging through him.

"What are you going to do with it?" she asked. "Sell it? I know people who would pay millions for this. Even small amounts of black market uranium have funded my people for years – and that is just uranium. But this..."

Jimmy didn't answer. He wasn't even listening. Instead he grabbed the radio from his belt and mashed the button on the side.

"You there, Stovorsky?" he barked. A second later came the reply.

"Go ahead, Jimmy." The reception was crackly because they were so far underground, but the words were still clear.

"Listen carefully," Jimmy snapped into the radio. "You've got twelve hours to radio me with evidence that my mum, my sister and Felix are safe. After that, I destroy this mine and everything around it."

Immediately he switched the radio off and thrust it into Marla's hand. "Take this," he ordered. "I don't want them tracking me."

"But what are you doing?"

"I told you," said Jimmy. "I'm working for me, not them. I have to make certain the French are going to do what I ask. The only way to do that is to have something they value. Something they really value."

He lifted the suitcase slightly. Marla backed away instinctively, even though the actinium was insulated now.

"They told me this actinium was valuable to them," he went on. "And I plan to make it even more valuable. They'll have no choice but to help me."

Together they started back up the stairs. At the top Jimmy hesitated. "You want to help me, right?" he whispered.

"I want to help you if you are against the French," replied Marla.

"Meet me at midnight in the dock," Jimmy said

quickly. Through his mind flashed the plans of the Mutam-ul-it complex – dozens of images every second. He hadn't even realised while he'd been looking at Stovorsky's laptop that these diagrams would take root in his head so strongly. "At the fifth pier," he announced. Marla nodded. "Bring a balaclava. And paper clips. Lots of them. Oh, and transport. Something fast, but small…"

"Wait," said Marla. "Midnight? That is only seven hours."

"I know. Counting is one of my special powers."

Jimmy turned and pressed his hand on the door, but Marla stopped him.

"What if that man radios with what you asked for? What if they take your family out of danger?"

Jimmy hesitated for only a second, then, just as he burst out into daylight, he announced his decision. "They won't."

"Evidence?!" raged Stovorsky. "Twelve hours?! How dare he!" He jumped up and down next to the off-roader, not caring that he was stumbling in and out of the shade and the top of his head was getting burned.

"But it's OK," urged his driver, trying to remain calm. "Zafi can make them safe, then we'll let Jimmy know."

"But what if she can't? We're not Jimmy's personal family protection force, we're the French Secret Service!"

At last Stovorsky stopped jumping. There was an uneasy silence. Then he ripped off his raincoat and hurled it into the back seat. The sweat marks on his suit made him look like a balding, angry panda.

"Send a message to Zafi," he ordered. "Get that evidence. We can't risk the mine."

"Tell her to get Jimmy's family to safety?"

"No!" barked Stovorsky. "I don't care whether she actually does it – as long as we can give Jimmy some kind of proof. Whether it's real or not." He stared blankly at his laptop screen. "We can't risk the mine," he whispered.

After a moment of thought, he tapped at his laptop again. The only way they could watch Jimmy was through the satellite aerial feed to the computer. Stovorsky studied the images. They were amazingly detailed, but large areas were obscured by the smoke still billowing from the mine compound across the desert sky.

"Where are you, Jimmy?" said Stovorsky, his voice rising with frustration. Then he launched a violent attack at the flies round his head. "Jimmy!" he yelled, flapping wildly.

"Calm down!" pleaded the young soldier. "We can still control what he does."

"Control him?" said Stovorsky. "He's gone rogue. You don't control a rogue. You destroy it."

Jimmy deliberately aimed for the thickest areas of the smoke. He knew they'd give him the perfect protection from the satellite imagery. He marched through the compound. When he reached the perimeter he didn't stop. The wire fence was over twenty metres high, but even with the fingers of his right hand locked around the handle of the lead-lined suitcase, he scaled it in seconds.

On the other side he waited just a few seconds, trying to read the gusts of wind that came in off the ocean and carried the smoke over the desert in a dense plume. That was his escape – his way out of Mutam-ul-it while Stovorsky was watching him from above.

He chose a moment when the smog was at its thickest and advanced. He stood as straight and as tall as he could, consciously making every step exactly the same length. And he counted each stride. *One, two, three, four...*

18 22,000 PACES

"Georgie!" Felix yelled over his shoulder. "There's a French super-assassin here to murder us. What should I do?"

Zafi couldn't help laughing. "You're lucky NJ7 can't hear a word we're saying right now, thanks to a wedge of your disgusting English cheese and a flock of pigeons."

She moved quickly into the flat, shut the door firmly behind her and brushed past Felix.

"*My* cheese?" Felix asked. "Whatever. I knew all that, you big... weirdo."

Georgie ran into the hallway. When she saw Zafi she froze in shock. The last time they'd seen each other felt like a lifetime ago – Zafi had once been sent to persuade Jimmy to join the French Secret Service and she'd delivered the message a little too violently for Georgie to remember the meeting fondly.

"What are you doing here?" Georgie asked sharply.

"Where's your mum?" Zafi replied.

"She's out. She's looking for..." Georgie stopped

herself and pointed around the corners of the ceiling. "Can they...?"

"We've got about two minutes before NJ7 have their surveillance back. So talk fast then I'll tell you everything you need to know. After that you call me Rhys and pretend I'm here to hang out with you. I might even need to stay the night."

"Why *are* you here?" asked Georgie.

"Have you found my parents?" Felix cut in. "I knew you'd do it! The moustache man got in touch with you, didn't he?"

Zafi pushed the hoodie from her head. Her hair tumbled down round her shoulders and she turned to smile at Felix. "I'm sorry, Felix; 80 per cent of the time I have no clue what you're talking about."

"It's more like 95 per cent for the rest of us," Georgie chipped in.

"I don't mind," Zafi added. "You're still cute."

Felix's grin nearly burst the sides of his cheeks.

"Would you hurry up and explain, please?" Georgie insisted.

"I was sent here by Uno Stovorsky," said Zafi quickly. "I have to protect you. That's all I know. If we need to move out of here, I'll take care of it. So relax."

"Is it..." Georgie looked across at Felix and broke into a smile. "It might be because of your parents, or it might be Jimmy."

"I just follow my instructions," said Zafi with a shrug.

"He's coming back, isn't he?" Georgie asked, growing more and more agitated. "To stop Britain attacking France, right? I saw it on the news: Dad said... I mean, the Prime Minister said the French blew up that oil rig. But it was Jimmy, wasn't it?"

"Jimmy blew up an oil rig?" said Felix. "He must be having so much fun while we're..."

"Don't worry, Felix," Zafi cooed. "We can have fun too."

Felix's mouth dropped open.

"You are so cool," he gasped.

Georgie was still thinking aloud. "But if Jimmy *did* blow it up and he comes back to prove it wasn't the French, he'll be putting us in danger. So—"

"Time's up," Zafi announced. "Get to know Rhys." She quickly wrapped her hair into a bundle and stuffed it back into her hoodie, which she pulled over her head again. "What is there to do around here?"

...Twenty-one thousand, six hundred and ninety-seven, twenty-one thousand, six hundred and ninety-eight, twenty-one thousand, six hundred and ninety-nine...

Jimmy had been marching for over three hours. The protection of the smoke had long since disappeared. Instead there were now vultures over his head. The landscape had changed gradually from the patchy tufts of low grass near the mine, to arid wasteland, and now he was deep in the rolling sand dunes, constantly shifting in the wind. Jimmy felt as if the sun had built a cocoon of fire around him and he was condemned to walk through it until he was a flame himself. His skin was screaming for relief. His mouth was totally desiccated.

Every injury he had suffered in his short life was coming back to remind him of the original torture – his left leg, where it had once been through an industrial shredder; his neck where he'd once plunged his own tooth into his flesh to escape from a strangling; his hands and feet, where the extreme cold of the Pyrenees had frozen him; his ribs, his back, his shoulders... and the physical memory of every blow Mitchell and Zafi had ever planted on his body.

But at the same time he never lost that feeling that there was something inside him driving him on. It was like an engine fuelled by the heat, not damaged by it. He didn't realise it, but his DNA responded to the desert conditions by controlling the dilation of his blood capillaries, the angle of the hairs on his skin, the flow of sweat from his pores... all to lessen the impact of dehydration.

Every five hundred strides he swapped the suitcase to his other hand, in case the weight imbalance made one leg stronger than the other. He didn't want to end up walking in a huge circle. And now he calculated he was almost fourteen kilometres from the mine. It would have to be enough.

He stopped dead on twenty-two thousand strides and marked the sand with his heel. This was the spot. He dropped the suitcase to the ground and fell to his knees. Then he started to dig.

He burrowed into the sand as if he was swimming a furious front crawl directly downwards. His skin was raw and the sand was hotter than he could have imagined, but he didn't slow down. His programming and his human mind were working in perfect unison, formulating a plan and accelerating the operating system within his body to carry it out.

His arms whirled like fans, opening up a gaping hole beneath him. The sand shifted so quickly it fell back into the space as soon as Jimmy had created it, so he worked even faster to stay ahead of it.

Eventually Jimmy stopped – he was more than a metre below the surface. The heat was still incredibly strong, but he could feel the air changing quickly. Soon the sun would go down and the temperature would plummet.

He jumped out of the hole and threw the suitcase in. The wind would do most of the filling in work for him, but he helped it along without even pausing to catch his breath.

Then he turned around to start the twenty-two thousand strides back.

19 THE FIFTH PIER

Georgie twisted past two defenders, sprinted to the top of the box and chipped the ball over the keeper's head. It glided into the back of the net.

"Goal of the century," she declared, throwing the console controller on to the sofa in triumph and dancing round the room. "Surely there's no way back now for poor old Felix Muzbeke."

She pouted and ruffled his hair, mussing it even further out of control than usual. She didn't bother picking up the controller again. In the final thirty seconds of injury time Felix just tried to get his players to run into each other, without success.

At the final whistle he couldn't stop himself beaming, even though he'd lost 4–1. He could hardly believe that he was enjoying himself so much. His parents might be missing and his best friend Jimmy was probably in mortal danger somewhere, but for one evening he remembered what it was like to relax and have a laugh. Maybe Zafi turning up had given him hope that things were going to change.

He didn't even mind that his only company was two girls. Zafi and Georgie sat on either side of him on the sofa, taking it in turns to beat him at FIFA Soccer. Felix always put more effort into getting his players to do tricks than score goals. He judged who won based on the teams' styles, not the score line.

"Don't you have any other games?" Zafi asked. She'd won her last match 9–3.

Felix and Georgie looked at each other, both knowing that the only decent ones they had were other football games. Everything else was just a British imitation of a banned American or Japanese game. They could both remember the time Felix had found what he thought was a real American game at a stall in Hackney Wick Market. But when he got it home, everything was in Dutch and one half of the screen froze up every five seconds.

"Let's stick to this one," Georgie suggested. "But we have to beat Felix by ten goals and he has to score with a bicycle kick."

"Bring it on," said Felix, gripping the controller with even more concentration.

They played on for a while, but the console itself was also a British copy of a foreign brand. It soon crashed.

"How about a board game?" Felix suggested. He jumped over to the cupboard and pulled out a pile of old boxes, balanced precariously on top of each other. Georgie and Zafi groaned.

Just then, Zafi drew her phone out of her pocket and read a new message.

"What is it?" asked Felix, his whole body electrified with excitement. "New instructions? Is it the moustache man?"

"Nothing," Zafi shrugged. She placed the phone on the coffee table in front of them, then announced brightly, "Let's play Monopoly."

"Is that what your message said?" Georgie asked, sarcastically.

"It said I should kill you, but it can wait until after a board game." There was a second of silence before Zafi burst out laughing. "What happened to your sense of humour?" she roared.

"Hilarious," said Georgie, not smiling. She grabbed the Monopoly set. "Right," she announced, tearing off the lid. "I'll be the little dog."

By the time Helen Coates arrived home a couple of hours later, she found three people engrossed in a very loud game of Monopoly. She waited in the doorway to the living room, watching.

"Your go, Felix," said Zafi. "I landed safe."

"You're not safe!" Felix roared. "I own that. And I have a house on it. You owe me gazillions of pounds."

"Can't I stay for free?" asked Zafi, fluttering her eyelashes.

"You might be playing some weird French rule,"

Georgie cut in, "but we're doing fine with the English version." She counted out the money from Zafi's pile and handed it over to Felix.

"Thanks, mate," said Felix, waving the notes in Zafi's face.

"Don't you have homework to do?" Helen interrupted.

Felix and Georgie looked up at her, then to Zafi, then back to Helen. Nobody needed to explain anything. The hoodie hiding Zafi from surveillance told almost the whole story. *She must be here to protect us*, Helen thought, studying what she could see of Zafi's face. *But from what?*

At the same time, Helen's sombre expression told Felix and Georgie that she still hadn't been able to find Christopher Viggo. She spent every day looking for him. While she pretended to be looking for a job, she tracked down old contacts and followed the trail of the ex-NJ7 agent, the man they needed to help find Felix's parents, or make the country safe for Jimmy to come home to, or change anything about Britain.

"Don't worry," Helen whispered. "I'll find something very soon."

Mutam-ul-it blended into the black of the desert. Boosted by his night-vision, Jimmy saw it as a mass of obscure blue shapes on the horizon. He staggered towards it, trying to maintain the regular beat of his steps, but fighting the stiffness in his legs and the dryness in his throat.

His teeth chattered and his skin felt like it was on fire, despite the sharp cold of the wind. At last Jimmy reached the perimeter fence. He climbed over it at the same spot he'd used before and lurched between the burnt-out buildings of the compound.

After another minute he'd found Marla's abandoned jeep and begun his rehydration with water from the engine, filtering it through a fist of sand. Now a little strength oozed back into his limbs. He was surprised at how quickly he felt the benefit of just a little water. Yet again, he was thankful for the incredible design of his body.

With new optimism he marched all the way through the compound to the other side, well over a kilometre away. Here the buildings were unaffected by the blasts from the British missiles. The rush of the sea grew louder as he approached and at last he reached the line of piers.

For a second he imagined how refreshing it would be to carry on walking, all the way to the end of the first pier and straight into the water. The only thing that stopped him was not knowing whether the water would soothe or irritate his ravaged skin.

His muscles interrupted his thoughts, clenching tighter. His programming was telling him to focus again. He couldn't stop now. His job was just beginning.

Giant storehouses loomed over him. This was where, normally, the minerals from the mine would have waited to be loaded on to ships and carried around the world. But the ships were missing. The whole of Mutam-ul-it had been evacuated – even this end. Now the whole dock was deserted.

Jimmy scurried along the seafront, counting off the piers, until he came to the fifth. The spray of the sea formed a thin mist across the dock. Up ahead, the soft light of a solitary security light filtered through the haze. In it, Jimmy saw a girl's silhouette, leaning against the pier's handrail and hugging herself to keep warm. He jogged towards her.

"Is that you?" Marla whispered, startled by the knocking of Jimmy's boots on the wooden slats. He was very close before she was able to make him out for sure. "What have you done with the suitcase?"

Jimmy wasn't in the mood to explain. "Did you bring what I told you to?" he asked.

Marla ignored him. "Where is the actinium?" she insisted.

"It's safe," said Jimmy, growing impatient. "Now, did you bring what I asked you?"

Marla reached into her pocket and pulled out a handful of paper clips. "I did not find baklava," she said sheepishly.

"Not *baklava*," Jimmy sighed. "That's a Turkish dessert. I said *balaclava*!"

Marla's face fell. "What is balaclava?" she asked.

"It doesn't matter," Jimmy reassured her. "And the—"

Before he could finish, Marla pointed across the pier, at a slim, matt-black motorbike leaning against the opposite handrail. French colours were just visible on the fuel tank.

Jimmy nodded, the specifications of the bike flashing through his mind automatically: *MZ 125 SX... 125cc... 4-stroke...* He had to shut his eyes to stop it.

"Can you walk back to town?" he asked, opening them after a few seconds.

Marla nodded. "What are you doing?" she asked. "Why did you need these things?"

"I'm going to make sure the French do exactly what I tell them to do."

Jimmy sounded so confident, but inside was a creeping uncertainty. He only had the vaguest idea of what his inner assassin was planning.

In short, sharp movements, he twisted the paper clips one at a time into bizarre shapes. Watching his hands was like watching a puppet show. Something else was in control – but he knew that the 'some will not obey you just because you threaten them. People have tried that before, you know?"

Jimmy ignored her and twisted the next paper clip with a vicious wrench. "Where's the radio?" he asked.

"I left it in town," Marla replied. "With a friend who is listening. You said you didn't want them tracking you."

"Good." Jimmy hesitated for a moment and Marla seemed to read his mind.

"There is no message," she whispered. "I am sorry."

Jimmy's face didn't flicker, but his heart gave a

twist of distress. He had hoped so hard that his intuition was wrong and that the French were actually going to help his family.

"But my friend will listen more, in case," Marla added brightly.

Jimmy avoided making eye contact. He placed a paper clip over each ear, twisting his earlobes up and tucking the tops of his ears down. It made his eyes water, but he didn't stop.

"This is for the security cameras," he explained as he worked. "Face recognition software reads your features even through a mask."

"Security cameras where?" asked Marla.

"On the *destroyer*," said Jimmy, as if it was obvious. "I can't let the British Government see that I'm still alive. Without a balaclava, I'll have to stay out of sight of the crew. But I'll be safe from the cameras."

"The British?" said Marla, confused. "What?"

"I'm going to deal with the British and the French at the same time." Jimmy stabbed the points of the paper clips into his skin and bent his ears to hold them in place. More paper clips went on his forehead – one over each eyebrow, distorting his face. With his skin already so damaged from his march in the desert, it hurt even more than it would have normally. But even with the damage they'd suffered, his hands moved with precision and confidence.

"The British destroyer is still anchored 16 kilometres

in that direction," he explained, pointing out to sea, into the deep blackness of the night. "Everyone wants to trick me into doing some mission. But this time it's going to be different. This time they'll have to take me seriously."

When he looked up Marla was horrified. "You look like a desert cactus." She stared at the paper clips sticking out everywhere. Jimmy let out a short huff.

"Go back to town," he ordered. "Is there a safe place there I can meet you?"

"Find Coca-Cola," said Marla. "You will be safe."

Jimmy bent down to unlace his boots and kicked them off.

"What are you doing now?" she asked.

"The swim will be easier without my boots."

"What?" Marla was shocked. "Jimmy, you cannot swim 16 kilometres there and 16 kilometres back."

"Don't worry," Jimmy replied brightly. "I'll get a lift back."

He gave a quick nod to say goodbye and ran to the end of the pier. He gathered pace, the boards resounding with the drumming of his socked feet. Then he leapt into the Atlantic.

20 *JIMMY COATES: DESTROYER*

Lieutenant-Commander Love sat alone in the command centre of *HMS Enforcer*. His head was in his hands. Then a voice crackled through his intercom.

"Sir, we're getting some irregularities on our system. Possible engine failure. Do you see that?"

Love snapped out of his reverie and studied his control panel. "It's not on my system," he said. "Are you sure about this?"

"We're sure, sir. We're going to have to abandon ship."

"Abandon ship?" Love scoffed. "That's ridiculous. It's probably a technical problem on your console. Or what if it's a trick? Those rebels could have worked out how to get inside the system and—"

"Nevertheless, sir, we need to follow protocol on this."

Love clenched his fists. "No!" he shouted. "We can't abandon ship until we've found a way out of this... situation. If we leave before I've secured the mine, I'll be discharged, or court-martialled, or... worse."

"Sorry, sir," came the response. "It's protocol. I'm issuing the alert now." Suddenly the lights in the command centre cut out and were replaced by a flashing red alarm, accompanied by a siren. "See you at the lifeboats, sir."

"I'm not coming!" Love roared. "You can't make me!" He ran to the door and locked himself in. "Cowards!"

As soon as he turned back to his console, the door crashed open behind him. Love spun round, but too slowly to catch sight of the intruder.

"Who's that?" he hissed, twisting to search the shadows of the room. His hand jumped to the service revolver on his belt. Before his fingers touched the handle, he felt a blow on the side of his head so strong that he thought one of the ship's missiles had been aimed at his brain. That was his last thought before he blacked out.

Love's limp body slumped to the floor. Standing over it was Jimmy Coates.

Love wasn't dead. In fact Jimmy hadn't even struck him that hard – just a sharp and precise stab with his fingertips into the occipital artery beneath Love's ear. The split-second surge of blood to Love's brain intensified the sensations of his nerves, then caused the blackout.

Jimmy waited a few minutes, until he could see from the control panel that all of the lifeboats had been launched, then quickly dragged Love out of the command centre. Within minutes he had placed three flotation aids on the Lieutenant-Commander, hauled him overboard and returned to the controls. *The cold water will bring him round*, Jimmy thought.

Now Jimmy stood alone in the command centre, the thrill of the mission rushing through his veins. The blood pumping in his head drowned out the sea, the wind and the rolling of the ship. His entire body was exhilarated. His eyes flitted over the vast desk of screens, thirsty for information. He was buzzing, but at the same time he felt supremely calm, as if his natural emotions were locked down.

The French had manipulated him for too long, just like the Americans and the British before them. Now was his chance to make sure nobody ever tried to take advantage of him again. At the same time he could make certain that Stovorsky brought his family to safety.

But his mother and sister faded further and further from Jimmy's mind. That thought throbbed in his head again: *Destroy.* At first he wanted to control it, but then he focused on it. He revelled in it. This is what he was here for.

His hands moved around the controls as easily as if he was answering an email on a home computer. He didn't understand how to control a Royal Navy destroyer, but he could feel it. His commands went straight from the deepest part of his subconscious directly into the operating system of the ship's navigational computer.

When the groan of the engines forced the huge vessel forward, Jimmy felt the power in his gut. *HMS Enforcer* quickly gathered speed.

"Any word?" asked Stovorsky's driver, hunched over the steering wheel with binoculars clamped against his face.

"Two units are on their way," replied Stovorsky, "but they'll be half an hour at least. Getting across this terrain at night is a pain."

"Two units? But he's just—"

"Don't you dare say he's just a kid. Don't be a fool." Stovorsky lifted his hands from his laptop to wipe the sweat from his face. "If I could call in twenty-two units I would. If that boy does anything to that mine, France will be plunged into economic chaos." He sucked a lungful of air in through his teeth. "Anyway, if I can get this signal to him we might not need the military support."

They were much closer to Mutam-ul-it now. As soon as it had been cool enough, they'd driven out of the town and taken a position a safe distance from the mine compound, watching and waiting for Jimmy to show himself.

"I think I've got it!" Stovorsky exclaimed at last. "How's this?"

He tapped a couple of keys and swivelled the laptop round on his knee to face the driver. A second later a voice recording rang through the speakers, as clearly as if the speaker had been sitting in the car with them. It was Felix.

"We're in a safehouse," said Felix's voice.

Then came Georgie's, adding, *"We're doing fine."* Then, after a short pause, *"The French rule."*

Felix again: *"We owe them."*

Stovorsky stopped the playback. He and the driver stared at each other.

"Is that it?" asked the younger man cautiously.

Stovorsky threw up his hands. "You want to try?" he roared. "Zafi sent me a two-hour recording of a game of Monopoly! This is all I could edit together that's even remotely usable."

"Nothing from his mother?"

"His mother must be a mute or something. She barely said a word."

They both thought in silence for a minute. Eventually Stovorsky asked gently, "Do you think he'll...?"

The driver shrugged.

"It's our only chance," announced Stovorsky. "I'm sending it."

He tapped a sequence of keys on the laptop then sat back, trying to seem relaxed – and failing. Straightaway his body snapped upright again and his eyes almost popped out of his head.

"Look at this." He turned the laptop screen to the driver again. "The British destroyer. It's moving. It's heading towards the mine."

"What are they doing?"

"They're not slowing down." Stovorsky frantically tapped

at the keys again, adjusting the contrast of the satellite feed. "They're going to crash straight into the dock."

"Wait, look." The driver pointed at the corner of the screen, to a cluster of dots on the map a little further down the coast. Stovorsky zoomed in. At first the dots were blurred and pixelated, but as Stovorsky tinkered with the settings, the shapes became clearer. They were lifeboats. And from those lifeboats figures streamed up the beach.

"It's the British crew," Stovorsky gasped.

"But if they're not manning the destroyer..."

Stovorsky was already scrabbling for his radio. "This is Stovorsky," he screamed. "Where are those two units?!"

HMS Enforcer powered through the waves like a charging rhino through tall grass. And the only soul aboard was Jimmy Coates. His eyes almost throbbed as he stared at the horizon. All he could see of the dock of Mutam-ul-it was the line of huge warehouses, black rectangles against the faint orange of the mine. Somewhere there must have been embers still glowing after the British attack.

Every few seconds Jimmy adjusted the navigational heading on the ship's computer. But when his fingers touched the controls he felt a rush of doubt. Who was making his decisions? He couldn't tell any more whether it was his programming acting to make sure he survived, or his human side pushing his programming out of control. All he knew was that his doubts were crushed by the urge inside him to destroy the Mutam-ul-it mine. He could feel it in his assassin's instincts. And *he* wanted it too. *It's the only way*, he thought, forcing away any hesitation.

He looked up at the dock. It was close enough to make out the individual lights on the piers now. He wiped the sweat from his face. Then his hand reached out to the controls again. There was still time to turn the ship and avoid a collision.

"No!" Jimmy shouted. "Force them." His voice cracked in every word.

In his head he pushed himself to think through the consequences: *Destroy the mine.* The ship plunged onwards, unrelenting. *Force Stovorsky to protect Mum and Georgie and Felix.* He was so close to shore now he could hear the growl of the ship echoing off the warehouses. *Go to London – finish their war.*

Now the *Enforcer's* warning system rang out an alarm – the water was too shallow and the shore was too close. The siren blended with the silent screams in Jimmy's head. Each side of his mind pushed the other towards destruction, while somewhere in the middle was a tiny voice that knew it was crazy.

But now it was too late anyway. Jimmy's ears were nearly ripped apart by a new noise. It drowned out the wail of the ship's siren and the fighting in his head – the keel scraping against the seabed. It sounded like the screeching of a thousand ocean monsters, grinding the bones of their victims.

Still the destroyer tore on: 7500 tonnes of iron crashed into the pier at over 30 knots. Shreds of wood and metal exploded into the sky. The momentum of the ship didn't drop. It smashed through the dock as if it was splitting the Earth itself in two. The impact knocked Jimmy off his feet. The vibrations and the noise quaked through his body, clattering every organ.

What's happening? he wondered, even though this was exactly what he had planned. He crawled across the floor, every centimetre a battle against the massive juddering of the ship's walls and floor. Now every instinct shouted the same thing: *Get out of here.*

21 NARNIA MUST BE CLOSED

"Faster!" Stovorsky roared.

His driver didn't respond. The Panhard PVP 360 was already going at over 110 kph. The tyres slipped in every direction across the wet sand, but still the young driver kept his foot fully planted on the accelerator.

"I thought you were a driver!" Stovorsky cried. "DRIVE!"

That moment, Stovorsky's wail was lost against an ear-splitting crack. The driver slammed his foot on the brakes. The off-roader skidded for 100 metres, spinning full circle before coming to a stop. Ahead of them, just visible in the darkness, was the compound of Mutam-ul-it. At one end of it were the charred skeletons of the bombed buildings. At the other were the giant warehouses of the dock. But ploughing through them, like a dog ravaging a house of cards, was the British Navy destroyer, *HMS Enforcer*. They were too late.

For a second they froze. Only the shaking of the earth brought the two men to their senses. The impact of the ship in the harbour shot tremors up the coast, creating huge clouds of ash, dust and sand.

"Turn around," Stovorsky ordered. "Get us out of here."

The driver was already doing it. In no time, they were speeding away as quickly as they'd arrived.

"They'll never hold," gasped Stovorsky.

"What?" shouted the driver.

"The tunnels."

Stovorsky peered over his shoulder. Within seconds his sight of the mine was lost in a huge black cloud. Another massive crash echoed across the beach. The miles and miles of tunnels snaking beneath Mutam-ul-it were collapsing.

"He's destroyed everything," gasped Stovorsky. He couldn't even hear his own voice beneath the sounds of obliteration.

Then a flash caught his eye. Against the huge black cloud that engulfed the landscape it looked like a diamond in a coalface. He strained his eyes to see what it was and scrabbled for his binoculars.

Racing across the sand, emerging from the blackness behind them, was the solitary headlight beam of a MZ 125 SX French military motorbike. Driving it, bent forwards over the handlebars so far his chin was between his hands and his backside didn't touch the seat, was Jimmy Coates.

"That way!" Stovorsky shouted. He shoved the driver in the shoulder and pointed wildly to the side. "It's him!"

* * *

Jimmy squinted against the wind and clenched his lips tightly shut. He didn't want a mouth full of wet sand. His heel never lifted from the accelerator. Even over the snarl of his bike's 15 crank-horsepower and the elements bombarding his face, he could hear the crashing of Mutam-ul-it collapsing behind him. Maybe his imagination exaggerated it, but he thought he could feel the rumbles in the earth as each tunnel gave way. *That place is finished*, he thought with a rush of hot satisfaction.

Straight away his blood ran cold again. Streaking towards him in a brown/grey blur was a Panhard PVP 360 off-roader. Stovorsky was leaning out of the side, aiming his gun.

This wasn't part of Jimmy's plan. He needed the chance to explain what he'd done if he was going to force Stovorsky to help him, but the man didn't look in the mood to talk.

Jimmy jerked his wrist to open out the throttle even further. The engine gave a kick as more petrol ignited in the chamber. Jimmy felt like he'd been thrown into the next dimension of speed. The wet sand offered a perfectly greased surface, with no friction to slow him down. What's more, the slightest bump in the ground became a launch pad, lifting Jimmy into the air for jumps that felt like short flights. He could almost feel the power of the machine underneath him infusing his limbs, as if they were just extra pistons.

But Stovorsky was racing to cut him off and the off-roader had a bigger engine than Jimmy's bike. Jimmy charged north up the coast, with the ocean on his left. To his right was Stovorsky, hurtling nearer, trapping him against the water.

The two vehicles tore towards a collision point, through a bank of smog and ash, their tracks scarring the sand. Jimmy flicked off his headlight. Why give Stovorsky a clearer target?

Then came the first shot. Jimmy heard the crack of the pistol and the whiz of the bullet over his head. He swerved to the left. The slightest nudge on the handlebars sent the bike spinning wildly off-line, until he was skidding along the very edge of the beach, the tide licking his tyres.

It was no good. The water slowed him down and Stovorsky immediately changed direction to compensate, speeding up even more. Jimmy would never outrun them like this. His bike was straining at 120 kph and there was nowhere to hide. Any second Stovorsky would be close enough to shoot the hairs off his head. *Get to the town*, Jimmy told himself, his inner voice calm and clear.

With a sudden jerk, he twisted the bike back away from the water – and straight towards Stovorsky. Jimmy charged on, ducking left and right every half-second in case Stovorsky fired again. The car was heading straight for him now. They'd seen him turn.

Within seconds there were barely fifty metres separating them. Then thirty, then fifteen... Before Jimmy could even think, he was close enough to see the lines on Stovorsky's forehead. And the barrel of his gun.

Jimmy didn't wait for the shot. His body was in the grip of his assassin instinct. The instinct to survive at all costs. The instinct that constantly tested his body, pushing his abilities to the very limits of what was possible.

The instant the bullet left Stovorsky's barrel, Jimmy let go of the handlebars and pushed with his knee to overbalance the bike. Still travelling at over 130 kph, it crashed to its side and slid along the sand, while Jimmy kicked off it, into the air.

Crash point. The two vehicles were on top of each other now – but they never touched. The tube-steel frame of the bike slid between the front wheels of the off-roader and right underneath it. Jimmy slammed into the front windshield and bounced back into the air. He soared right over Stovorsky's head. As he flew, he rolled and kicked out one leg to push himself off the back of the car.

He reached out, in blind faith, clutching for something without even realising what it was. Then he landed on it – his bike spinning out from under the car. In a split-second, Jimmy grabbed the handlebars, but kept spinning, like a puck across ice. At the perfect moment, he gave one more kick, jamming his heel into the sand and heaving with his forearms.

The bike jumped on to its back wheel like a trained animal leaping to its feet. Stovorsky's driver braked hard and swirled round in a giant U-turn, showered in sand. By the time they were in pursuit again, Jimmy had a head start. It wasn't huge, but it was enough. He willed the motor to spin even faster and his wheels to find some grip on the sand. He didn't dare look round to see how close Stovorsky was.

At last the terrain became more solid. There was the vague outline of a track and the occasional building. A few seconds at top speed and suddenly Jimmy was in the heart of Tlon.

What a difference from the open landscape. The narrow streets twisted like the branches of a desert tree. Jimmy careered up the main street, but then abruptly skidded to a stop and twisted 90 degrees. He kicked off again straight away, firing himself between two buildings. He just caught sight of the off-roader close behind him before he disappeared into the alley. The buildings were so close together Jimmy could have touched the walls on either side of him at once. There was no way the car could follow.

At the other end of the alley he was spat out into another wider road. Jimmy's pace hardly dropped. Stovorsky was tearing round the corner at the top of the street. They'd worked out where he would emerge. Jimmy didn't have time to think. He slammed his heel down and charged straight towards the wall of a house.

All he could see was the white plasterwork plunging towards his face. One image flashed into his head: his brains going splat against the building. But his body had a plan. Immediately he cut the engine and redoubled his grip on the bike. The front wheel hit the wall with a bone-crunching shock. Jimmy's chest clenched and he pulled with his arms. The back end of the bike was thrown into the air and Jimmy with it – straight through an open window directly above the point of impact.

Jimmy was aware of a woman's scream. He tumbled over himself, still attached to the bike. The world became a whirl of colour, then *CRASH!*

Darkness. He'd flown through a window into a couple's bedroom, right over the bed and smashed into the wardrobe. But still Jimmy's body didn't stop. He stood up, brushed the splinters of the wardrobe from his front and hauled his bike out of the pile of gaudy pink and orange dresses. *With clothes like that*, he thought, *they don't deserve a wardrobe.*

The couple were sitting up in bed, with books in their hands and their mouths hanging open. Jimmy gave a small nod, then jumped on to his bike and drove out of the room. He let himself out of the front door of the apartment and sped along the hallway, building up enough speed to make another jump, this time out of the window at the end of the corridor, back into the open.

Any shadow of Stovorsky giving chase in the all-terrain PVP was gone.

'All-terrain' obviously doesn't include wardrobes, Jimmy thought to himself with a smile.

22 JOSH BROWDER

The quicker Jimmy was off the streets, the better, so he kept up his speed. The last thing Marla had said to him was lodged in his mind: *Find Coca-Cola*. It didn't take long before he realised she hadn't meant he should buy himself a drink. He snaked his way through the labyrinth, sticking to the darkest corners, until he saw the Coca-Cola billboard. It was torn at two of the edges and the red was faded, but nevertheless it glowed under a line of spotlights – probably the brightest thing in the whole town that night.

Jimmy climbed off his bike and stared up at the swirling white letters. He'd seen the logo in New York and France, so he was beginning to get used to it, but it would always look foreign to him. There were no Coke logos left in Britain.

The billboard covered up the whole side of the building – three storeys – but next to it was an old blue door. *You will be safe*, Marla had told him. Jimmy felt his gut churning. Was it natural nerves or his programming telling him to be wary?

It didn't matter. He didn't have a choice. He couldn't stay on the streets. Any minute, Stovorsky or somebody working for him could come round the corner or spot him on satellite imagery. If this was where Marla and her friends were based, this was where Jimmy had to go.

He hid the bike under an empty market stall and approached the door, checking over his shoulders and scanning the buildings for surveillance cameras. There didn't seem to be any. Marla and her friends had chosen this spot well.

Jimmy reached up to knock on the door, but before he could touch it, it swung open. He found himself staring up at a huge man with a machine gun and a wide, round face, like a black moon. Three round pearls shone from his mouth – his only teeth. At first Jimmy felt a jolt of anxiety. But he quickly put himself at ease – the machine gun was safely stowed over the man's shoulder and he moved back to welcome Jimmy inside. As he stepped in, Jimmy noticed the click of the guard's false leg.

Slowly Jimmy shuffled sideways, keeping his back close to the wall in case of an ambush. Then a door on the other side of the room opened. Light flooded in, dazzling him for a second. When his eyes adjusted he saw the silhouette of a tall, muscly man in the doorway.

"I never thought I'd get the chance to meet you, Jimmy."

The northern English accent set off sparks in

Jimmy's head. It felt like the ringing of a thousand alarms. Jimmy peered closer to make out the man's features. A ball of curly red hair filled the top quarter of the doorway and cast the man's pale, freckled skin into shadow. His beard was also red and bushy, like an upside-down reflection of the hair on his head.

But Jimmy's eyes continued downwards – to the thin black tie round the man's neck; to the lapels of his black suit; to the green stripe. *NJ7*, Jimmy thought in horror. The people who had created Mitchell and Jimmy. The people who undid their mistakes with murder.

At once, Jimmy dropped to the floor and kicked his leg out to the side. He hooked his foot round the guard's false leg and jerked it towards him. He moved so fast nobody else had time to draw breath, let alone react. The guard fell with a clatter, landing on his gun. Jimmy grabbed the end of the metal leg, then rolled forwards, twisting into a double somersault.

The metal pole unscrewed from the guard's knee as Jimmy rotated. Jimmy landed on his feet, the false leg swinging in his hands. He knocked out the guard in his backswing then stepped into the redhead, pushing him up against the doorframe. He shoved the pole up under the man's chin.

"Where did you get that suit?" Jimmy could feel his fists throbbing as they gripped the metal pole.

"It's just a suit, Jimmy," the man told him softly. Was he smiling? Didn't he realise Jimmy could do anything he wanted with him before he even had time to know what was happening? "I'm Josh Browder. I used to work for NJ7."

Jimmy's blood seemed to fizz at the mention of those initials. His eyes flashed with anger and he dug the pole into the man's neck a little harder. Still the red, bearded smile didn't fade.

"I said *used to*, Jimmy," Browder whispered. "Not any more. Relax."

Jimmy could feel so much heat and tension inside his head that he wanted to use the metal rod to tunnel into his own skull and release it all.

"Jimmy!" came a cry from behind Browder, inside the brightly lit room. It was Marla. "Stop wasting time. I told you about Browder."

"No, you didn't," Jimmy barked.

"I said I knew a man you should meet."

Jimmy tried to think back. Was it possible that all this time Marla had been working for NJ7? No. It made no sense.

Jimmy slowly lowered the false leg, then tossed it behind him, where it landed on its owner.

"Sorry about your friend," Jimmy mumbled.

"Don't worry about him," shrugged Browder. "Let's hope you knocked some sense into him. Come and sit down."

He guided Jimmy into the inner room and closed the door. It was a much smaller room and furnished like an old-fashioned study, but a very messy one. One wall was covered in books and magazines, another in old computers and communication equipment, all strung together with a muddle of wires in every different colour. In the middle of the room was a small round table with half a dozen chairs squashed around it. Marla was already sitting, and there was somebody else as well – a young boy. Jimmy thought he couldn't have been older than about nine.

"What is this?" Jimmy asked.

Browder sat at the table and pulled out a chair for Jimmy. "Put the kettle on," he ordered, to nobody in particular. "Let's have some tea."

"I don't want any tea!" Jimmy roared. He slammed his fist on the table. "I have to get a message to Stovorsky. I have to tell him that if he wants his actinium he has to help me, not shoot me."

Browder stared at him. "You've got your father's temper," he murmured.

Jimmy went cold. Of course – if this man used to work for NJ7 he had probably known Jimmy's parents. But did Browder mean the man Jimmy had always thought was his father – who was now Prime Minister of Britain? Or did he know who Jimmy's biological father was?

Forget that, Jimmy told himself. *Focus*. But putting those thoughts out of his head was harder than he expected. And by the time he did it, he found himself sitting at the table, arms folded, while Browder offered more explanation.

"I work for the Capita," announced Browder proudly. It

meant nothing to Jimmy. "Heard of the Mafia?" Jimmy nodded. "Heard of the black market?" Again Jimmy nodded. "Well," Browder went on, "when Britain became a Neo-democratic State and cut off more and more of the legitimate trade with other countries, the black market exploded. Demand went through the roof for all of those things you weren't allowed to buy any more: European designer clothes, American DVDs..." He paused and jerked his thumb over his shoulder with half a smile. "...Coke."

"You smuggle Coke?" Jimmy asked, confused.

"No," Browder replied. "Let me explain. None of the old black market organisations could cope with the new demand. At first it was chaos, but eventually a few of them joined forces. You know, like, merged. Became more organised. More hi-tech. More like a proper business."

"And it's called the Capita?"

Browder nodded.

"And you left NJ7 to work for them?" Jimmy went on.

"You're smarter than you look, Jimmy," Browder grinned. "No offence," he added quickly. "A lot of people tried to quit NJ7 at the same time. Most of them got killed, either then or since, and the ones that survived had to make a living. Years working for the Secret Service had left me with certain... skills. So I put them to use."

"That's all this is?" Jimmy waved his arm round at the room. "A way of making money?"

"For me – yes. I can't deny it. We can't all be like Christopher Viggo, Jimmy."

Jimmy stared. Every word seemed to reveal an extra piece of Jimmy's past.

"Yes, I knew Chris too," Browder explained. "Not very well, but well enough to see that he was stuck with some stupid ideas about making the world a better place. I suppose he'd call them ideals."

"While you just wanted to make money, right?"

"Well, you can't eat ideals."

"So what about Marla?" Jimmy asked, feeling his anger rising again. "What about her friends? You charge them money for helping them?"

"Hmm. Maybe you aren't so smart after all."

Jimmy was about to lash out, but Browder grinned and winked. The glint in his eye disarmed Jimmy for the moment.

"It's a simple business arrangement," Browder continued. "I'm here to provide certain training and, um, hardware to these people, which they buy using a few grams of uranium smuggled out of the mine by workers on the inside. And of course, as the middleman, the person organising the whole arrangement, I take a certain percentage."

"Which you take back to these people – the Capita?"

"Mostly." Browder's beard creased into a grin again. "What's a few grams between friends?"

"He is a good man," Marla cut in.

"Don't be silly, Marla," Browder protested. "I'm a man making a profit." He was suddenly serious again.

"I'm part of a business. A massive, efficient, multinational business that, well, happens to be illegal."

Jimmy couldn't help scowling. Didn't the man care that hundreds of people had just been killed in the attack on Mutam-ul-it? Browder must have read his thoughts.

"Look at it this way," the burly redhead explained. "At least you'll always know where you stand with me – wherever there's money to be made, that's my side." He shrugged and grinned. "It's straightforward and it's honest."

Against his will, Jimmy could feel himself slowly beginning to like this man, despite his lack of morals. There was something so warm about his smile – he looked like a ginger version of Father Christmas.

"You'd sell me your own grandmother," Jimmy muttered. "Wouldn't you?"

"The poor woman's dead," Browder snapped back, before beaming his biggest smile yet. "Which means I can offer you a great price." He leaned back and let out an expansive sigh. "Can I put the kettle on now?"

Jimmy couldn't help giving a dry chuckle.

"Whatever," he said. "But I'm not paying for my tea."

23 *VOICES LIKE FRIENDS*

Browder waved his hand at the young boy, who scurried back into the other room. Through the door, Jimmy caught a glimpse of the tall, one-legged guard sitting up on the stone floor, rubbing his head.

"Now, Jimmy," said Browder, leaning forwards and furrowing his brow, "I think it's your turn to explain a few things."

Jimmy's words tumbled out in a rush, as if they'd been queuing up to escape. "I need to get back to Britain to stop them going to war with France."

"You have the power to do that?" Browder raised one eyebrow. The bristling of the red hairs looked like a fox dancing on his forehead.

"It's a long story. I need to sort out a... misunderstanding."

The detonation of Neptune's Shadow oil rig crashed through his mind once more. For a second it was all he could see. Then it merged with the thunder of Mutam-ul-it crashing to destruction.

"War is never a misunderstanding," Browder said.

"What?" Jimmy glared at Browder, who just shook his head and waved for Jimmy to continue. "Um," he faltered. "Well, if I turn up alive in Britain again, NJ7 will..."

"People you cared about are still there, right?" Jimmy nodded. "And you convinced Stovorsky to use one of his agents to get them to safety by threatening to destroy Mutam-ul-it."

"How did you know?"

Browder jumped up from the table and set about the wall of the computers. "Marla left your radio with the boy," he explained while he clicked through several screens on one of the monitors. "He's very thorough. He spent every second scanning for a signal."

Suddenly a fuzzy white noise filled the room. Jimmy turned to face the speakers, half-knowing what he was about to hear. Then came the voices – crackly and distant, but instantly recognisable.

"We're in a safehouse."

Felix's voice brought a hot lump to Jimmy's throat.

"We're doing fine." It was his sister. *"The French rule."* She spoke softly, but cheerfully. The words burned Jimmy's ears. His eyes stung.

"We owe them."

Georgie's voice again. Jimmy's throat went more dry than when he'd been dying of thirst in the desert.

"When did..." The rest of his question was lost in a succession of sharp coughs. He steadied himself on the table and wiped his eyes with the back of his sleeve. "What are they...?" His voice still didn't come out properly. It seemed to jump in his chest then die in his mouth.

"Does it sound genuine?" Marla asked gently. "Is it really their voices, I mean?"

All Jimmy could do was nod quickly. In his gut his programming swirled, constantly suspicious. Jimmy grimaced and crushed his doubts as simple paranoia.

"They sound... nice," Marla added. "Like friends."

Jimmy held his head in his hands. He wanted to collapse on the floor and curl into a ball. His head was reeling. A sudden click stabbed his consciousness. It was just the door opening. That young boy, his eyes wide and staring, shuffled into the room, carrying a tray of tea. He bit his bottom lip in concentration and the light bounced off the liquid in the mugs, shimmering in his features. Jimmy couldn't work out if he looked like an angel or a demon.

"It doesn't sound right," Jimmy panted at last.

"Why?" asked Browder.

"What are they trying to tell me?"

"That they're safe," replied Browder, matter-of-factly. "And that the DGSE helped them."

"But..." Jimmy thought for a second. "They must have tried to put in a coded message, or instructions, or something. Something that would tell me *where* they were, or..."

"It's possible they did, but the French spotted it and cut it out," Browder suggested.

"And why is there nothing from Mum?" Jimmy felt his chest tighten and his breath squeeze into a ball. "What if she..."

"You can't assume anything, Jimmy." Browder rested his hand gently on Jimmy's shoulder.

"This means it worked," said Marla. "Do you see? You made them do what you wanted. It is amazing. You are controlling them."

Jimmy forced himself to breathe deeply and sit upright. He closed his eyes for a second to try and sort his thoughts into some kind of order. There was so much chasing through his head. His programming seemed to be spinning his brain at 1000 rpm, while he desperately tried to understand what it was making him feel. Fear? Suspicion? Relief? He knew very well what his human self was trying to express: panic.

"They did what I wanted," he said under his breath. "But I still destroyed their mine. I never expected them to..." He stopped himself, overcome by a surge of anger. "I need to get a message to Stovorsky!" he choked.

"Calm down," Browder said firmly. "You're with us now. You don't need Stovorsky."

"But I need to get back to Britain," Jimmy insisted. "I'll make them take me. I'll force them, just like I did with the mine."

"I'm not sure they'll be so keen to help you this time, Jimmy," Browder chuckled. "You can't destroy their mine twice, can you?"

Jimmy drew himself upright, sitting with his back absolutely straight, and spoke in a quiet, flat tone. "Actinium," he declared. "I've buried a case of it in the desert. All that they had in fact. They'll help me or they'll never get their precious actinium."

"Ah," Browder exclaimed. "Now we get to it." He sat down and reached for two cups of tea, placing one right next to Jimmy's hand. "If you have the actinium, Jimmy," said Browder softly, "maybe you don't need the DGSE."

Jimmy glanced at him quizzically.

"You see, the mine workers were never able to smuggle out any actinium. And Marla was just trying to work out a way to bring it out safely when you turned up." He leaned forwards and dropped his voice to a whisper. "There are plenty of people in the world who can smuggle you back into Britain in return for a case full of actinium."

Jimmy stared into his tea. A clump of powdered milk that hadn't dissolved swirled to the surface.

"Drink your tea and we can talk business," Browder continued. "That's my speciality."

"Your speciality is tea?" Jimmy quipped, bringing the steaming mug up to his lips. He took a long slurp.

"No," replied Browder, completely straight-faced. "Business."

Suddenly Jimmy saw the room swirl around him. His stomach lurched with disgust and terror. He swayed to the side, half falling from his chair. Then his senses were bombarded with everything at once: his tea cascading into his lap, burning his thighs; Marla screaming; the click of a metal leg on stone; a bag thrust roughly over his head.

And one crushing realisation: *That wasn't powdered milk.*

24 MESSAGE FROM THE SEWER

Stovorsky's laptop whirred on the table in the centre of the room, while he stood at the window, staring out. His two support units had turned up only minutes after he'd lost Jimmy in the streets of Tlon. He'd sent them away almost immediately, but only after borrowing enough equipment to set up a temporary operations base in the top flat of a derelict block.

The only thing he hadn't been able to requisition was an air-conditioning unit. Instead all of his equipment was gradually heating up the room. Opening the window only seemed to add to the furnace.

"I thought nights in the desert were cold," he grumbled to himself.

He knew he had the option of changing out of his suit, but this was work. And while he was at work he would be dressed appropriately. It helped him to separate his personal opinions from his professional duties. He was serving his country. He should never forget that and it helped to have a length of polyester knotted around his neck. His raincoat was on the back of the door and his suit jacket was draped over a chair.

He looked down to the alleyway and watched his driver in the dim pool of a streetlight, making the necessary repairs to the PVP. Then his laptop 'pinged'. With a sigh, he went over to it and brought up a small video window, in which the head and shoulders of a man were waiting for him.

The image wasn't perfectly clear and the movements were jerky, but the man was instantly recognisable. His face was almost perfectly round, his mouth emphasised by a neat blonde moustache.

"Clear channel?" he said sharply.

Stovorsky picked up a small black rectangle from the table and roughly slotted it into the USB drive. "Clear," he announced wearily. "Go ahead."

"I've met with Helen Coates," said the other man, speaking quickly and evenly. "Standing as a charity representative, I made contact and determined that her appeal for help on behalf of her friends, the Muzbekes, was genuine. If we do decide to help her, her gratitude could be useful in the long run."

"I know all this," Stovorsky groaned. "It was in your report. Emails do reach Africa, you know."

"But there's been a development."

"Well?" Stovorsky slumped back and roughly rolled up the sleeves of his shirt.

"I've been contacted by Christopher Viggo."

Stovorsky stopped what he was doing and leaned over the keyboard.

"He wants a meeting," the moustache man went on.

"Did he say where?"

"King's Cross. At an old ice house on Wharfdale Road."

Both men sat silently for a few seconds. Only the hum of the laptop filled the room.

"We could set up the meeting," the moustache man suggested eventually, "then trade the information with NJ7. Miss Bennett would be very grateful to us. It might even prevent further British attacks on French assets. It could—"

"Wait!" Stovorsky snapped, "I'm thinking!" He slowly dragged both hands over his scalp, smoothing down the thin wisps of hair, soaked in sweat.

"No," he announced at last. "Nothing would give me more pleasure than to dump that man into severe trouble, but Viggo's not stupid. He knew this request would come back to me. He's testing us. He wants to see whether we'll support him when he tries to overthrow the British Government."

"And will we?"

"How do I know?" Stovorsky barked. "The point is we can't betray Viggo. Not yet. He'll know it's a possibility and he'll protect himself against it somehow. It wouldn't work. We'd gain nothing from NJ7 and Viggo would never come to us again."

"So what do you suggest?"

"A powerful man is asking for our help."

"He's not powerful," scoffed the moustache man.

"Not yet," Stovorsky corrected him. "But he could be soon. He could be the future of Britain, and if he is, we want him to be grateful to France."

"So should I meet him?"

"No." Stovorsky held up a finger to emphasise his point. "He's powerful and he's dangerous."

"But you just said—"

"Someone should meet him, but not you. We can't trust him. I'll send someone who can defend themselves if there's trouble."

The man with the moustache was indignant. "I'm a trained agent!" he protested. "I'm highly dangerous!"

"I can only see your head and shoulders," replied Stovorsky, "but you still manage to look overweight." He shook his head in exasperation while his colleague glanced down to examine his waistline and tried to suck in his belly.

"I'm sending Zafi," Stovorsky announced. "Jimmy's family isn't going anywhere – NJ7 will make sure of that. So she can leave them for now, meet Viggo, then go back later if she needs to."

"What do you mean?" The moustache man stared into the camera. "About the family?"

"Nothing." Stovorsky sighed. "It's just we're having a slight... problem. Jimmy's... it doesn't matter. You can leave this with me. I'll take it from here."

They ended the conversation quickly and in under ninety seconds Stovorsky was decrypting an email attachment containing details of a proposed meeting with Christopher Viggo. With new energy, he straightened his tie and rolled his shoulders several times. Then he opened a fresh document. It was time to send Zafi her new instructions, then get out of Africa. Somebody else could run about in the heat for a change.

Zafi snapped out of her sleep with a flood of images in her head – the flat where she was staying the night, a rough schematic outline of the whole estate, the light on her mobile phone softly glowing in the darkness... For a second they were outshone by the brightest of them all – a flash of something from her dream. But then it was gone, forgotten forever. Her dreams always vanished like that.

She rolled off the sofa, slipping out from under the blanket. Still she didn't let her guard down and kept her hoodie covering her face. It was cold and the only noise was the occasional *thrum* of a car or night bus going past the window. The lights flared through the gap where the curtains didn't quite meet.

Zafi grabbed her phone and felt a knot of anxiety forming in her chest. A new message. Her thumb hovered over the button. Was this the kill order? A part of her thrilled to the idea, while the rest wanted to shut it out completely. If it was, she would obey. She had always followed orders and always would. *It's how I'm made*, she told herself. At the same time she knew that somewhere out there was a boy made just the same way as her, but who didn't follow orders when he didn't like them.

She opened her message. The seemingly random sequence of letters and numbers jumped into her head, taking new form as it travelled, as if to her it was written in 3-D and could dance to form new shapes.

Viggo? She was suddenly awash with a strange mixture of confusion and relief that she didn't want to admit existed. *And not to kill, but to talk?* It seemed simple enough, but Zafi didn't like it. Why was the DGSE using her as a messenger all of a sudden? She thought she was their most potent weapon. Recently they'd sent her to try to kill the British Prime Minister. Were her doubts stronger than she thought? Had they started to show?

No, she reassured herself. *Impossible. They'll want me to kill somebody soon. Everything will go back to the way it was.* Even as she gave herself this pep-talk, there was a growl of terror in her heart.

A second later she was up and could feel new strength pumping through her. She was about to dash out of the front door, but stopped herself. She stood, frozen, staring at the half-finished Monopoly game still set out on the coffee table. What if the DGSE did send her a new kill order? And what if the targets were the other people asleep in this flat?

* * *

The iron lattice gate on Wharfdale Road rattled as Zafi climbed over it, but at 4.00 a.m. there was nobody around to notice. She hurried to the end of the narrow alley, where there was an opening in the brickwork and a dark stairway.

Years ago there had been an Ice House Museum here, offering an experience of London's Victorian age, when ships brought Norwegian ice up the canals to this spot. Some of the museum paraphernalia still survived. Zafi hurried down, past the welcome signs and broken fittings, all thick with dust and cobwebs.

The further down she went, the more she shivered and the more the stench in the air grew. At some point since the museum had closed the drains must have leaked into the ice house. *Smells like British cheese*, she thought. She felt a faint buzz in her head as her night-vision came into operation.

She jumped off the last step and landed with a slight splash at the bottom of the ice house. Now she could appreciate why visitors had once paid to see the place. It was much bigger than she'd expected, with Victorian graffiti carved into the brick walls.

"Chris!" she called out playfully. "Viggy!" She loved the way her voice bounced around the pit.

Suddenly a hand clamped over her mouth. "Are you alone?" came a hiss in her ear. The breath was hot.

Zafi's muscles jolted as if her veins were carrying

lightning. She dropped into a perfect splits, her heels sliding through the slime. In the same moment, she grabbed the wrist of the hand at her mouth and rotated her shoulders with the torsion of an aeroplane propeller. A black heap rolled over her shoulder, but instead of landing with a splat, the man controlled his fall and skidded across the mud.

"You move well for an old man, Viggo," Zafi called out. "And yes – I'm alone."

"Keep your voice down," came the whispered reply. Then there was the groan of a battered man getting up from the floor. "We'd better move."

A few seconds later they were walking through a tunnel complex that no visitor to the museum had ever seen – low underground passages that had been used to transport the ice across London to the major railway stations. Some of the tunnels were severely dilapidated and they were squirming with rats, but it was obvious Viggo had recently cleared certain areas to make them passable.

"I know people who are looking for you," Zafi told him, following a few steps behind Viggo. "Apart from the Government, I mean." She wasn't sure, but Zafi thought she saw Viggo shrug. "Helen Coates," she said.

"Is she...?" came a croaky whisper back up the tunnel. But then it died. "They mustn't come," he said in a stronger voice. "You mustn't..."

"It's not why I'm here."

They walked on in silence. Zafi counted the paces as

they walked, calculating the distance as well as noting every slight shift in direction. Without her even wanting it, a map of their route was taking shape in her head. On top of that, her imagination superimposed a map of the streets above them. *We're heading for King's Cross Station*, she realised.

Only a few minutes later they came out into what looked like an empty storeroom. They'd entered through the back entrance and there was another door on the opposite side of the room. Zafi worked out where it must lead: an unoccupied retail concession at St Pancras International terminal.

It was warmer in here and the lights were on. It was also a relief not to have to put up with the smell any more. Zafi wasn't surprised to see that Viggo had furnished his new home with the essentials. The empty shelf racks were pushed against the walls to make space for a heater, a large mattress and several blankets laid across the floor.

Zafi looked straight to the mattress. There, sitting up against a rack, with a blanket across her lap and her arm in a sling, was Viggo's girlfriend.

"Saffron Walden," Zafi gasped. "I heard you were dead."

The woman smiled calmly and it was one of the warmest smiles Zafi had ever seen. Her dark skin seemed to glow. The harsh strip lights emphasised the fullness of her lips while her tousled black hair framed her face in an oval.

"I nearly was," she said softly, and Zafi couldn't help smiling at the richness of Saffron's voice. "I was shot by an NJ7 agent at the French Embassy."

"I know," Zafi answered quietly. "I was there."

Viggo and Saffron stared at her. "You were there?" Viggo asked in amazement.

Zafi just shrugged.

"So much for history," she said, then carried on quickly. "Shouldn't you be in a hospital?"

"I've healed well enough, thanks," said Saffron firmly. "I'm not as frail as I look." She raised an eyebrow and lifted her good arm from under the blanket. She was clutching a rifle.

"Going on a hunting trip?"

"Kids!" cried Viggo, with a grunt of exasperation. "Why did they send a child?"

"They didn't," Zafi protested. "They sent an agent."

She studied Viggo's face. He looked more rugged than in images on the news or surveillance photographs. His soft brown eyes seemed to glint a little more and his stubble was a little more unkempt. His hair was longer too. For a second Zafi was distracted by thinking about how she would disguise his strong features.

Saffron's voice pulled her out of her thoughts. "We need to know we have the support of the French," she said.

"I'll pass on the message," Zafi replied casually and turned to leave.

"No," Viggo blurted. He grabbed Zafi's shoulder and

spun her round. "You'll pass on *this* message: Britain's Neo-democratic Government is going to come to an end. Soon. I'm going to end it. Whether you French like it or not, this country will soon have free and democratic leadership. I plan for it to be me, and when it is I'll support French interests – trade, diplomacy, migration... everything." His eyes burned into Zafi's. "That will happen much more quickly if I can count on French support now. Tell Uno Stovorsky to forget what happened between us in the past. Like you said – it's history, right? We have a common enemy now. I need France as my friend."

Zafi waited for the silence to fill the whole sewer. She held Viggo's intense gaze. "That's a long message," she whispered at last, raising one eyebrow.

"Will you pass it on?"

Zafi shrugged very slowly and shook off Viggo's grip.

"I might forget it," she whimpered. "I'm only a child, remember?" She gave her sweetest smile, then brushed past Viggo to the other exit. "I'll find my own way out, thanks."

25 *THE CAPITA*

Jimmy felt consumed by heat. Sweat crawled all over him. His mind was a mess of colours and shadows. *I'm not dreaming*, he told himself. *I don't see my dreams.* He didn't feel asleep, yet he knew these visions weren't reality.

It's a drug, Jimmy finally remembered. *Where am I?* The parade of images flashed faster and faster, and the colours became objects: a mug of tea, a black K, a green stripe, a paper clip, Marla's face, the fuel gauge of an aeroplane, his old bedroom, the freezer from the kitchen at home... they all spun into each other. Then suddenly they vanished and Jimmy saw a clear, hot, blue sky.

It's not real, he told himself. *It's still not real.* But he wasn't sure any more. He saw that he was lying on his back in the desert. And bent over his middle, their heads dipped, was a flock of huge brown vultures. Jimmy wanted to shoo them away, but couldn't move. Then that urge melted and he felt a strange new feeling rush over him. Was that gratitude? Were these vultures trying to help him?

Wake up, Jimmy screamed inside his head. The cry was lost in the heat and the sounds of the birds pecking. That noise grew louder and louder until finally the largest of the birds lifted its head and stared straight at Jimmy.

In his delirious apparition, Jimmy felt genuine horror. This bird wasn't like the others. It was a deep black, not brown, and where the others had eyes like glowing blue pebbles, this one had no eyes at all. And yet Jimmy still felt it staring. Then he saw its beak – a thick, green hook. From it hung a smooth pink ball, dripping with blood.

Jimmy realised that the birds had ripped open his belly and were consuming the contents. The black bird was eating Jimmy's stomach. It opened its beak, while the entrails dangled out of the corner, and let out a squawk. Jimmy had never felt such terror. The noise exploded from the bird's throat and seemed to form a word that blasted across the desert:

"Lies!"

Jimmy screamed. He felt it in his chest and almost ripping the lining of his throat. His eyes shot open. His heart was hammering. He couldn't see anything – just the inside of a black linen bag and a bright white light behind it.

"*E svèglio,*" said a man's voice.

Jimmy's mind absorbed the words and understood them without him even realising they were Italian. *He's awake*, they'd said.

Yes, Jimmy thought. *I think I am now.*

He tried to move, but discovered his hands, ankles and knees were fastened to the wooden chair he was sitting in. He strained them again. They were held tight. He poured everything into breaking free. He shook his whole body violently, letting out a great roar of effort. He could feel the cuffs stretching against the arms of the chair, which told him they must be plastic hand ties, but they refused to snap. The attempt had only made him hotter.

It seemed that the heat in his hallucination had been real, even if it wasn't from the desert sun. Jimmy guessed that if he'd been able to remove the bag from his head, he'd have seen a huge halogen lamp about 30 centimetres from his head. An old interrogation tactic. The question was, who was interrogating him and what did they want to know?

"Where am I?" Jimmy cried. His voice caught in his throat, it was so dry. "Who are you?" Then, unexpectedly, that force swept up his neck and surged through the muscles in his face, like black honey pumped at a thousand miles an hour. He felt his lips moving and his voice emerging: "*Dove sono?*" he said, repeating his questions in Italian. "*Chi sei?*"

There was no response, but Jimmy heard his voice echoing back to him. He repeated himself, but not for answers this time – to listen to the echo. As the words bounced back to him, he felt lines forming in his head. His mind's eye was constructing the shell of a building, estimating the size and shape of his surroundings based on how his voice rebounded off the walls.

A high ceiling, Jimmy thought, seeing it take shape in his head like an architect's drawing. *Probably about a hundred metres up, possibly domed. Stone walls, but enclosing a narrow space, like a long hall.* And there was something else... Jimmy shouted again. His breath was hot against the inside of the bag – almost stifling – but he focused his concentration. His hearing broke down the echo into hundreds of separate components, including the tiniest sub-echoes that would be lost to normal ears. *That's it,* Jimmy thought in triumph. *A line of pillars on either side of the hall.*

Then Jimmy started to listen to the breathing of people around him. Their presence had affected the echo too and now he started to place them around him, like dolls in his mental dolls' house. *Five of them? Six?*

Jimmy was only wearing socks, so he could feel the texture of the floor. It was rough. *Flagstone?* The floor was cold too, despite the heat coming from the lamp. It was obvious to Jimmy he wasn't in Africa any more.

Memories rushed back to him – first the face of Josh Browder, then, more importantly, what the man had said about the organisation he worked for: that the Capita had grown out of old organised crime networks.

Now Jimmy was ready to make his guess. "Rome has such beautiful churches, doesn't it?" he announced.

There it was – a barely audible response. Somebody

behind him had changed their breathing pattern. They'd stifled a gasp. Jimmy smiled.

Suddenly the bag was whipped off his head. Jimmy was almost blinded by the white light blasting into him from the spotlight.

"Are they coming?" asked an English voice softly. Jimmy recognised it as Josh Browder's.

Jimmy squinted and ducked his head to lessen the intensity of the light on his face. "I came to you for help, Browder," he said calmly. "What do you want from me?"

"Are they coming?" Browder asked again.

"I think I need another cup of tea," Jimmy snapped back.

Browder laughed. "Your nice cup of tea wore off a long time ago, Jimmy," he chortled. "We've injected plenty of other things into you since then."

Jimmy squirmed again, pulling at the ties that bound his wrists to the chair.

"It's nothing serious," Browder added. "Just something that will help you tell us the truth. Now..." He enunciated every word as slowly as possible. "Are... They... Coming...?"

Jimmy couldn't see him, but the man's voice was circling him.

"I don't know who you're talking about," Jimmy insisted. "If you think somebody's coming to find me, search me for a tracking device."

"We did," Browder replied immediately. "We found nothing."

"So this is all just for fun?" Jimmy asked quietly. He could feel his anger stirring in his head, mixing with the whispers of the invisible figures around him. How many were there? Then the image of the vultures chewing on his digestive system lurched back at him through the glare of the light.

"We're not playing games, Jimmy," said Browder slowly. Then he exploded with rage. "ARE THEY COMING?"

"WHO?!" Jimmy bellowed back, fighting off the torment in his mind.

"The DGSE? NJ7? CIA... ANYBODY!?"

Jimmy clenched his jaw and rocked ferociously, battling away the beaks of the vultures. The chair rattled on the stone floor. "Nobody's coming!" he cried, squeezing out every scrap of strength his body could push through his muscles. "Nobody!"

At last Jimmy felt a blast of power. He slammed his feet down on to the floor, thrusting his whole body backwards and the chair with it. The wooden back landed with a clatter, sending a judder through the structure. At the same time Jimmy wrenched his arms upwards, straining against the plastic ties. They didn't break – but the chair did.

In a shower of wooden struts and splinters, Jimmy jumped to his feet. The remains of the chair scattered about him.

Immediately the people around him pounced. Jimmy was out of the spotlight now, but its glare had left him temporarily blinded. All he could see was a black void and random flashes of dim colour. He felt the first hands on his shoulders and swivelled sharply to throw them off. He felt his hand chop into a man's elbow, heard a crack then a yelp of pain.

Still unable to see, Jimmy listened. He pinpointed every attacker's position by the tap of his step, the shuffle of his heel or the sharp intake of breath before action. Every time, Jimmy struck with minimum movement at the last possible moment. His core stayed almost motionless while his fists and feet swung around him like a dancer's, connecting with the impact of a cannonball.

But there was one noise Jimmy dreaded. And there it was: the swish of metal on leather. Someone had drawn a gun from a holster. Jimmy ducked and swerved. Which way was the exit? Then came the click of the revolver. Jimmy had to find a way out.

"*Basta!*" The new voice was barely above a whisper. It was almost drowned out by the sounds of the fight, but it carried around the church and seemed to stab straight into the hearts of every one of Jimmy's opponents. They all froze. Suddenly there was near total silence – except for the heavy breathing of half a dozen men, the blood rushing through Jimmy's own body and something else – a tiny buzz and the squeak of rubber on stone. What was that?

Jimmy squeezed his eyes tight shut. His vision was starting to clear. Somebody was approaching, but they were directly in front of the spotlight. Jimmy shielded his eyes and peered closer. All he could make out was the outline of a person sitting down. Where had the second chair come from? Then Jimmy realised – the buzz he'd heard was the tiny motor of an electric wheelchair.

"Who are you?" Jimmy whispered into the shadows.

The response was even quieter. A man's voice – old, with a strong Italian accent – ever so softly announced, "I am the Capita."

26 A GOOD HEAD FOR A DEAL

Jimmy leaned in towards the man to hear the words more clearly.

"It means 'the head'," said the voice, still quiet and a little croaky. "And a head is all I am. My body gave up a long time ago."

"I don't understand," Jimmy whispered. "I thought the Capita was an organisation."

"It is," Browder cut in, still panting from the fight. "Large, rich and powerful."

"And it's mine," said the husky Italian voice. "Most of the people who work for me don't even realise that the Capita is a single person. But here I am, Jimmy."

Jimmy could feel his hands trembling. Why did this person make him so nervous? He took a deep breath and demanded, "What's your name?" Everybody around him laughed.

"Just call me the Capita," replied the man in the

wheelchair. "Or if you're not a fan of Latin, I don't mind if you call me the Head."

Jimmy craned his neck to try to avoid the light and get a better look at this man. His vision had cleared now and he could see that he'd been right about the building – he was standing in the central aisle of an old church, between the rows of battered wooden pews. There was a medium-sized dome above him, a row of columns along each wall and stained-glass windows higher up, letting in very little daylight. But there was only one thing Jimmy was interested in seeing and that was the man in the wheelchair. He edged closer.

"Stay there, Jimmy," said the Head. His tone made Jimmy stop dead. "You don't need to see my face. You never will. And I know you could end my life easily, but I know you won't try. You need my help too much, just like I need yours."

Jimmy could feel his breathing getting heavier. Were there still drugs in his system, or was it fear?

"I'm sorry I had to put you through that examination," the Head continued. "I had to make sure you weren't still working for anybody else. I know now. If you were working for someone you wouldn't have tried to escape. You would have taken everything – even torture – and waited for them to track you."

"I told you," Jimmy insisted through gritted teeth, "I'm not being tracked. I can't be. It's how I was..." His voice dropped, as if the thought didn't want to come out aloud, "...designed," he added under his breath.

The Head ignored this. "What you did at Mutam-ul-it, Jimmy..." The man's voice never rose above a whisper and he pronounced the name of the mine with a strong Italian lilt. "It was very impressive. And it probably did a lot of good – for you. But for us, it created one big problem. We're not a charity, Jimmy. We don't help the people of Western Sahara because we love them or because we feel sorry for them. Our training and hardware is in return for small amounts of smuggled uranium that made us large amounts of money. When you destroyed the mine you cut off a very profitable revenue stream."

"So now you want the actinium," Jimmy said, almost to himself.

"Where is it?"

Jimmy felt his tension ease slightly. "You can have it," he announced brightly. "It's buried in the desert."

"The Sahara is a big place, Jimmy. You'd better give us co-ordinates."

Jimmy thought for a second, a smile creeping over his face. "Then you'd better use your large, rich, powerful business to get me to England." Jimmy couldn't disguise his excitement. Only a few minutes before he had been feeling despair and desperation. Now he was buzzing with power.

"Sounds like you're a businessman," announced the Head after a long silence.

"Sounds like we have a deal," Jimmy replied. He tried his best to keep his voice calm, while inside he was leaping with joy – he was going to make it back to the UK to find his mum, his sister and Felix. And he was going to stop Britain attacking France.

"My people will take you to the English Channel," the Head agreed.

"What about getting into England?"

"We'll arrange that too. We have a good network for moving people around without immigration services. But that will only happen when you've given us the co-ordinates of the suitcase. Joshua Browder will escort you as far as the Channel. Tell him the co-ordinates when the time comes."

"When do we leave?" Jimmy was beaming. He looked around to find Browder. The big redhead was directly behind him, smiling back. Jimmy couldn't help feeling positive towards him, despite what the man had put him through. He could well understand the Capita's eagerness to protect their privacy, as well as their longing for the suitcase of actinium.

Then Jimmy was distracted by the tiny sound of an electric motor. But by the time he'd turned round, the Head was already disappearing through a door at the side of the altar. All Jimmy saw was the back of a very large wheelchair, with a strange glass dome sticking out of the top of it. *Maybe he really is just a head*, Jimmy thought, trying to work out whether that was even possible.

The rest of the Capita's men filed out through a different side-door, taking with them the remains of Jimmy's chair, the power cables for the spotlight and the lamp itself. For the first time, Jimmy got to see the men properly.

They were a strange collection of people and most of them were limping or holding their heads after the fight with Jimmy. They were all different heights and ages, but all were packed with muscle and scowled cruelly. As they left, Jimmy was sure he saw that one of them was in an NJ7 suit, the same as Browder.

Now only Browder was left, waiting at the front entrance to the church, leaning against a pillar. Jimmy was about to go to him, but something caught his eye. He stared into the dim corners of the building, through the streaks of multicoloured dust picked out by the stained glass. Sitting in the penultimate row of seats was a dark face with long black hair.

"Marla?" Jimmy called out, hardly believing it. "Is that you?" He ran up the aisle towards her.

"Do not come too close!" Marla shouted. "I might..."

Jimmy slowed to creeping pace, but didn't want to stop. "You don't need to worry about that, remember?" he said softly. "I'm..."

"Oh yes," Marla gave a little laugh. "Of course."

Jimmy was close enough to see her properly now and shuffled along the bench towards her.

"I am so used to it," Marla explained. "They made

me travel in a separate car with a driver who does not know about what happened to me. They are all scared they might become poisoned by being near me."

"I don't mind." Jimmy tripped over his words as he sat down next to her. "Being near you, I mean. But not, you know..."

"It is OK." Marla smiled and reached out to pat Jimmy's hand. He flinched at her touch, but not because of the radiation poisoning. It felt so strange to be touched when it wasn't part of a fight. The tenderness was unfamiliar.

Marla pulled her hands away and clasped them under a roll of her jumper. For the first time, Jimmy saw evidence of her illness in her face. Her eyes seemed hollow and the colour in her cheeks was much less intense.

"I am so sorry, Jimmy," she said, looking down at her lap. "I did not know they were going to treat you like this. I told Josh you had taken the actinium and he said he was going to help you."

"It's OK," Jimmy reassured her. "He is helping me. But what are you doing here?"

"The Capita was grateful for everything I did for them and has agreed to find a doctor who can treat me. If I get better, they think perhaps I am useful in training other people. And they say they are always short of girls. Especially black girls."

Unknowingly, she raised her hands to push her hair

away from her face. Jimmy noticed something. He grabbed Marla's wrist and studied her fingers. Straight away, she pulled her hand back, but not before Jimmy had confirmed what he'd seen: the base of her fingernails was tinged with blue.

"Is that...?" Jimmy gasped.

"It is fine," said Marla harshly. "The doctor will help me."

"But—"

Jimmy was cut off by a shout from the main entrance of the church.

"I'll start the car, Jimmy." It was the cheerful northern brogue of Josh Browder. "Don't try going anywhere without me. The exits are manned."

He stepped outside and Jimmy and Marla were left alone, staring at each other.

"Do not trust Browder," Marla whispered. "He does not believe in anything."

"Except money," Jimmy replied. "That's why I can rely on him."

"For now."

"Now is good enough. I'm not marrying him. I just need him to get me to England."

"Be careful, that is all."

Jimmy gave a quick nod, but he couldn't concentrate. All he could think about were the blue patches on Marla's fingernails and the poison attacking her body.

"Time to go," Browder called out, startling Jimmy.

"Good luck, Jimmy," said Marla.

"You too." He stood up. There was a lot more he wanted to say, but the thoughts jammed in his brain. Marla gave him a small smile, which sent a lurch of excitement through him. He smiled back and went to Browder. When he looked over his shoulder, Marla had turned away. He looked a second time, but she was sitting in the deepest shadow.

He couldn't tell whether she was looking back or not.

27 THE MAN WHO DIDN'T RUN

Jimmy Coates and Josh Browder travelled swiftly and quietly. Browder drove them to Rome Termini Station, where there were already tickets waiting for them. Jimmy wondered whether any visitor to Rome had ever seen less of it than he just had. The efficient workings of an international criminal organisation had whisked him through it. He longed to hold on to the noises, the colours, the traffic, the smells... and the snatched glimpses round street corners of columns and white stone ruins: the kind he'd never realised existed in real life.

Without a word, they boarded the huge Artesia Express, moments before the train pulled away. The carriages were gleaming silver with tinted windows and a distinctive red stripe all along the length of the train.

Browder collected a duffel bag from the rack by the door and thrust it into Jimmy's arms. He pointed to the toilet and grunted, "Get changed."

The tone of his voice told Jimmy there was no point asking questions. A couple of minutes later, Jimmy emerged in an old tracksuit and trainers with a baseball hat pulled down low. His sweaty, stained desert camouflage and borrowed boots had undoubtedly attracted attention at the station.

Browder was just finishing a phone call, so Jimmy slipped into the seat next to him. *Probably setting up the next stage of the journey*, Jimmy thought. He was already starting to feel more at ease. He was on the move and finally going in the right direction. Still in silence, Browder produced a loaf of ciabatta bread and a block of provolone cheese, as if out of nowhere.

"Sorry," he grunted, concealing a smirk. "No wine."

Jimmy grinned and tucked in. *I think I'm going to be OK*, he thought.

They changed trains at Milan, then settled in for the main leg of the fourteen-hour journey. Before long, Jimmy was watching a snowscape flashing past him. *So these are the Alps*, he thought, shuddering at the memory of his mountain ordeal. The vibrations of the train window throbbed through his forehead and when he sat up he saw a trail of drool down the glass.

"Did I fall asleep?" he asked, stretching and rolling his shoulders.

"For twenty years," said Browder with a totally

straight face. "You're in your thirties with a wife, three kids and a job cleaning drains."

"Drains?" Jimmy scoffed. "At least invent something realistic."

"Don't worry," Browder added, "your wife loves you. Even if she does come round to my house quite a lot."

Jimmy sighed and shook his head. "I knew one day I'd marry a zookeeper."

"Hey!" Browder protested, barging Jimmy with his shoulder. Jimmy laughed and snatched a crisp from an open packet Browder had on the flip-down table in front of him. It felt so good to be laughing again. It reminded him of Felix and his life before NJ7 had come for him. Maybe one day life would be like that again. Jimmy dwelt on that hope. He promised himself that he would never let the people he loved be out of his thoughts.

But since leaving Rome there had been another person Jimmy hadn't been able to stop thinking about.

"Josh," Jimmy said quietly, "do you know what the effects of radiation poisoning are? The type you get from uranium or actinium, I mean."

Browder didn't look at him, but replied immediately. "I know what you mean." His expression darkened. "Forget Marla, Jimmy. She'll be dead within a week. Two at the most."

Jimmy was shocked by Browder's bluntness. "You don't know that," he insisted. He could feel his chest tightening again – that heavy fear that he'd felt slowly dissolving since he got on the train.

"Radiation poisoning isn't like chicken pox," Browder mumbled.

"Well, can I—"

"There's nothing you can do," Browder cut in. Now he turned and grabbed Jimmy by the shoulders. "And you shouldn't have to either. It's a tragedy, but it isn't your fault." He stared into Jimmy's face, as if he was searching for something. "You didn't do that to her."

Jimmy crumbled in Browder's glare. He felt as if every breath he took was bringing blackness into his body, where it grew and came to life, consuming him from the inside. And Jimmy knew the one thought that was fuelling it. *I didn't do it to her*, he heard pounding in his head. He pictured the British rockets speeding through the air and penetrating the mine complex with deadly precision. *Ian Coates did.*

"*He* did it," Jimmy snarled.

"Who?"

"MY DAD!" Jimmy screamed it at the top of his voice. As he yelled, he thrust the palm of his hand into the back of the seat in front, powered by the mountain of aggression growing in his system. The flip-down table snapped like a cracker.

"*Excusez-moi!*" came a high-pitched squeal. It was the lady sitting in the seat in front. She half-stood and twisted to look over the top of the seat, down her nose

226

at Jimmy. Her face was a picture of elderly indignation – all creases and smudged purple eye-shadow.

"I'm sorry," blustered Browder in stilted French. "It's time for his medication." The old woman turned again and sat back down. As soon as she did, Browder slammed his elbow into Jimmy's head, twice. "Take two of these, son," said Browder, deliberately loudly. "You'll feel much better."

Jimmy took the blows without flinching, too enraged to fight back. He slumped in his seat, fury boiling under his skin.

"Risk your own life, boy," Browder growled, "but not mine."

Just then a conductor moved through the carriage, checking passports. When he reached Browder and Jimmy he kept moving, winking as he passed by. Jimmy tried to smile, but he felt like he'd left all of his joy behind in Italy.

In Paris, Jimmy and Browder hurried away from Gare de Lyon. "There's a contact waiting for us with a van at the Sorbonne," said Browder in a hushed voice. "It's ten minutes' walk. He'll drive us north, to the boat."

"What's wrong with the train?" Jimmy asked, trying to sound curious rather than suspicious.

"Are you running this operation or am I?" Browder asked. He said it with a smile though and glanced down at Jimmy with a sympathetic nod. "Eurostar security," he explained. "It's tight these days. And the roads aren't watched so heavily."

The explanation sounded valid to Jimmy, but still he could feel doubts mounting. He'd been betrayed too many times before – once already by Browder. His programming was growling inside him and he couldn't think of any reason to resist what it was telling him to do.

Jimmy stopped suddenly. "Call the contact," he ordered.

"What?"

"Change of plan. Tell him to meet us there." Jimmy pointed across the water, a little way ahead and to his left, to the Île St-Louis. It looked as pretty as ever – an island in the River Seine with about seven blocks along a narrow main street. Jimmy had been there once before, in very different circumstances. He knew the island was packed with DGSE safehouses – it was the last place on Earth the Capita would try to ambush him.

"But that's not the plan," Browder protested. "How about I let you—"

"Do I look like I'm negotiating?" Jimmy's voice was low and firm.

Browder threw up his arms in exasperation and swivelled 180 degrees. "OK," he declared at last. He was still shaking his head while he unflipped his mobile phone and sent a text. The reply came in less than a minute. "Let's go," he mumbled, and marched off towards the island.

As they crossed the Pont de Sully, Jimmy's head was

an electrical storm of conflicting urges. Heading into a nest of DGSE safehouses was good protection from the Capita, but it was a risk. He felt his muscles preparing for every possible kind of attack. At the same time his imagination incorporated each of the six bridges off the island into a different escape route, plus a few more through the water.

Suddenly his muscles tightened. He looked up. As the sun set behind them, it glinted off the windows further down the street. But one glimmer seemed out of place. It connected with something at the core of Jimmy's brain, which spun it round and spat out a picture: the long, thin, silver barrel of a sniper's rifle.

Jimmy turned and ran.

"Hey!" Browder shouted.

Jimmy shut it out. He didn't care whether Browder had planted the sniper or somebody else. He just ran across the cobbles with the power and speed of a Formula One Ferrari. His leg muscles felt like they would split his skin.

He rounded the corner, but three black four-wheel drive Mercedes hurtled towards him, their tyres squealing like animals at a slaughterhouse. One mounted the pavement in front of him, barely squeezing between the bollards that lined the street.

Jimmy didn't hesitate. He jumped up on to a bollard, balancing on top like a circus gymnast on a pole. In strong, precise leaps, he flew from one bollard to the next, slipping between the cars. Mid-flight, he pushed himself off the wing mirror of one of the Mercs, then raced for the other end of the side street.

BAM!

A massive blow crunched into Jimmy's right hip. He was thrown up into the air in a giant arc. For a second he lost all sensation in his right leg, then he landed cruelly, hitting the stone kerb with his shoulder. But he couldn't stop. He could already see the huge black motorbike that had hit him. It was turning to come back and finish him.

Jimmy staggered to his feet with only one choice: he limped back towards the main street, eking more speed out of his battered system with every step. He knew there would be snipers waiting, but the fear only powered him to overcome his pain. He flashed past Browder.

"Wait!" the man yelled, his voice betraying genuine panic. "What's happening?" He stayed rooted to the spot.

Suddenly there was another shriek of car brakes. Ahead of him, Jimmy saw a dirty white van jerk to a halt. The side door slid open. This was his chance.

"The van!" Browder bellowed. "GO!"

Jimmy could hear the motorbikes behind him, growling like a pack of panthers, and he could almost feel the snipers' targets hovering around the back of his neck, waiting for that one clean shot. He lurched towards the van. Out of the blackness came a white hand, reaching for him. The driver gunned the engine.

Jimmy pushed all of his strength into his last few paces,

caught the outstretched hand and dived into the back of the van. The door slammed shut behind him. He wiped the sweat from his forehead while the van roared away.

Jimmy's eyes were watering from the pain in his hip and his shoulder. He could tell there were other people in the van with him, but his head was foggy and there was no light. He wheezed for a few seconds, rolling on the bare metal until he could calm his body.

Slowly his programming was able to drive away most of the pain – for now at least – and his night-vision hummed into action. Two men crouched in front of him, leaning against the back of the driver's seat.

Then the van stopped. *What's happening?* Jimmy thought desperately. The words set off a chain of vivid memories – Browder standing in the street asking the same question. *Why didn't Josh run?* Jimmy could feel his brain clearing. Questions attacked him with as much ferocity as the French special forces. But one stood out: why would Browder shout for Jimmy to escape without him, before finding out where the actinium was buried?

Jimmy pulled himself upright into a seated position on the floor. He pushed himself back, but felt the knees of somebody crouched behind him and smelt the musty reek of the man's breath. The door of the van slid open. Light streamed in across the faces of the men opposite him.

One of them he had never seen before. He was young, muscular and dressed in a paint-spattered boiler suit. And he was clutching a large black rucksack that looked full, but Jimmy didn't know of what. Next to him was Uno Stovorsky.

"*Bonjour, Jimmy,*" he said softly, his expression blank. He was sitting on the floor awkwardly, with his knees up and the tails of his usual grey raincoat gathered in a pool underneath him. His hands were at floor level, by his waist, and in one of them he gripped a revolver. The barrel never wavered from Jimmy's stomach.

Now another man appeared at the door of the van. Jimmy's gut lurched when he saw who it was.

"Sorry, Jimmy," declared Joshua Browder brightly. "It's just business."

The young Frenchman closer to the door rolled the rucksack out of the van, into Browder's arms.

"However much money you've got in that bag," Jimmy croaked, his voice barely under control, "the actinium is worth a thousand times more."

"But the actinium was going to the Capita," Browder replied, a smile emerging on his lips. "This," he heaved the rucksack on to his shoulder, "is all for me."

Jimmy opened his mouth, but no words came out.

"Business, Jimmy," Browder repeated, reaching out to close the van door. "Goodbye."

"You idiot!" Jimmy yelled, finally finding his voice. "You betrayed me *and* the Capita? They'll kill you!"

"They'll never find me." Browder gave a nod of thanks to Stovorsky and hauled the door shut.

"*I'll* kill you!" Jimmy raged. He made a grab for the

van door, but Stovorsky stuck out his foot and shoved Jimmy in the chest. At the same time the man behind Jimmy grabbed his shoulders and pushed him down. They were back in darkness for only a second before Stovorsky turned on some dim sidelights.

"Sometimes," he explained, still not smiling, "all you need to do to get what you want is to make the highest bid."

28 THE SECOND THING

Jimmy's whole body was throbbing with fury. Stovorsky's face seemed to distort into a grotesque monster. Jimmy clutched at his temples. What was happening to him?

He nodded towards Stovorsky's gun. "Are you just playing with that?" he asked under his breath, his French coming to him as naturally as his anger. "Or are you going to shoot me?"

"Do I have reason to shoot you?" replied Stovorsky, also in French.

"You seemed to think you did in the desert."

"I only shot at your bike, Jimmy. Never at you. I'm not a killer and I know you're not either."

How could Stovorsky so casually announce what Jimmy was or wasn't? *You don't know what I might do*, Jimmy wanted to scream. That urge came with a flood of terror. He realised that he himself didn't know what he might do either. The horrors of being led into this trap now felt like nothing compared to the torture in his mind.

"I'm here to make a deal with you," Stovorsky explained. "Just like Browder made a deal with me to bring you here."

"Business," Jimmy scoffed. "Right?"

"Right."

For a second Jimmy thought he saw a hint of pity in Stovorsky's eyes, but that made no sense to him.

"The trouble is," Stovorsky went on, with a sigh, "I made a deal with you before and you broke it straight away." Jimmy stared straight at Stovorsky, not flinching in his glare. "So I'm going to make this very simple."

"You want the actinium?" Jimmy was doing everything he could to appear calm and not give away any sign that inside he was almost falling apart.

"That's the first thing."

"What's the second?"

"That you never go back to Britain."

"What?" The shock felt like a blast of cold water to Jimmy. "But you know I have to go back. I have to show the Government I'm still alive. And the British people." The words poured out of him, his thoughts finally beginning to fall into order. "This is the only way to prevent a war!"

Stovorsky let out a derisive laugh. "The war's started!" he shouted. "Get over it, Jimmy. If NJ7 found out now that you're still alive, only one thing would change: they'd know Zafi was still alive as well."

Jimmy didn't understand. What did Zafi have to do with this? He waited for the explanation, but Stovorsky just stared at him and waited.

Go back, Jimmy told himself. *Think. The oil rig…*

He could almost feel the flames on his body. He would never forget it. The smell of the oil and his own flesh burning. The explosion rocked his head again. He had to close his eyes and force his mind under control. *No*, he told himself. *What about after that?*

Then it came: that flood of guilt he'd felt when he first realised the British were going to blame the French for the explosion. They'd seen a child at the rig and assumed it was Zafi. *Of course!* Jimmy couldn't believe he'd been so stupid. NJ7 thought Zafi had been killed. So now she was carrying out operations in England without surveillance and without suspicion. For the French, it was the perfect cover. And Jimmy turning up alive in the UK would blow it.

"So you were never going to let me go back to Britain?" Jimmy asked, already knowing the answer.

Stovorsky narrowed his eyes. "If we're at war," he said, "I need Zafi in Britain and I need NJ7 thinking she's dead."

"And what's your end of the bargain?" Jimmy asked, drawing himself upright, trying to fool his own body into being confident again.

"In return for your two things," Stovorsky announced, "I give you two things. The first is a place to live. We'll let you stay here in France, or I can arrange a helicopter to escort you anywhere in the world – except the UK, of course."

"I don't need an escort," Jimmy interrupted.

"It's part of the deal."

"Then you don't get the actinium."

Stovorsky clenched his jaw, but kept his frustration in check. He thought for a moment. "OK," he said at last. "Then instead of an escort, I'll give you the helicopter. Satisfied? I assume you'll work out how to fly it. You give me the actinium and fly anywhere except Britain."

"The actinium is buried in the desert," Jimmy explained quickly. "In a lead suitcase. As soon as I have the chopper, you can have the exact location."

"Good." Stovorsky nodded and seemed to relax a little. Jimmy didn't want him to relax too much.

"What's the second thing?" he asked.

"Oh yes, the second thing." For the first time, Stovorsky's eyes dropped from Jimmy's. He cradled the gun in his lap and fixed his gaze on that.

"The second thing," he said softly, "is a list of specialist doctors who can help you."

"Doctors?"

Jimmy had no idea what the man was talking about. Help him with what? Then Stovorsky lifted his eyes, but not to Jimmy's face – to his hands. Jimmy looked down, following Stovorsky's line of sight. What he was looking at, Jimmy didn't believe. Instead, once again he saw that flock of vultures crowding around him and he felt the pain of their talons on his skin.

"I'm sorry, Jimmy," Stovorsky whispered.

"But... but..." Jimmy stuttered. He finally forced away the images in his mind to focus on his fingers – and the blue tinge around the base of his nails.

"You were the only one who stood any chance," said Stovorsky. "We didn't know for sure you'd be affected. We hoped you wouldn't be of course. And then you..."

He didn't have time to finish. The ice in Jimmy's gut erupted into thick, black flame. It rose in his chest and detonated.

Jimmy sprang forwards. The DGSE agent behind reached out to stop him, but Jimmy kicked both his feet into the man's stomach with the force of a charging rhino. Then he flicked his heel up into the man's head. It connected with the pressure point just between his eye and his eyebrow, sending such shockwaves through the man's brain that he instantly blacked out and slumped against the back door of the van.

But now Jimmy was stuck in a press-up position and Stovorsky lifted his gun, while the other agent planted his huge hands on the top of Jimmy's back and held him down. Jimmy didn't know what his own body was doing. His muscles fizzed with the combination of his programming and his rage. His body was a primed and finely tuned combat instrument.

Jimmy punched his left hand into Stovorsky's wrist. It knocked the gun off target, forcing Stovorsky's finger against the trigger. The blast shook Jimmy's brain and set his ears ringing. The bullet, however, lodged in the other DGSE agent's shoulder.

Blood sprayed everywhere. Jimmy rolled to the side and slammed his knee into the man's chest, then caught Stovorsky's wrist and gave one sharp twist. The bone snapped with a loud, deep crack and the gun dropped to the floor.

Stovorsky didn't make a sound. Jimmy looked into his face – bright white and contorted in horror and shock. But Jimmy hadn't finished with him. He pounced on the man, pinning his chest to the floor under his knee and gripping his throat.

Jimmy felt like his mind was coated in tar. He watched his limbs moving, but couldn't feel where they went. Every action was a slow, blurred composite of light flashes and blocks of colour. He could hear Stovorsky gasping for air, but didn't know what it meant. He saw Stovorsky's cheeks grow even paler, his lips fade to purple. He even stared at the red marks on the man's throat where the tips of his fingers dug in, but all he saw were the blue crowns growing up his own nails, like ten tiny sunrises painted in negative.

"Jimmy..." Stovorsky tried to gasp, but only the faintest noise emerged.

Jimmy! screamed a voice inside his own head. Somewhere, deep down, he was battling for a moment of control. His own name echoed around his head a thousand times, in the voices of every person he knew. Each time, it blended with the sounds of violence – the oil rig exploding, mixed with his mother's voice; the British destroyer powering into the mine complex, mixed with the terrified cry of his sister. Finally he heard his name once more, but this time it cut through all the other chaos in his mind. It sounded cruel and stern, but at the same time it was unmistakably pleading. It was the voice of his father.

With a sudden snap, Jimmy twisted his shoulders. He jerked as if his muscles didn't want to obey him, but with just enough power to dislodge his grip on Stovorsky's neck. Then he threw himself backwards, hitting the side of the van with a sharp slap.

Stovorsky doubled up in a wild fit of coughing, gasping for air. He rolled on to his front, clutching at the floor of the van for support, then collapsed again, blinking fast.

Jimmy couldn't bear to watch. He shrunk into the corner of the van, hugging his knees. There was nowhere for him to look. In every corner was another slumped body, semi-conscious or just struggling to come round. Even on the ceiling was a thick spatter of blood, some of it dripping off into pools on the floor.

Jimmy wheezed and retched. The danger inside him hadn't faded. He clutched at himself, clawing his chest and throat, desperate for some way to control this force inside him. He felt his lips crumpling and scrunched up his face. He wanted to cry, but his eyes refused to well up.

At last Stovorsky was strong enough to sit up against the side of the van. He leaned at an acute angle and stared at Jimmy. He forced out his words with venom, having to catch his breath again between each one.

"Do... we... have... a... deal?" he panted.

Jimmy closed his eyes and let out a huge wail from the very base of his gut.

"UUURGH!"

All his strength seemed to die with the noise of his scream. He opened his eyes, still breathing hard, and forced his voice out, as loud as his body could manage.

"Yes. We have a deal."

29 PANDORA SHOULD HAVE PACKED LIGHT

Jimmy could hardly believe how quickly things could change. Less than an hour ago, he and Stovorsky had been trying to kill each other in the back of a van. Now Stovorsky was helping him into the pilot's seat of an old Fennec AS550 helicopter at Sauvage Military Airbase, 60 kilometres northeast of Paris.

"I'm trusting you, Jimmy," Stovorsky shouted over the wind that howled across the tarmac.

The sun had gone down fully by now, but the airfield was brightly lit. A ring of stadium floodlights reached out of the earth like huge claws, and there was line upon line of ground lights, criss-crossing the landing field.

"I have your chopper," Jimmy replied, adjusting his helmet. "So you have my word. I won't go to Britain."

"If you head in that direction we'll have to shoot you down. We can't risk our asset."

Jimmy nodded. In his head was the steady thud of the memory of what Stovorsky had told him back at the detention centre in the Pyrenees: *Lies work. Lies kill.*

"Write this down," Jimmy ordered.

Stovorsky reached awkwardly for the inside pocket of his suit, lifting his right arm out of the way and adjusting his sling. Jimmy noticed him wince a little as he pulled out a mobile phone.

"Write it down?" he repeated bitterly. "I'm right-handed." He flipped open the phone. "Speak into this instead." He mashed a few keys and held up the handset. "I've got a hazardous materials response unit waiting in the Sahara."

"Hello?" Jimmy shouted into the phone. A response crackled back, so Jimmy continued. "The actinium is buried in a lead-lined suitcase, exactly 13,765 metres due east of the eastern corner of the perimeter fence of the Mutam-ul-it mine compound." He glanced up at Stovorsky. "OK?" he asked.

Stovorsky shrugged and pulled the phone away, studying the screen. "We'll see."

Jimmy turned to the controls of the helicopter. The on-board computer was ready. The multi-function display was spread across two LCD screens. Everything seemed to be fine. Jimmy still felt a rush of wonder at the fact that he understood all of this. Every digit, chart and dial threw up meaning, but always on the edge of Jimmy's consciousness, like a memory he didn't know he had.

He glanced sideways at Stovorsky. The man was still focused on the screen of his phone and he'd turned slightly so Jimmy could see it too. It was a live satellite feed from the hazmat team, on board their helicopter in the Sahara. The image was jerky, but Jimmy could at least make out that they were all in total insulation suits. It gave their bodies a weird, alien shape. For a second Jimmy seethed with frustration – if only he'd worn one of those himself.

Now his eyes jumped back to the helicopter's controls – straight to the push-button ignition. The button that would start his escape from France. The button that would start his journey home.

"What about the list of doctors?" Jimmy shouted, still staring at the controls. His fingers were trembling, impatient to get moving.

"Don't worry about it," Stovorsky replied, not taking his eyes from the screen. The hazmat team had just landed. The blades of their chopper were creating a mini sandstorm.

Jimmy gulped. He knew he'd never get to see that list of doctors. *It's OK*, he told himself, trying to stay calm.

"I'll flash it to your on-board system when you're in the air," Stovorsky went on, totally engrossed in what was going on in the desert, 1500 km away. "As soon as the radar boys have determined your route."

Anybody can find a doctor, Jimmy reassured himself. *They're not wizards.*

He glanced at Stovorsky's screen. Three men were operating hand-held sand-diggers, with a spinning wheel that scooped out litres of sand with every revolution. In seconds they were half a metre down. *Time to go*, Jimmy thought.

He plunged his thumb on to the ignition button. Stovorsky whipped round to watch him, his eyes wide with surprise. Jimmy was dumbfounded too – because nothing had happened. No engine roar, no whip of the rotors. The helicopter remained motionless.

Jimmy prodded the button again. Still nothing. He felt panic swirling in his lungs. Was he not doing this right? He searched for guidance, trying to draw up his programming from deep inside – but it was already there, telling him to try the ignition, then telling him this chopper was never going to leave the ground.

"Why won't this start?" Jimmy demanded.

Stovorsky held up his hand. He was staring at his phone display again. Jimmy saw the men pull the suitcase from the sand.

"I need a chopper that works!" Jimmy yelled.

The desert sand blew off the suitcase in the gusts from the hazmat helicopter. One of the team turned to the camera and gave a thumbs up.

"Come on!" Jimmy cried. He slapped his hands against the control panel. Still Stovorsky ignored him. Jimmy felt his programming throbbing up his neck, whipping round his skull like a tornado. He looked all around him. There was nowhere to run. The helicopter was perfectly placed – right in the middle of an empty acre of asphalt. The terminal building was 500 metres away. The same distance in the other direction was the control tower. *Snipers*, Jimmy heard in his head.

He knew instantly he would never make it if he ran. When he looked harder he made out the shadows of DGSE agents posted at every possible escape route. He was trapped. He punched his thumb into the ignition button again and again, harder and harder. Eventually the plastic covering cracked and fell off, so Jimmy punched the control panel instead.

"Let me go!" he shouted.

Stovorsky moved closer to him, still watching the screen, but looming over Jimmy. There was excitement all over his face. This was the most animated Jimmy had ever seen him. The glow from the phone's screen lit up his teeth as he bit his bottom lip in anticipation.

On the screen, the hazmat team hauled the suitcase to the surface. They dumped it on its back. Its weight lodged it in the sand. Two of them crouched over it, while the others stood back, some of them holding Geiger counters or other pieces of kit. Jimmy had no choice but to watch. He'd lost. Stovorsky had fooled him with a trick as simple as a dummy helicopter.

The hazmat agent opened the suitcase. He paused for a second. Whoever was holding the camera-phone hurried towards him. The other agent spun the suitcase round.

It was empty.

30 MESSAGE FROM A CONDIMENT

Stovorsky and Jimmy stared at each other. Stovorsky's face was white again. He squinted against the wind and the corner of his eye twitched rapidly.

"Where is it?" he bellowed. He held up the phone, thrusting it towards Jimmy's face. "Where's the actinium?"

Jimmy couldn't help smiling. "Where's my helicopter?" he countered firmly.

"OK," Stovorsky announced. "New game. It's called: tell me where the actinium is or I send the order to kill your family."

He mashed the buttons on his phone and put it to his ear. Jimmy's heart stabbed into his chest. Was the man bluffing? Could Jimmy risk not taking him seriously?

"Get a message to Zafi," Stovorsky shouted.

Jimmy glared at him, wishing poison would somehow pour from his eyes into Stovorsky's blood.

"Don't make me a killer, Jimmy," said the DGSE man.

"You already are one!" Jimmy screamed at the top of his lungs. He held up his hand and wiggled the tips of his fingers. "You sent me into that mine unprotected. You knew what you were doing. You even *hoped* it would kill me to protect Zafi's cover!"

Stovorsky ignored him and yelled, "Where's the actinium?"

"I tell you and you'll shoot me," Jimmy replied, suddenly wishing he could trust the man enough to reveal to him the location of the mineral without being shot immediately.

"You listening?" Stovorsky said into the phone, his determination showing in his jaw. "The message is this..." He hesitated, staring at Jimmy, his eyes wide. Was that fear that Jimmy saw? Or was it pride? "Make them dark," Stovorsky ordered and snapped the phone shut.

Jimmy felt a cold sweat break out all over him, but he couldn't understand what was happening. His head couldn't catch up with his body. It was as if his brain had deliberately obscured all the information it received. Yet his hands still trembled and his eyes were hot with dread.

"You've no idea what you're putting me through," Stovorsky whispered, his words barely carrying to Jimmy in the wind. "You think if you tell me where the actinium is I'll shoot you? Well, try this..." With his good hand, he flicked the tail of his jacket away and pulled a gun from his hip. "Your family's as good as gone." He levelled the gun at the base of Jimmy's neck. "Tell me where it is or you're gone too."

Jimmy felt tears creeping to his eyes. He tensed every muscle as hard as concrete. *I'm gone anyway*, he told himself. The silence was too long for Stovorsky.

"WHERE IS IT!?" he screamed. His voice tore through the wind, blustering round the whole airfield. If Jimmy told Stovorsky now, he might still have a chance – to stop his family being killed and even to find a doctor who would save him. But at the same time he braced himself for the bullet. Finally he opened his mouth to give the answer – *the honest answer*, he insisted to himself.

Before he could form the words, another voice carried across the tarmac.

"It is here!" came a shout.

Jimmy looked past Stovorsky. It was Marla. He thrilled at the sight of her, but could see the effects of her illness had got worse. Her colouring was less intense and her hair, which flew around her face like a lion's mane, looked much thinner. She moved slowly towards them. Her arm was stretched out in front of her and in her hand she grasped the top of a black linen bag. A soft blue light glowed through the linen.

Stovorsky spun round as if the wind had knocked him off-balance.

"Do you want me to bring it closer?" Marla shouted, taking another step forward.

"NO!" Stovorsky jumped backwards and aimed his gun at Marla.

"You know you cannot shoot at me," she explained calmly. "Do you realise how unstable this is?" She gently waved the bag backwards and forwards. "And how poisonous?" She jumped forwards another sudden step. Stovorsky lurched back again and dropped his gun to the ground. "OK, OK," he panted. "Just stay back."

"And make sure your gunmen know they cannot shoot also. A bullet at the wrong angle, in the wrong place..." again she waved the bag, almost taunting "...and the whole of this airfield becomes a cloud. Probably all of Paris too."

Stovorsky raised his hands high in the air and turned full circle, waving to every corner of the airfield and giving the signal to lower every weapon. "How did you get here?" he asked, astounded. "There's a cordon of my men. This whole place is locked down!"

"Perhaps I have the key," Marla replied, a huge grin on her face. "And it glows, no?"

Jimmy loved the image of Marla skipping past a ring of DGSE agents, threatening them with her deadly, radioactive bag. She and Jimmy were the only people who had nothing more to fear from it.

"Come, Jimmy," Marla ordered. "There is a helicopter waiting over there." She pointed towards the other side of the airstrip. "Perhaps one that works."

Jimmy didn't need asking twice. He jumped out of the chopper and raced over to Marla. Together they backed away from Stovorsky, towards a waiting helicopter.

"Don't go to London, Jimmy," Stovorsky pleaded. "It's no good. You can't save your family. You can't stop the war. All you'll do is make it easier for Britain to win."

Jimmy could feel a seething passion inside him. *Keep going*, he told himself. *Keep control.*

"You're only exposing Zafi," Stovorsky went on, his arms still raised. "Do you really want to give NJ7 that advantage?" He shouted at the top of his voice now, shrinking smaller and smaller as Jimmy and Marla edged further and further away, leaving the man alone in the middle of the concrete desert. "It's Britain or France, Jimmy!" he yelled. "Don't you want to help France?"

"I'm going off France," Jimmy muttered.

At last they turned and ran, moving together silently. In seconds they were in the cockpit of a new chopper – a Tiger Hellfire IV. It was a much smaller vehicle, with only two cramped seats in the cockpit and no other cabin space, but the rotors were spinning and the drone of the engine sounded like music to Jimmy.

"Do you know how to...?" Marla started to ask, but she didn't finish. Her answer was in the speed and confidence of Jimmy's movements.

A cushion of air drew them upwards, perfectly stable. Jimmy held the chopper level about twenty metres up, ran his eyes over every centimetre of the two control and display units to double-check the readings, then leaned on the flight stick to send them soaring forwards.

They flew directly over Stovorsky. They were easily

close enough to make out the purple rage bursting from every pore in his face, but they couldn't make out his words over the whine of the chopper.

The second they passed directly over Stovorsky's head, Marla threw the bag out of the open door of the cockpit.

"Wait!" Jimmy shouted. But he was too late. "What did you...?" He stared across at Marla, but her enigmatic smile revealed nothing.

The black linen bag dropped like a tiny bomb from the helicopter – and with lethal accuracy.

"NO!" Stovorsky screamed. He flapped at the bag with his one good arm, swatting it away as if it were a wasp. It bounced off his elbow and crashed to the concrete half a metre away.

Stovorsky instinctively raised an arm to shield himself from the radiation, even though he knew that was useless. But now he lowered his arm and stood straighter. He stared at the bag. It wasn't glowing.

Tentatively he shuffled towards it. Then he grew bolder. If he was poisoned already, looking inside the bag could hardly make things much worse. He picked up the bag, slowly opened the top and peered in.

It took him a second to work out what he was looking at, but then he realised: the broken pieces of an old mobile phone. The glow of its screen had died as soon as it had hit the ground.

Stovorsky erupted into a fit of frantic laughter. For a full five seconds he hopped around in a jig of relief. A moment before he'd been facing an agonising death sentence. Now he knew that was a lie. An act. A clever charade by a devious girl from Western Sahara.

As suddenly as it had appeared, the smile on Stovorsky's face vanished. *I don't have the actinium*, he thought. *But neither do they*. In a frenzy, he pulled out his own phone again and dialled two keys.

"Shoot him down!" Stovorsky bellowed in French. "He's on his way to London. Get two jets in the air and BRING HIM DOWN NOW!"

Felix had been disappointed to wake up and find that Zafi had disappeared. He puzzled over it all day at school – she'd said she'd come to protect them, then just left. Didn't they need protecting any more?

He tried to snatch a minute with Georgie to talk about it, but it was impossible. They were being watched every minute, either on the school security cameras or by certain 'teachers' who weren't trying very hard to disguise the fact that they were NJ7 agents. Felix knew anything he said within the school walls was being monitored.

Now he was at home and his mood was swinging violently. There was joy that maybe Zafi had left because she'd found out something about his parents, there was misery about pretty much everything else and there were a thousand emotions in between.

He stalked from room to room, desperate for a distraction from the mess of his thoughts. He had already consumed four slices of cheese on toast, so now he whipped up a plate of salami and anchovy mush – one of his specialities. He took his time over it and squeezed the last dribble from the ketchup bottle with a little too much enthusiasm. It spattered across the kitchen counter and on to the floor. *Eat first, clear up later,* he told himself. *Maybe.*

Georgie had stayed at school for football practice. She and Helen wouldn't be home for hours, so there was no reason to keep the place tidy. Felix threw himself on to the sofa and flicked on the TV. What he saw ruined the first bite of his snack. Instead of a distraction, he got what felt like a slap in the face.

On the screen was a grainy close-up of an old school photo of Jimmy. It was the same image that the news programmes had been recycling for weeks now, but it still froze Felix's muscles and stole the flavour from his salami mush. He found he couldn't change the channel.

The camera zoomed in on Jimmy's eyes, bright, almost laughing. Felix remembered the day when that photo was taken. He'd spent all morning trying to draw a face on Jimmy's tie without him noticing. Now he wanted to be sick. He was mesmerised by the screen, which seemed to linger on the image of Jimmy's face forever.

At last the programme switched to showing two grey-faced old blokes in suits, stuck in a studio somewhere discussing Britain's "security challenges". They were supposedly experts and they were rattling on – something about how NJ7 had successfully tracked down the psychotic boy who had assassinated the old Prime Minister.

Felix was finally able to flick over. He found a cookery show. A man with a shiny head was slicing through a mushroom with rapid, heavy chops. Felix let the images wash over him, trying to steady his breathing. Suddenly more tired than he could imagine, he lifted his feet and plonked them on to the coffee table, right in the middle of the Monopoly set.

He was still there a couple of hours later, breadcrumbs and bits of salami all down his front. He couldn't even remember what he'd watched on TV. He didn't care about the programmes – just the feeling of numbness that watching gave him. The way it dulled all of his thoughts.

Then he heard a crash. Something smashing on the floor of the kitchen. His body shook with an eruption of adrenaline. He slowly got to his feet and edged towards the kitchen. Who was in there? His imagination burned with the possibilities – an NJ7 assassin come to kill him, or just a regular robbery? Viggo coming to make contact at last, or Jimmy? His mum or his dad? He couldn't hold himself back. Despite the danger, he shoved the kitchen door open.

The room was empty. Felix blinked hard and looked again. Still empty.

The floor was covered in the shards of a broken plate and underneath the pieces was a dull, red smear. Ketchup. The smell was unmistakable. But Felix wasn't worrying about clearing it up. He was staring at what was smudged into it. He crouched to move the pieces of plate out of the way to reveal a message. It was written in large finger-writing through the ketchup, across the kitchen floor.

Felix's throat seized up in shock. At first he just stared at the letters:

FLAT NOT SAFE. GET OUT. 40 SECONDS.

It was signed with a loopy Z, followed by a curly heart.

Felix felt an intense chill stab right through him. It was chased by a thrilling tingle. Zafi had been back. Felix jumped over the message to the kitchen window and pressed his face to the glass. Was she out there? He couldn't see anything in the darkness. Then he realised the window was still locked. How had she got in? And how long had she been in the flat?

Felix's mind was racing. *She could have broken into a different room*, he thought, *and crept past me to get to the kitchen*. He couldn't believe it was possible and yet here was the evidence. And how had she got out? *She is so cool*.

His heart was thumping so hard he thought he was going to collapse. Finally the words of the message sank in: *40 seconds.* Felix felt a jolt of horror. *How long have I been standing here?*

He bolted out of the kitchen. He tumbled over the coffee table in the living room, but kept going through a shower of tiny green houses and fake money. He raced for the front door, counting off the seconds in his head, but still with no idea how long he had, or even what was going to happen when his time ran out.

He scrambled to open the front door, but the catch kept slipping through his fingers. On his fourth attempt, he finally burst out into the open. He ran to the pavement, relishing the cool air against the sweat on his forehead. Then:

BOOM!

Felix was blasted off his feet. Heat roasted his back. All he could see was an intense orange flash and he felt like his eardrums would burst. He crashed to the pavement on the other side of the street. It knocked all the air from his lungs and for a second he couldn't breathe. Then he rolled over and looked back towards the flat.

The explosion was small, but devastating with its precision. Through the smoke he could see the jagged outline of where their flat had fitted into the building. It was a ripped black hole. Felix staggered to his feet. He couldn't stand properly and nearly fell three times, finally leaning back against the wall of the Gregor's Elbow pub. His eyes took in the scene piece by piece, as if together it was too much for his mind to cope with. The heat...

the flames dancing inside... the glass that was still falling around him, along with black confetti.

After a few seconds, Felix became aware of the sirens, then the clusters of people gathering to watch. A couple of kids started throwing stones into the burning shell.

"Felix!"

He heard his own name, but didn't respond.

"Felix!" It was a woman's shout. The next thing he knew somebody was clutching him to her chest. Still he couldn't take his eyes off the devastation. Then his thoughts changed. Who was hugging him? It felt good – almost like his mum.

Slowly he came to his senses.

"Felix, thank God you're OK." It was Helen Coates. Felix's brain wasn't processing any of the words, but he loved the soothing sound of her voice and the reassuring smell of her clothes. "Come on, we've got to go."

She took him by the hand and dragged him up the street. By this time there was a different kind of chaos in the street: fire engines, police cars, people evacuating from the neighbouring flats. Felix stared as long as he could, craning to peer over his shoulder. He hardly blinked. Finally he managed to mouth a single word: "Boom."

Zafi felt her shirt clinging to the sweat on her back. What was happening to her? She sprinted through the back streets with as much speed and grace as ever, but it felt like she was carrying a weighted pack on her shoulders.

The explosion rumbled through the air only a few hundred metres away, but she didn't look back to see the smoke rising above the buildings. Instead she pressed on, harder and faster.

What have I done? she heard herself thinking. Her imagination played out two scenes simultaneously – in one, Felix made it out of the flat alive. In the other, he stumbled at the door and was lost in the flames.

There were sirens piercing the air now, but to Zafi they may as well have been in her head. She reached Camden and climbed over the railing of the canal bridge. She stared into the water, crouching in the wrought-iron curls of the bridge like a gargoyle at Notre Dame.

How long would it be before Stovorsky found out that Jimmy's mother, sister and friend had survived? That Zafi had failed. Would he ever find out that she'd failed deliberately? *No*, Zafi told herself. *It wasn't deliberate. I tried to blow them up. I failed. That's all.*

But she could feel her left index finger trembling. She tried to look away, but it seemed to catch the light, almost flashing. There was still ketchup on the tip. *I didn't write the messages*, she pleaded with herself. *I didn't.* She shivered and closed her hand into a fist to hide her fingertip. *If I did, I went against orders... If I did, I disobeyed my nature...*

"If I did," she whispered, "I'm not a killer."

A spark ran through her blood. It flared into her brain. In the murky water beneath her she saw Felix's smile. Then it melted into the shapes of her targets' bodies. Were they alive or dead?

If I'm not a killer, what am I?

Finally she closed her eyes and sprang into a powerful dive. A tramp was woken by the splash, but in the darkness there was no way he could have seen the shadow beneath the surface. It cut through the water with the power of a shark.

She didn't surface for miles.

31 LAST ORDERS AT THE GREGOR'S ELBOW

Helen Coates and Felix stopped half a mile from the flat, just outside a greasy spoon café. The light from inside was enough for Helen to give Felix a quick examination. She studied him up and down, staring into his eyes and his ears, rolling each of his limbs, asking what hurt.

"I'm fine," Felix insisted, pulling away. "I promise. I'm just bruised."

"You were nearly blown up," Helen said sternly. "And I'm not taking you to a doctor, so at least let me check you over."

Felix narrowed his eyes and let her carry on. "No doctor?" he asked softly. They exchanged a glance. Both of them knew the Royal Free Hospital was just round the corner. "You think the explosion means they've lost us on the surveillance?"

"It means either NJ7 is trying to kill us, or somebody else is trying to kill us and managed to get round NJ7 surveillance – possibly even shut it down temporarily, like Zafi did. Either way, we need to get into hiding as quickly as possible."

"It was Zafi," Felix blurted. Helen gave him a puzzled look. "In the flat," he went on, excited.

"Did you see her? Was she...?"

"No, no, but there was a message from her: that the flat wasn't safe and I had to get out."

"What's she doing?" Helen said, almost to herself. "Why blow up the flat, but warn you about it so you don't get hurt?"

"Hey," Felix protested. "I am hurt a little bit." He put on his saddest face and rubbed his shoulder.

"Get over it, sunshine."

Felix shrugged. He didn't mind the lack of sympathy. Really he was just relieved to be in one piece – he knew how lucky he was not to have been hurt more seriously.

"Where's Georgie?" he asked.

Helen pointed through the window of the café and tapped on the glass to her daughter. "We were lucky," she explained. "I bumped into her on the way home at the top of the road, We both saw the explosion. I told her to come straight here and wait for us."

Georgie rushed from the café and wrapped her arms round Felix. "You OK?" she asked, squeezing him hard. "We saw what happened. How did you get out in time?"

"Zafi left me a warning. You didn't know I could fly, did you?" he joked, squirming out of Georgie's bear hug.

"And such a graceful landing too," Georgie quipped back.

"So are we grabbing a bite before we go into hiding?" Helen rolled her eyes.

"Actually, Mum," Georgie cut in, "I just ordered some toast"

Before Helen could reply, Felix reached into his pocket.

"Great plan, Georgie. Get some for me too." He pulled out a few coins and was about to count them, but something else came out of his pocket too – a small card. Georgie picked it up off the pavement where it had fluttered down and brought it close to her face to study it in the light.

"So you're sitting at home," she began, "you get a warning from some weird French assassin girl that you're about to get blown up and the only thing you grab on your way out is a property card from the Monopoly set?"

"What?" Felix screwed up his face. "Let me see that." He snatched the card from her. "I have no idea how this got..." He stopped himself mid-sentence and his mouth fell open because when he saw what was written on the front of the card, he suddenly knew who had put it in his pocket. "How did she...?" he gasped.

"What's going on, Felix," Helen asked seriously. "Is it another message from Zafi?"

"What's it mean?" said Georgie. "How do you know it's from her?"

At first Felix couldn't take his eyes off the card. "The warning in the flat was written on the kitchen floor in ketchup," he explained. "Smell this." He shoved the card up to Georgie's nose, then to Helen's. "So either there's suddenly a whole community of people who've given up emailing and decided to send tomato-sauce messages instead, or this is from Zafi."

"Slow down, Felix," Helen told him. She knelt down and rested a hand on his shoulders. "Are you sure you didn't have it in your pocket already."

"Maybe you took it with you to school this morning," suggested Georgie.

"Oh yeah, maybe trading Monopoly cards is suddenly a massive new craze – especially the stations." He pulled a face of maximum disbelief. "And maybe when *I* hit the pavement *you* lost some of your brain." Before Georgie could react, he rattled on. "Why would I write myself a heart in ketchup? Did I die and come back as a freakoid?"

Now it was Georgie's turn to pull a face. "Wait," she said, "that's not a heart."

"Of course it is," said Felix, waving the card in front of her nose. "I think me and Zafi, we've got, like, a little thing going on." He gave a cheesy wink. "Don't be jealous."

"Felix," Georgie cut in. "That's a V."

She took the card from Felix's fingers and flicked it round to show the face to the others.

"King's Cross Station," gasped Helen. "V for..."

"Victory?" Felix suggested, looking more puzzled by the second. "Vertical? Vomit?"

"Felix," Helen announced, "this message isn't just for you. It's for all of us. Especially me." She stood tall and glanced around, checking whether anybody might have been watching them. "Sorry about your toast, Georgie," she said. "We'd better get going."

She took Georgie and Felix round the shoulders and marched them off towards Camden.

"Er, vaccination?" Felix muttered. Helen and Georgie ignored him.

"But how did she find Chris?" Georgie asked her mum.

"Chris?" said Felix. "But Chris doesn't begin with..." Suddenly the realisation struck him. "Oh, *Viggo!*" he exclaimed.

"Smart work, freakoid," laughed Georgie.

"This has to be Christopher Viggo," Miss Bennett muttered under her breath as they sped through Camden. She glanced across the back seat to Eva, but seemed to look right through her. Eva recognised the expression on her boss's face. It usually meant she was plotting something.

Eva shifted uncomfortably, wishing she could move out of Miss Bennett's glare. But she had no room to move and her knees were scrunched right up by her chest because William Lee was in the passenger seat directly in front of her. *People that tall shouldn't be allowed in cars*, Eva thought to herself. He'd pushed himself right back for a superhuman amount of legroom.

When they reached the incident scene, a line of

police tape marked a blockade, but an officer saw the long, black car with its distinctive but subtle markings and lifted the tape in good time for them to sail straight through. The driver slowed to a crawl.

Eva stared at the flashing blue lights that bounced off the old walls and lit up the faces of the onlookers. It made the whole place look like a scene from a bad TV drama, but this was real. She peeked between two of the huge fire engines to see the gaping black hole where an hour before there had been a flat. Once again she felt the wild lurch of emotion she'd experienced when she'd first heard the news: One burnt-out Government flat. No bodies.

The intensity of the relief and excitement made her want to throw up. She couldn't allow herself to reveal any hint of how she felt – the terror that her friends might have been hurt, the sheer joy that they'd survived and the exhilaration at the thought of them being on the run again. Bottling it all up made her guts boil, but she had no choice.

"Doesn't look like an accident, does it?" announced William Lee, dipping his head so that he could examine the disorder in the street. "Look – none of the other flats has been touched. It takes skilled manipulation of the flow of gas and the temperature of the ignition to control an explosion as accurately as that." He didn't wait for any response. "How do you think he sabotaged our surveillance operation this time? More cheese? Or coffee and chocolate perhaps?"

Eva saw him snatch a glance in the rear-view mirror to check Miss Bennett's reaction. The woman didn't move a muscle. Then all she said was, "We'll know."

"When?" Lee barked. "When will you know?"

Miss Bennett gritted her teeth and narrowed her eyes. The car pulled up in the middle of the junction opposite the estate and the driver jumped out to open Miss Bennett's door.

"All the evidence is in there," Miss Bennett insisted, jerking her head towards the Gregor's Elbow pub.

The three of them marched past a line of fire fighters, policemen and Secret Service agents who were scurrying in and out, fetching all of the surviving contents of the flat. Eva was nearly knocked over by two burly men with a charred sofa.

Inside the pub, everything had been neatly set out on the bar and along the tables. New material was coming in all the time and there was a team sorting through it all. Everything was given a little white label, photographed, prodded and discussed by a forensic team. At first Eva didn't see any faces. All she saw were the dozens of hands going about their work, all of them a lifeless beige because of the way the pub lighting struck the latex gloves.

Eva scampered after Miss Bennett and William Lee, ignoring the questioning glances from the police and Secret Service teams. When Miss Bennett and Lee took latex gloves from a box, Eva took a pair for herself as well, instinctively trying to fit in.

"And does it matter how he did it?" Miss Bennett whispered to William Lee as they surveyed the rows of evidence. "The fact is he's done it – he made contact with the family, he extracted them from the flat and now he's probably taken them into hiding with him. The question is: why?"

"No," Lee snapped back. "The question is, where have they gone. It doesn't matter why – if you find them and kill them."

"Don't tell me how to do my job, Lee." Miss Bennett turned on him and her fist closed around the blackened remains of a cuddly stuffed cow. A pool of foam oozed out as she squeezed. "I've already called Mitchell. He's on his way."

"You think he'll find something in all of this that the rest of us can't see?" Lee snatched one of the charred objects from the bar and gestured with it. Eva thought it might be the remains of a games console. "There's nothing in here that tells us a thing about where they've gone," he said. "The fire service was here in under two minutes. The forensic team wasn't far behind. They've saved or reconstructed every piece of data storage equipment that was found in the flat."

"Calm down," said Miss Bennett. "They'll find something."

"They've found nothing!" Lee declared bitterly. "No message. No signal. Nothing. They've even rescued every fragment of card or paper in case there were hand-written notes. Look! They saved the stupid board games, for crying out loud." He pointed to the end of the bar. "But still nothing!"

"Then they'll keep looking," Miss Bennett countered. "There has to be something."

"And nobody saw them leave!" Lee exclaimed.

Miss Bennett spun round and addressed everybody in the pub.

"Is there no surveillance information?" she demanded. She was met by blank stares and glances of concern. "Nobody saw a thing?!" she yelled. When nobody responded she turned back to Lee. "He must still be nearby," she hissed. "There's a ring of agents round the whole area. Viggo can't possibly get past them."

She ran her hands through her hair in exasperation. When she realised she was still wearing latex gloves and she was spreading small bits of ash all over her hair, she tore them off in frustration and stormed towards the exit. "Eva!" she bellowed. "Stay here and take notes."

Before she could leave, the door burst open and there was Mitchell, in a heavy duffel coat with the collar turned up around his ears.

"Where've you been?" Miss Bennett barked.

Mitchell shrugged and nervously looked around. "Looking for my target," he said meekly.

"Well your target's been busy blowing up Government

property," Miss Bennett replied. "Find out where he is and deal with him." With that she stomped out, and Eva heard her shrill voice splitting the quiet of the night. "Who's in charge here?"

32 *THERE IS NO EUSTON*

Eva and Mitchell exchanged a glance of sympathy. The tension in the room seemed to dissolve now that Miss Bennett was gone and everybody carried on with their jobs.

"I was so close to him," Mitchell grumbled to Eva. "I'd tracked him to somewhere round King's Cross. I thought I had anyway. Then I was called in about all of this."

"She's been nuts since that guy turned up," said Eva, nodding towards William Lee. The man was stooped over a table, scrutinising a melted lump of red plastic. The white tag on the table read 'ketchup bottle'. "She wants me to watch him. Find out about him."

Mitchell shrugged. "You can do that," he said. "You're good at all this secret stuff. It's perfect for you."

Eva's heart jolted.

"You've gone red," Mitchell chuckled.

Eva couldn't answer. She was burning with a violent mix of pride and horror. Was working at NJ7 really the perfect job for her? She couldn't even work out how she'd feel about that if it was true.

After an awkward moment of silence, Mitchell became embarrassed himself and shuffled across the room to find a seat. Eva fought to block out her thoughts. *Act normal*, she scolded herself. Eventually she followed Mitchell and they sat together in the darkest corner, behind one of the evidence tables.

"It's so weird," Eva said, almost to herself, fiddling with some of the items on the table.

"What is?"

"To think of Felix and Georgie using all of this stuff." All of the pieces of the board games had been carefully set out and listed on a clipboard on the evidence table. The boxes were mostly burned, but the pieces were still there and recognisable for what they were – chess, Cluedo, Scrabble... Eva flicked through the Monopoly money and turned the little dog over in her fingers.

"Maybe even Jimmy," she added, a croak in her voice.

"Jimmy's dead," said Mitchell sharply.

Eva felt it like an alarm call. She sat more upright and pretended she was studying the little dog. "Yeah, of-of course," she stuttered. "I'm just saying, you know. That's weird. That he's dead, I mean. And Felix and Georgie play with all this stuff."

She threw a smile up at Mitchell. She knew that would distract him. She rarely smiled at him and whenever she did he became like an obedient little puppy. She put the little dog down and rolled the dice.

"What do think that is?" she asked when they landed. The cubes had melted out of shape and some of the spots had burned off.

"Who cares?" Mitchell asked. "You can't play when half the pieces are just bits of soot..."

"No, look," Eva protested. "You can still make out what it says on them. Anyway – you got anything better to do?"

Mitchell shrugged. "Guess not," he muttered. He peered round the room then dropped his head again. "I've got to wait around here for all these boffins to do their... boffining."

"I think it's called forensic investigation."

"Looks like boffining to me." He rolled the dice and picked up the battleship playing piece. "Double four," he announced, moving the piece round the board, over black patches and smears of melted plastic.

"That's not a four," said Eva. She dusted some of the ash off the dice, but it didn't make it any clearer.

"Whatever," Mitchell shrugged. He rolled again. "You meant to be taking notes on all of this?"

Eva picked up her notebook and pretended to write.

"9.41 p.m." she announced in mock seriousness. "Mitchell Glenthorne rolled a double four, followed by a double one million." She picked up his battleship and zoomed it round the board as fast as she could. "Pass 'Go' and collect £200." They both collapsed into giggles and had to control themselves when some of the forensic team eyed them with disapproval.

"You can't play with that," hissed a technician from across the room. "It's evidence."

"Yeah," Mitchell groaned. "Evidence that Felix and Georgie have no life." He grabbed a fistful of the Monopoly property cards and waved them in front of Eva's face. "All mine," he announced.

"You wish," Eva said with a smile.

"Aw, poor Eva. OK then, you can have the stations." He flicked through the cards and picked out the four stations: Liverpool Street, Marylebone, Fenchurch Street...

"Where's Euston?" he asked.

"There is no Euston, you idiot. It's King's Cross." Eva grabbed the cards from him. "Let me have a look." She dealt them out slowly, deciphering the fragments of print on the surviving portions of the cards.

"Forget it," said Mitchell. "It's not there. It probably went up in flames."

"That's stupid," Eva protested. "Why would just one of the cards burn up when every other one is here?"

"It was probably lost before the fire then."

Eva ignored him and placed the cards around the board next to their property spaces. When her hands were empty, she prodded her finger into King's Cross, the only property without a card on it.

"Where'd it go?" she asked again, raking over the objects on the table and checking the floor around them. When she looked back at Mitchell his expression had changed. His arrogant smile had faded into uncertainty, as if he was puzzling out a maths problem.

"What's up?" Eva asked softly. She tried flashing a smile at him again, but he wasn't looking at her. His eyes were flicking rapidly all over the Monopoly board. Then they fixed on King's Cross Station.

"Gotta go," he said, rushing to his feet. He nearly knocked over the whole table.

"Mitchell," Eva called out. "Wait..."

It was no good. She watched him say just a couple of words to William Lee, then they both dashed for the door. Eva was left alone, staring at the Monopoly board, with the feeling, deep in her stomach, that she'd done something terrible.

Jimmy and Marla seared through the night sky like a comet – but one with 1200 kW turboshaft engines and two Mistral missiles.

"How did you find me?" Jimmy asked over the noise of the chopper.

Marla picked up the helmet from behind her seat, put it on and spoke into the headset. "I followed from Rome," she explained. "I told you not to trust Browder. But I did not think you were listening."

"But—" Jimmy stopped himself. "Thank you," he said. He looked across at Marla and tried to smile, but it didn't come out right. His mouth became a wiggly mess.

"What's the matter?" asked Marla. "You're fine now. You can go to England, just like you wanted."

"I'm not fine." Jimmy's face darkened and he pushed all of his strength into the flightstick of the helicopter, powering them onwards even faster. "Stovorsky sent the order to kill my mum, my sister and my best friend."

"I am sorry, Jimmy." Marla's voice was suddenly sombre.

"And there's more," Jimmy added. "Worse."

"Worse? What can be worse?" Marla looked at him in astonishment, but he looked away, concentrating instead on the controls of the helicopter. Marla stared at him hard. The light from the LCD screens lit his expression, a perfect mix of courage and terror. Then her eyes ran down his arms. She saw his fingers. She saw the growing blue stains. At first she thought it was the light from the controls, but she quickly realised the truth.

"Jimmy, your hands..." she gasped.

Jimmy didn't react.

"I thought..." Marla couldn't finish her sentence.

"Stovorsky lied," Jimmy explained quietly.

"But, but... why? Why would he do that?"

"Because lies work," Jimmy whispered, barely audible.

"So you are..." Marla couldn't bring herself to say it. She looked at her own fingers and her face hardened. The sympathy disappeared and in its place came pure determination. "You will survive, Jimmy," she declared.

"Not just perhaps – for sure. You will find a doctor. Like me also." Jimmy was shaking his head gently, but Marla pressed on as if she was issuing a stream of orders. "And your poison is much less than mine. I lived near that place, remember. The poison killed my parents."

"It killed your parents?"

"Many years ago, yes. They worked there. For the French." She looked down at her lap. "But you were only perhaps two hours. No more. You will survive."

"It makes no difference," Jimmy said, his tone flat. "It's deadly, Marla." Steadily his voice rose. "I put my hands into it. Like it wasn't enough to be near to it – I put my hands right into the actinium! Then I..." He stopped himself suddenly.

"What?" Marla asked.

Jimmy's eyes filled up with tears. "I thought I was going to be able to save them," he said. "Georgie, Mum and Felix." His words started to slur into each other. "But I couldn't anyway. And now I'm finished."

"Jimmy, do not say it. You can still get to them in time."

She reached across to put a hand on his shoulder.

"Don't touch me!" Jimmy snapped, pulling away. "Everything that comes near me..." He tailed off. "I was built to kill and I can't stop it. Even if I fight it. Can't you see all I do is cause destruction?"

"What?"

"I destroy life!" His voice boomed over the din of the flight. "I destroy everything!"

"Jimmy, stop!" Marla yelled. "You have to be strong. You do not destroy! You save! You are not a killer!"

Jimmy didn't react. His fists squeezed the flight-stick and his lip trembled.

"You saved me, no?" Marla shouted. "And you are going to save your mum and your friend and your sister also!"

"How can I?" Jimmy yelled back. "When I can't even save myself?"

"What?"

"Nothing. Forget it. You can't help me. Nobody can."

Marla stared at him. Jimmy could feel her eyes on his face. A part of him wanted to look back, as if just seeing her sympathy would take away his troubles. But he knew he couldn't. He forced himself to look only straight ahead, out of the cockpit.

Then his senses were pricked by a new noise – a warning beep. He glanced down at the LCD and tapped through several different screens, sucking the information into his brain before he was even aware of what he'd seen.

"They're coming," he announced grimly.

"What?"

Jimmy slammed his fist into the control panel. Then he pointed at the screen to show Marla the two flashing red dots steadily closing in on the black one in the centre.

"That's us," Jimmy explained in a gruff tone. "And that's two French fighter jets." Then there was another beep, more shrill this time, and all of the controls lit up red.

"And what does that mean?" Marla asked.

Jimmy raised an eyebrow, flicked his eyes over the dials in front of him and said, "It means hold on tight."

33 ONLY LIKE THE BEST HUMANS

Felix, Georgie and Helen moved through King's Cross Station with their heads dipped, scanning everything for another sign from Zafi. Felix and Georgie had no idea what form that would take.

"I can't think with all this noise!" Georgie muttered. Four station cleaners were pushing large mopping machines across the main concourse in an area that had been roped off after some kind of accident with two of the stock carts. There were pools of liquid across the floor. "Should we check the card again?" she whispered. "Maybe it has another clue on it?"

"No," replied her mother. "What do you smell?"

Georgie and Felix looked at each other.

"I dunno," Felix muttered. "Smells like... station stuff."

Georgie shrugged, but after a second her face changed. "Wait," she said. "Smells like breakfast or something."

"It's milk and fruit juice," said Helen.

"Milk and fruit juice?" Felix mouthed to Georgie. "I think your mum's lost it." He tapped a finger against his temple. Georgie suppressed a giggle, but then looked across the forecourt and her expression changed.

Felix followed her eyes. The cleaners in the centre of the concourse were scurrying around two stock carts – the small electric vehicles that carry merchandise to the refreshment outlets in the station. The carts were lying on their sides about five metres from each other, their engines burnt out and their shelf units mangled.

"Looks like they exploded," Felix suggested.

"Explosions are popular tonight," muttered Helen.

Felix looked again. One of the carts had obviously been carrying milk, while the other must have been loaded with red fruit juice of some kind. There was a huge pool of each spreading across the floor, merging in the middle into pink slime.

"It's just a red pool and a white pool," said Georgie. "It's not a message or a sign."

Helen pointed to the part of the floor just next to where the cleaners were working. It was outside the partitioned area, so it was thick with commuters, but for a second they cleared to reveal the bigger picture.

The pool of juice formed a red streak. The milk had spread into a white one. But next to that was a third colour – a permanent band of blue in the pattern of the floor tiles.

Three stripes: red, white and blue.

"It's the French flag!" Felix gasped.

"But it's—" Before Georgie could finish, the three of them were running through the station. Because of the way the carts had fallen, the liquids had spread out in two balloon shapes to form a giant arrow, with the point aimed in one definite direction: the passage through to St Pancras International Terminal next door.

St Pancras was surprisingly busy, despite the Neo-democratic Government's restrictions on who could travel in and out of the country. Helen, Georgie and Felix tried to blend in, but there weren't many other children around.

"Where now?" asked Georgie. She and Felix couldn't help lifting their heads to gawp at the amazing terminal interior. It was dominated by a huge new statue of Ares Hollingdale, the last Prime Minister, who'd been assassinated. Several commuters stopped to take photos of it on their mobile phones. It was over thirty metres high, reaching nearly all the way up to the wall of glass and steel that loomed over everything.

About fifteen metres directly above the statue was the ornate station clock. Felix was mesmerised by the huge gold arms that seemed to flash in the light like mediaeval swords.

"Get your head down," Helen ordered. "It's this way." She pulled Felix and Georgie towards the end of the concourse where there were two refreshment outlets. One consisted of just a few tables and chairs around a stand pretending to be an old English pub. The other was shuttered up.

Felix was confused at first, but when he looked again it was obvious: underneath the day's specials chalked on the pub blackboard there was a small 'Z'.

"She thinks she's Zorro, doesn't she?" Georgie sighed.

"Who's Zorro?" asked Felix.

"Never mind."

They tried to slip round the pub stand, but the server cut them off. "Can I help you?" she barked.

Before Helen could respond, there was low, deep voice.

"It's OK, Steff. They're with me."

Jimmy's hands flashed across the dials and switches. He was amazed to see himself moving so calmly and with such control, while at the same time his insides were on fire with anger, confusion and fear.

He dipped hard, taking them close to the rooftops of Northern France. He knew the fighter jets would never fire at him if he was so close to French civilians. The red flashing light in the cabin went solid for a moment, then beeped off. The missile launch detector in the electronic warfare software suite showed that the jets had cancelled the missile lock on Jimmy. They were waiting.

Jimmy pulled up rapidly. The chopper leapt high into the air and pitched backwards. The two fighter jets ripped past them. They'd have to circle round to make another pass.

In the corner of Jimmy's eye was Marla. Despite the danger, she was perfectly still, staring at Jimmy as if he was a puzzle to be solved. "Jimmy," she said softly, "if the actinium is not in that suitcase you buried in the desert, where is it?"

Jimmy stayed silent. He pretended not to have heard her and concentrated on manoeuvring the chopper.

"Where is it, Jimmy?" Marla pressed.

Jimmy took a deep breath, but couldn't stop the rage bubbling inside him. "I thought I was immune, OK?" he shouted. "I didn't know!"

"Where is it?"

Marla was shouting now too, matching Jimmy's anger with her own strength of will. Still Jimmy wouldn't say. Marla didn't ask again. Instead she reached all the way across and grabbed Jimmy by both shoulders. Jimmy's shock rattled through him like the vibrations of the helicopter. Marla twisted him round to face her, ripping his hands from the controls. She stared into his eyes for a second.

What's she doing? Jimmy thought desperately. *Does she want us to crash?* He knew the chopper would stay stable for a short time, but they had less than a minute before the French jets would be back to fire at them. Then, with a deep breath, Marla slammed her fist into Jimmy's stomach.

All the wind burst from his body. He bent double over Marla's arm, clutching at his belly. His instincts fizzed inside him. His hands twitched, ready to counter-attack. It would have been simple, he knew that, as both sides of the cockpit were still open. His mind had already visualised the move – *twist away*, it told him. *Grab her. Throw her out.* But Jimmy didn't move. He didn't want to.

He wheezed hard. It felt like he would never breathe again, but he didn't make a move to fight back. Marla punched a second time, this time with her knuckles extended. The blow came sharper, harder and aimed precisely at his stomach. She pressed deep into him, as if she was trying to reach inside and rip out his guts.

Jimmy had no breath left to give. He forced himself to move his hands away. *Sit up*, he ordered himself. *Give her a target. If she wants to hit you, let her.* He extended his arms out to the side as far as he could in the cramped cabin and presented his front to Marla. There were tears in his eyes from the pain, but he wasn't going to give in.

Marla pounded her fists into his stomach: left, right, left, right... each time harder and harder. She was crying now and with each blow she let out a furious grunt. Jimmy held up a hand to stop her. She'd done enough. He could feel it. He didn't know how she'd worked out what she had to do, but there was no way he could hide it now.

Jimmy crumpled in two and pitched forward until his head rested on the control panel. Then, with two gut-wrenching heaves, he retched violently. He turned his face to Marla, barely able to see her through the water in his eyes, and puked at her feet. Marla didn't flinch. This was exactly what she had intended and Jimmy knew it too.

He had hardly eaten in the last twenty-four hours, so at first nothing came up. But then, coated in thick yellow bile from Jimmy's stomach, came a shower of glowing blue stones: the actinium.

Jimmy was almost on the floor of the cockpit now, barely able to stay in his seat. The helicopter rocked from side to side. The cabin shook. The rotor over their heads rattled. But Marla and Jimmy were frozen. They looked at each other, then to the pile of actinium at Marla's feet.

"Why?" Marla mouthed, unable to get her voice out.

Jimmy couldn't answer at first. He was still finding it hard to breathe and he knew there was a higher priority. He pulled himself back into his seat and planted his hands firmly on the control panel, just as the helicopter threatened to dive. He snatched the flightstick and hauled them back under control.

"You don't understand," Jimmy wheezed. He wiped the back of his sleeve across his mouth, spreading strings of yellow saliva. His words came in lurches, his sentences chopped up between huge gulps of air. "I needed Stovorsky to think... I'd hidden it in the desert... so he would get Mum... and Georgie to safety."

Marla couldn't take her eyes off the actinium. She pressed herself back in her seat, trying to avoid touching it, even though she knew it was already too late for her.

"This was the only way..." Jimmy went on, gradually getting his voice back. "So I didn't poison everybody around me... my body would insulate it... like the lead suitcase..." He leaned all of his weight on the flightstick, plunging them forwards, accelerating rapidly.

"You idiot!" Marla screamed. "You protect everybody else, but poison yourself!"

"I thought I couldn't be affected!" Jimmy tried to shout, but didn't have the strength.

"You forgot you were human."

"I'm not human!"

"Yes you are!" Marla shoved him in the shoulder, tears streaming down her face. "You might be different from the rest of us, but... but... look at you! You act and think and feel like every human I have ever met. No – that is not right. You are only like the best humans." Jimmy couldn't help glancing across at her, but she looked away. "You are human. If you forget that, you destroy yourself."

Jimmy didn't know what to say. Her words washed through his mind. Outside the darkness closed in around them. They were over the water now, leaving the lights of the French towns behind them. Fog rushed past them like ghosts escaping from hell. Jimmy gritted his teeth and punched a few buttons on the control panel, employing the Saphir-M chaff and flare dispenser – the Tiger's missile countermeasures.

"But my DNA..." he whispered, almost to himself.

"Who cares about your DNA?" Marla screamed.

"I DO!"

His cry was lost in the roar of an explosion. A French missile tore through the debris trailing the chopper and detonated barely two metres from them. The helicopter banked wildly to the side and Jimmy lost control.

From behind the pub stand at St Pancras Station emerged a tall man dressed in a shabby brown coat and big trainers with a cap pulled down low.

"Viggsy!" Felix whispered.

Christopher Viggo couldn't stop his harsh expression melting into a smile. He held up a hand and Felix gave him an athletic high five.

"I knew I couldn't keep you lot away forever," said Viggo.

"Why keep us away at all?" Helen wasn't smiling. "Do you know what we've been going through trying to find you?" She gave him a shove in the chest. He stumbled backwards and held up his hands in self-defence.

"I was protecting you," he protested quietly, all the time checking the station concourse to make sure they weren't being observed. "You should be getting on with your—"

"Protecting us?" Helen shoved him again, harder.

"He's in so much trouble," said Felix softly, shaking his head.

"You don't have a clue, do you?" Helen went on, only

keeping her voice down with difficulty. "You think you can change the world on your own? Do you even realise that Felix's parents have been taken?"

"Taken?" Viggo was shocked. "By who? Where?"

"Exactly!" Helen shoved him again, even harder. Viggo caught her wrists and pulled her round the back of the pub stand. Felix and Georgie followed. "We need you, Chris," whispered Helen. She stared into his eyes. Her voice softened. "And you need us."

"What good do you think you being here could possibly do?" Viggo seethed. "Even if Felix's parents have been taken. The only way to put that right is to get rid of this Government. And I can't do that with kids around."

"Hey!" Felix protested.

"He's right," said Georgie. "We're just going to get in the way."

"But it's not as if we can go anywhere else, is it?" Felix ranted. "Somebody tried to blow me up tonight."

Before Viggo could react, Helen cut him off. "*Is* it the kids?" she asked bitterly. "Or is it me?"

Viggo was stunned into silence. They looked at each other, Viggo still holding Helen by the wrists. His grip melted. "I'm sorry," he whispered, his voice hoarse. "How's..."

"Jimmy?" Helen shook her head. "I don't know." She dropped her eyes to the floor. "He did some amazing things so that we could come back here and live without Miss Bennett trying to kill us."

"Doesn't sound like that lasted too long." They looked intently into each other's faces, barely centimetres apart, as if they were having a whole conversation without speaking.

"So," Felix chirped, "when you're not single-handedly fighting evil, you like to lurk about behind fake pubs, right?"

Viggo tried to laugh, but it came out as if he was about to choke.

"How's Saffron?" asked Georgie, directing the question to Viggo, but staring at her mum.

"She's—" Viggo froze. He'd heard something. He peered round the side of the stand and his eyes widened. "Were you followed?"

"No," said Helen, the tension in her throat forcing her voice out too loud. "I—"

Suddenly one of the small metal tables came flying towards them. Viggo shielded his head just in time, but the table crashed into him and knocked him to the ground.

"Get out of the station," he shouted. "Now!" He pushed himself up and sprinted away towards the centre of the concourse. Felix peered after him and was stunned at what he saw. The customers in front of the pub backed away in shock. In their centre was a burly thirteen-year-old boy, brandishing a metal chair.

"Mitchell!" Felix gasped.

Viggo powered towards the assassin, who stood firm, waiting for the perfect moment to swing, like a baseball player poised to smash a fast-ball out of the park. Mitchell whipped the chair towards Viggo's head. At the last instant, Viggo bent his knees and leaned backwards, but carried on gliding across the floor. He was at such an extreme angle that his body was almost horizontal. He slid through underneath the chair, leaving a look of shock and confusion on Mitchell's face.

It was a second before Felix realised that Viggo's trainers were heelies, with wheels in their soles. "That is so cool," he whispered.

"Come on," said Helen. "Let's go."

34 TERMINAL CLIMB

Jimmy felt like the whole world was fighting to break into his skull, while his brain was bursting to get out. He'd been thrown out of his seat, but he wasn't sure where he was – somewhere sprawled on the floor of the cockpit. At last he regained focus and found himself face to face with a pile of actinium. The dread charged through him again.

"Jimmy!" he heard. "Help me!"

He looked up. Marla was wrestling with the flightstick and flicking switches in panic. But Jimmy's mind was sluggish. Something was holding him back – slowing his thoughts and draining the energy from his muscles. *It's the radiation poisoning*, he told himself. *It's killing me and I can't stop it.*

But at the same time he knew that couldn't be true. Not yet. He could feel his body fighting with itself. His assassin's instinct kicked and writhed in his chest. It would never give up. The only thing stopping him was this feeling of utter hopelessness that swamped his heart.

"Come on!" yelled Marla.

Jimmy heard it as a distant cry. He closed his eyes. He couldn't stop seeing the faces of his sister, his mum and Felix. What was happening to them? Then he saw another face – his father's.

"Jimmy!" Marla screamed. "You've got to get to Britain!"

Jimmy jumped back to the controls. Out of the front of the chopper he watched the waves, coiling like thousands of huge black serpents jumping up to bite them.

He threw the flightstick up and to the side, suddenly reversing the direction of the lift in the rotors. The bank of air rolled the helicopter over on to its side then, just at the right split-second, Jimmy jammed the heel of his hand into the flightstick and the whole machine flipped back the right way up.

"You OK?" Jimmy shouted.

Marla was clinging to her seat, but she was smiling.

"I'm going to get them off our tail," Jimmy called out, sending the chopper swooping low to the water. He didn't need to check the systems to know that the two planes were close above them and ready to fire again. Jimmy flicked the cover off one of the rocket launch switches and before Marla could respond, he clicked the switch.

A rocket burst out from the left side of the chopper. In less than a second it dived into the water. Three seconds later it detonated on the sea bed. A wall of water erupted in front of them, but they carried on straight into it. The upsurge lifted them higher. Jimmy never lost control.

"What are you doing?" Marla cried out.

"I'm going to get as close to the planes as I can," Jimmy replied. "I want them to see me."

Mitchell spun round and hurtled across the station concourse towards Viggo. He powered through onlookers like a giant bowling ball.

Then he came face to face with a policeman.

"Clear the area!" the man shouted. Mitchell stopped and looked around. The police were closing in on the centre of the concourse like a net, hurrying bystanders out of the way. Viggo was trapped in the middle, but already he had seen his escape route. Hardly slowing his pace, he climbed the huge Ares Hollingdale statue towards the wall of steel and glass above.

"What's on the other side of that glass?" Mitchell yelled.

"You have to clear the area!" the policeman repeated.

Mitchell gritted his teeth and pulled up the sleeve of his coat. On the underside of his wrist was a small tattoo, still raw where the skin was healing: a green stripe.

"I said, what's on the other side of that glass?" he shouted again.

The policeman's demeanour was transformed. "It's

just the roof of the next building and the ladder for the clock," he said quickly.

"So shoot him down!" Mitchell ordered. "If he reaches the clock he'll jump out of the service door and get away."

"Shoot him?" the policeman huffed. "In front of all these people? People with camera phones? We'll make him a martyr. He'll be more popular than ever."

"Just do it!"

"Sorry, but—"

"But what?" Mitchell looked past the policeman to see Viggo nearing the statue's head.

"I'll need clearance from the top," said the officer.

"I *am* the top!" Mitchell roared, but the policeman was already dipping his mouth to his walkie-talkie.

"It will take less than two minutes," he said to Mitchell. "We'll shoot as soon as—"

"We don't have two minutes."

Mitchell raced to the statue and clambered up the pedestal. In no time he reached Hollingdale's waist, but Viggo had already made the leap higher to the glass underneath the clock. Then, in the corner of his eye, Mitchell saw Helen, Felix and Georgie leaving the station, unnoticed by the police.

Mitchell realised how clever Viggo was. By creating a scene in the centre of the concourse he had pulled the focus of the security cordon, allowing his friends to slip away. *They can wait*, Mitchell reminded himself.

Viggo is the target. Now finish the job. The desire felt like an overwhelming thirst.

Mitchell's fingers dug into every fold of bronze, his limbs clambering up with a regular and rapid beat. At the top he stood on Hollingdale's head. He could hear the shouts and gasps from the crowd below, but didn't hesitate. He leapt up and caught the first steel strut in his fingers, then pulled himself on to it.

Viggo was directly above him, climbing up the glass panes towards the clock. Each pane was about thirty centimetres high in a thin wooden frame. Mitchell could climb this as easily as if it was a ladder.

Within seconds he could reach Viggo's ankle, but the man knew he was there. Viggo kicked out at Mitchell's grasp. Mitchell responded with a burst of speed. Viggo was only centimetres from the bottom of the clock, but Mitchell clambered up to be level with him and slammed the base of his palm into Viggo's face.

Viggo's head rocked back. His cap tumbled down to the crowd below and blood spurted from his nose, spattering red on to the white and gold of the bottom half of the clock face. He lost his footing and only held on to the wooden frame with his fingertips. The back of his head was exposed and easily within Mitchell's reach. It may as well have had a target sign painted on it. *A single blow*, Mitchell told himself. *Complete the mission. Finish him.*

He lifted his arm for the kill, but Viggo wasn't giving

up. He kicked both legs up to the side, crunching his knee into Mitchell's solar plexus. Mitchell crumpled in two. His fingers slipped. But his body responded with a jump and he was able to grab hold of the decoration round the bottom edge of the clock itself.

He was above his target now. And Viggo had swung round with the impetus of his kick. He was only holding on with one hand, his back to the glass, the front of his body totally vulnerable. Mitchell hauled in a deep breath and raised his right arm above his head.

"Right here, isn't it?" said Viggo suddenly, pointing to the base of his throat. His words seemed to echo around the whole terminal hall. "That's how we were trained, isn't it?"

Mitchell could feel the blood fizzing through his fingertips. He clenched his hand, ready to chop, and fixed his eyes on that square centimetre of flesh just above Viggo's collarbone. One strike and he could cut off the oxygen to the brain.

"Come on," Viggo taunted, pulling his shirt collar down and thrusting out his chest to bring the target closer to Mitchell. "Right here. End it."

Mitchell's eyes flickered up to Viggo's face. What was this man doing? Didn't he want to survive?

"Without me the Government will go on forever, won't it?" Viggo hissed. "Long live Neo-democracy and war whenever you feel like it."

Mitchell stared into the man's eyes. There was no

fear there. Mitchell had never seen such contained passion – such calm fury.

"It won't happen, Mitchell," Viggo went on. "Not once you've shown everybody down there what this Government can do."

Stop this, Mitchell ordered himself. *Time to finish it.* He could hear his brain telling him he may never have a better opportunity. And yet it felt like there was concrete running through his veins, slowing his movements, fossilising his thoughts.

"Look down there," Viggo whispered. "I fight for what I believe and I'll die for what I believe. But Britain doesn't need me to fight for them. After this, people will know without me telling them. They'll see for themselves. They'll fight for themselves."

Mitchell tried to shut out the words. He didn't care about the politics. This was his job, his mission. NJ7 was his life. Without it, there was nothing for him. This was what he believed in.

At last he forced a burst of heat into his muscles. A spark flew up his arm then exploded into pure strength.

"People know nothing," Mitchell grunted. His arm whipped downwards. Viggo closed his eyes.

But in that hundredth of a second, the crack of a rifle echoed through the terminal. A bullet flew past Mitchell's ear. His hand veered off target. *Miss Bennett sent clearance to shoot!* he thought.

CRASH!

The glass shattered. Mitchell saw Viggo fall backwards through a shower of glass, wooden splinters and blood. The man's eyes were still closed. After a split-second he disappeared into the darkness.

Mitchell's footholds in the wooden frame had collapsed. He dangled from the clock with one arm and looked below him. On one side, the station concourse was in chaos. People were bleeding from the dropping glass, others were screaming, running, or just gaping up at Mitchell, while the police tried to control them all.

On the other side, Mitchell could see the roof of the next building.

"Where are you?" he whispered.

But there was no movement. All he could make out were shadows.

"You want them to see you?" Marla was shocked at what Jimmy had said.

They soared higher, darting through the clouds until they were level with the cockpits of the two fighter jets.

"Take the flightstick," Jimmy ordered.

"What?" Marla gasped.

"Just hold it steady. That's all you need to do." He took off his helmet and scooped the actinium into it.

"What are you doing?" Marla shouted, grabbing the flightstick in panic. "I think they are going to shoot again. The lights are—"

Jimmy was already climbing out on to the arm that held the missile launch mechanism. There was one on either side of the chopper, sticking out like stubby wings. He had to force himself to hold the strap of his helmet in his teeth so his arms were free to grip the chopper. He could feel the strain in his shoulders, the muscles gripping the bones in their sockets. He mentally counted off every injury he'd suffered, each one weakening his system a little more, making it more likely he'd lose his grip and plunge to his death.

His helmet dangled against his chest. In the dim light, with the spray and the fog, the actinium stones glowed like beacons. He thought he could feel them burning through the metal, through his shirt and into his skin. *Forget that*, he told himself. It couldn't harm him any more than it already had. But it could help him get to Britain.

When he reached the rocket, he cracked open the casing, working with one hand while he gripped the chopper with the other. Inside, the rocket was a jumble of wires and metal slots, but Jimmy's mind highlighted certain parts, picking out the routes of the circuits and the details of its workings. The wires were reduced to the simplicity of a fast-food menu.

Jimmy unclipped the explosive charge – a red and blue cylinder that resembled a large battery – and dropped it into the fog. Then, still with one hand, he carefully poured the stones into the empty space in the rocket.

When he had finished, he swung back to the side of the chopper. Even at this altitude he could taste the sea salt in the air. He pulled himself into the cockpit, dropping the helmet at his feet, and took back the controls of the helicopter.

"Do you think he saw me?" he panted, peering through the fog towards one of the fighter jets.

"I think you are crazy," Marla shouted back. "I think we are trapped, we have no defence and they will shoot us."

Jimmy looked from Marla to the plane and back again. The warning lights from the control panel flashed against Marla's skin, red on black. The chopper was locked in as a target.

"So why haven't they fired yet?" Jimmy asked quietly. "What are they waiting for?"

High up in the control tower of Sauvage Military Airbase, Uno Stovorsky clutched a mug of coffee. His hands were still shaking. In front of him a team of three flight controllers monitored the progress of events over the Channel.

But Stovorsky's thoughts were far away. He stared blankly at the wall above the computers in front of him and simply nodded when the engineers updated him. A portrait of an elderly man looked down at him – Dr Memnon Sauvage. The man this airbase was named after. A Secret Service hero who had died protecting

French secrets. The man who had designed Zafi.

Stovorsky's head throbbed and his eyes were heavy with tiredness. All he could hear was his own voice buzzing round his head. Jimmy's mother, sister and best friend... He'd given the order to kill.

Two children, he told himself. He took a sip of coffee, but couldn't wash away the bitterness rising in his throat. *He made me do it*, he thought, but it didn't alleviate the stabbing pain in his skull. He couldn't take his eyes off Dr Sauvage's stern expression bearing down on him. "It was the only way!" he shouted in English.

The other men in the control tower spun round to look at him. "Sir?" one of them muttered, using English even though he hardly spoke a word. Whatever language his boss addressed them in, that's what he would use, if he could.

Stovorsky shook his head, embarrassed at his outburst. Then came a crackle through the radio.

"This is Hawk 7," came the voice of one of the pilots in French. "We have a clear shot on the target and are ready to deploy again."

Stovorsky jumped to his feet. It could end now. But the pilot knew his orders – why didn't he just fire? At the same time, Stovorsky could hear words pounding through his head – *two more children*.

The pilot continued his transmission: "Target is implanting something into his second rocket. It appears to be a number of glowing rocks. Possibly a radioactive substance. Please advise."

The radio crackle stopped and left silence in the control tower. The three controllers looked to Stovorsky for a response. Stovorsky was motionless.

"How did he..." he muttered. "He must have... somehow..."

"What is it, sir?" asked one of the engineers. "Should they shoot him down?"

Stovorsky was shocked out of his thoughts. "*Non!*" he shouted. "*Non!*" He pushed the engineers aside and bellowed into a microphone in French: "Pull back! Do not fire!" Sweat dribbled down his neck. "Repeat: abort operation! Return immediately and DO NOT FIRE!"

"Understood," came the response.

Stovorsky slumped back into his seat.

"But he'll make it to England," protested one of the flight controllers.

"The boy is loading radioactive material into a rocket," Stovorsky explained.

There was a slight pause, but then the controller pressed his point. "It might still be safer to shoot him down. It takes very precise equipment and delicate engineering to cause any kind of nuclear reaction. Even with highly unstable materials..."

Stovorsky cut him off. "This boy isn't... normal!" He clutched his head in his hands. "Who knows what he can or can't do?"

"But what about Zafi? The Brits will work out she's still alive. She'll—"

"So be it." Stovorsky stormed to the door. "I'm not NJ7," he announced, his head hanging low. "I'm done killing for today." He was about to leave, but paused in the doorway. He glanced back over his shoulder at the portrait above the computers. "Better tell Zafi to get herself into hiding."

He left without waiting for a response.

35 MESSAGE FROM A GHOST

Helen, Felix and Georgie hurried up St Pancras Road. The street was packed with people, some rushing towards the commotion to see what was going on, others running away.

That's when they heard the shot.

Georgie and Felix stopped dead.

"What was that?" Georgie gasped.

"Come on," Helen urged them. "We've got to move."

"Was that a gun?" asked Felix.

The three of them looked at each other, the fear bouncing between them. Then they heard shouts from the station. At first they were hard to make out, but a woman rushed past them and her scream was clear: "They shot him!"

"NO!" Felix yelled.

His senses swirled and seemed to swallow each other. He was hardly aware of anything happening around him, except Georgie crying, his feet running on the pavement and Helen pulling him up the street.

At last they ducked into the shadows of the railway bridge behind the terminal building. Through his tears, Felix saw Georgie slump against the wall. Helen knelt down and held her, reaching out for Felix to join them.

"Don't worry," she said, barely holding back her own tears. "We don't know for sure."

"But what if he's..." Felix was stunned into silence. A woman's silhouette appeared in the arch of the bridge. Felix crept towards it, unable to believe his eyes.

"Saffron!" he gasped.

Helen and Georgie's heads snapped round to look and Saffron Walden stepped forward into the light. Her arm was still in a sling, but otherwise she looked strong and stood tall, in a long black coat.

"Saffron!" Helen exclaimed. "Are you OK?"

Felix rushed towards Saffron, but froze half a metre away. Her coat flapped open in the breeze and Felix caught a glimpse of metal: the long metal neck of a rifle.

"You..." he said, barely able to get the words out. "You shot Chris?"

Saffron beamed at him. "Don't worry," she said softly. "He might recover."

"What?" snapped Helen, jumping up to stand with Felix. "Saffron? It was you?" Before she could even ask why, there was a footstep behind them. They spun round and Felix thought his head was going to explode with confusion.

Standing there, rubbing his neck and slightly out of

breath, was Christopher Viggo. When he saw Felix's expression, Viggo let out a raw laugh. Felix did too, but with shock as well as happiness.

"You cut that pretty fine, didn't you?" Viggo called out to Saffron, "If I'd climbed any higher I could have broken my neck in the fall."

"Sorry." Saffron replied. "A little warning about what you were going to do would have been nice. I'm a little out of shape." She lifted her sling slightly.

"You don't look it," muttered Helen, wiping her cheeks. "You both look wonderful." She didn't know who to hug first, and in the end Felix got squashed in the middle of a clinging huddle.

"So good to see you," Helen whispered.

"Good to see you too," Saffron and Viggo replied at the same time.

"You don't have to shoot so close to me next time," Viggo added, pointing a finger at Saffron.

"Next time?" Saffron let out a derisive laugh. "If you even think about doing anything like that again I'll aim right between your eyes."

"So what happens when they look for your body?" Georgie asked, brushing the mud from the back of her trousers.

"I expect they've already searched the roof where I landed," replied Viggo, wiping a slow trickle of blood from his nose. "And they'll know it wasn't a police rifleman that shot me."

"That shot *near* you," Felix corrected him.

"Come on," Viggo declared, with a reluctant chuckle. "It means we can't stay here." He led them all up the street.

"Where are we going?" asked Felix

"Don't worry," replied Viggo. "I know a place. Now, what's all this about you getting blown up?"

"Oh, it was so cool, right. I was sitting there and I felt a bit hungry..."

Felix's reply lasted, uninterrupted, until they were well away from King's Cross, fading into the London night.

The two French fighter jets seemed to drop out of the sky. In reality, they dipped and turned, disappearing into a bank of thick fog, then wheeled round to return to Paris. Marla and Jimmy exchanged a smile, but Jimmy didn't feel any triumph.

"What are you going to do?" Marla asked quietly.

Jimmy couldn't hear her because he hadn't put his helmet back on, but he knew what she was asking.

"We have to deal with it," she went on, shouting this time. "We cannot go near any other people until we have. We have to destroy it or bury it or something... What are you going to do?"

Jimmy's breath caught in his throat. He felt like the black fog outside the chopper was invading his body, creeping through him and spreading darkness. Destroy – the word fuelled Jimmy's anger. He knew the actinium couldn't be destroyed and at the same time he pictured the obliteration it could cause. He could still feel the heat of the stones... the burning of the explosion at the oil rig... the thundering annihilation of Mutam-ul-it...

Destroy.

His arm reached out suddenly for the rocket switches.

"No!" Marla gasped. She caught his hand in hers.

The touch seemed to shimmer through Jimmy's body. It felt soft – too soft for the situation. Jimmy could feel a frost in his chest melting. "It won't detonate," he rasped. "I removed the charge. If we get low enough we can fire it into the seabed. The rocket will bury itself."

He heard the words and knew they made sense, but at the same time he realised that's not why his fingers had darted to the rocket switch a second before.

"I will not let you," Marla insisted. She reached for the parachute fastened to the back of her seat and strapped it over her shoulders.

"What are you doing?" Jimmy asked in wonder.

"Go to England, Jimmy. Find your family. I am going to take those rocks away. Far away."

"But where? What will you do with them?"

"I do not know." Marla clambered over Jimmy, to the side of the chopper which still held the remaining rocket. The hair that hung below her helmet brushed against Jimmy's face. Her closeness took Jimmy by surprise. He wished it could last longer. Then he caught sight of raw, red burns on the back of her neck.

"Perhaps I bury it," she went on, "like you should have." She held herself on the edge of the cockpit, then carefully climbed out, along the missile arm, just as Jimmy had done. Her legs swung beneath her, floundering in the wind.

But before she could go very far, Jimmy reached out and grabbed her shoulder. "They've killed you," he shouted. "Don't you want to—"

Marla shook her head. "Not yet, Jimmy," she smiled. "They have not killed me yet."

"But we're both poisoned. We're going to..." Fear hurtled through Jimmy's bones. He felt the back of his neck, searching for burns. His body was shaking and his lip trembled.

"If I die," said Marla, "I will die for a cause. You did that for me, Jimmy." Her huge brown eyes glimmered in the lights of the helicopter. They seemed to expand to swallow Jimmy up. He wished he could stare into them forever. "You made sure that I will not die for nothing," Marla went on. "You destroyed Mutam-ul-it and now my people can rebuild for themselves. France and Britain will not control us any more."

Jimmy opened his mouth to protest, but nothing came out. The cold air blasting into the chopper seemed to cut through to his heart. *Don't go*, he wanted to scream. *Save me.*

Marla pulled herself further out, hand over hand, then looked back one more time to see the panic in

Jimmy's eyes. "Do not waste what you have," she shouted, her words almost smothered by the constant storm of noise. "Live or die for a cause, Jimmy."

Jimmy dropped to the floor of the cockpit. He searched for some kind of emotion inside him, but there was nothing. He felt completely hollow and it was terrifying. He couldn't even cry.

After a few seconds, Marla was hanging not from the chopper, but from the missile itself. Jimmy let his hands move about the controls, hardly aware of what he was doing. His movements were detached from his brain. Then, without firing it, the claws of the helicopter let go of its remaining rocket.

Jimmy looked across in time to see Marla fall with the missile. She plummeted from the helicopter, embracing the rocket with her arms crossed over her chest. Just as the canopy of the parachute burst open, she disappeared into the fog.

"Good luck, Marla," Jimmy whispered.

The beach at Hastings was dark and deserted. The wind ripped across the sand leaving scars that became rivulets when the sea rushed in up the slope. A hundred metres away from the water, the beach front parade of restaurants was also quiet. Only a few elderly couples braved the evening drizzle, stabbing at soggy fish and chips with pointed wooden spatulas.

But then a rumble cut through the wail of the wind. One couple stopped and huddled at a bus stop, scanning the sky.

"It's nothing," grumbled the man, stuffing another chip into his mouth.

"No," replied his wife. "Look."

The husband held his cap down on top of his head and craned his neck… listening… watching. There was a steady *chop-chop-chop* and it was growing louder. Then out of the black clouds came a dot of light. The noise increased to become an insistent drone. Another couple joined the first at the bus stop. Then a gaggle of teenagers appeared and stood nearby, in the rain.

Gradually the light emerged from the fog and took on a shape. The rotors of a helicopter blasted away the cloud, sinking closer and closer.

"Let's go," growled one of the old men to his wife. "It's just a footballer."

His wife grabbed his arm. Her fish and chips fell to the pavement with a greasy splat. Everybody clung to their coats and hats. They squinted against the shower of sand being blown up by the rotors. The chopper touched down delicately on the beach.

By now there was a larger crowd – perhaps fifty people. Certainly more than the restaurant owners had seen on the street any evening for several months, so they too came out to see what was going on.

"That's not a footballer," gasped the old lady.

A ripple of confusion went through the crowd. They spilled out from under the shelter now, not caring about the rain, too absorbed in the sight in front of them. Marching up the beach, in a ripped tracksuit, his face partly obscured by grime, was a boy who didn't look much older than twelve.

As he approached, a murmur began. His eyes were fixed on the people in the crowd and his jaw was held high. Still several metres away, he wiped some of the grease from his cheeks with the back of his sleeve. The determination in his eyes seemed to light up the beach.

There was a gasp in the crowd. "It's that boy off the news!" shouted the first old lady. "The one who killed the Prime Minister!"

The people edged back, but the boy kept advancing up the beach. The murmur of the crowd grew.

"She's right, it's him," said one man.

"That face – I saw it on the TV too," cried another. "A killer, they said."

"But... they said he was dead."

Suddenly the boy's face seemed to darken and he stopped. "Do I look dead to you?" he shouted.

"No, but... but..."

The crowd edged back, terrified but mesmerised at the same time. The boy took a deep breath and the people fell silent. "Look at my face," he ordered. "Phone everybody you know and tell them you've seen me." His voice trembled with fire. "Tell everybody you meet. Tell them I'm alive. And tell them that before I die, there are going to be changes."

Now he turned and sprinted back to the helicopter. The crowd was so stunned they couldn't move before the boy was back in the cockpit. The rotors zoomed into action. The Tiger skimmed across the sand, straight towards the crowd. It lifted at the last instant, almost knocking the cap from the old man's head.

As it sailed past the tops of the people's heads, Jimmy Coates leaned out of the cockpit and roared, "Tell them I'm back."

Jimmy's world is about to go BOOM!

SNEAK PREVIEW...

The metal shutter slammed down on to the concrete, cutting off the last sliver of daylight and sealing Jimmy in the car park. Strip lights cast soft shadows around the rows of cars, lined up between huge supporting pillars. Jimmy stood up and dusted himself off, but the first thing he saw made him feel like his knees were going to give way.

Next to the entrance was the booth for a security attendant. A cup of tea was perched on the ledge inside, still steaming. But the only thing left of the attendant's head was an explosion of bone and brains on the back wall. Jimmy lurched to the side. He looked away and tried to breathe, but every lungful of air was thick with the stench of fresh blood. He tried to cry out, but the noise he made was only a desperate gasp.

He staggered back from the booth, clutching at his mouth and nose, as if he could pull out the taste of what he'd seen. After a second that seemed like a lifetime, his insides swirled with the force of his programming. It gushed up through his body, blasting away the shock, but it was too late to stop Jimmy retching up the measly contents of his stomach.

A part of him wanted to curl up in a corner and catch his breath, but he knew that wasn't an option. He pulled himself up to his full height and rushed back to the booth. This time when he looked his eyes ignored the blood, even though it was still pumping from the security attendant's neck in a thick dark fountain. He scanned the area, searching for a phone or walkie-talkie. Both were there. Both had been smashed beyond usability – presumably by the same man who had blasted the attendant's head off.

I saw him, Jimmy realised, the nausea returning. *He drove past me on that moped. I could have stopped him.* He felt faint, but his programming seemed to crank up a gear. It was like a belt fastening a notch tighter inside his skin, pulling his thoughts into calm, emotionless order.

First he found the van. That wasn't hard – it was parked in the central row, right next to one of the pillars. The rear doors were locked, but Jimmy jabbed his elbow into the catch and pulled them open.

The vehicle was completely full of crates, stacked up three high and covered in a thick grey blanket. Jimmy pulled back one corner and nearly threw up again. It was even worse than he'd expected.

When he'd first smelled the nitroglycerin, he'd assumed

that one or two crates might contain volatile bomb-making equipment of some kind. But here were dozens of crates, and every single one of them was packed with slim glass tubes of a clear, jelly-like solid, all connected by a network of black wires. The whole van was one giant bomb.

Jimmy wanted to run straightaway to warn people. He thought of all the residents in the tower above him, and the children in the playground alongside the building. They all had to evacuate. But Jimmy's feet wouldn't move. Instead he remained rooted to the spot while his eyes darted over the contraption before him. He traced the lines of wire as if following the map of a labyrinth, examining the piles of crates for precious seconds. How long did he have before the whole thing blew up?

Come on, Jimmy told himself, feeling the sweat crawling down his neck. *There's no way you can defuse a bomb.* There was no ticking clock, no red digits showing him a countdown. There certainly wasn't anything that looked like an 'off' switch, and all of the wires were the same colour – black.

Jimmy thought his eyes were going to bulge out of his head, they were flitting around so fast without blinking. He noticed the condensation on the glass tubes. *Of course. Nitro freezes at thirteen degrees.* The chemical was usually a liquid, but Jimmy realised it had been cooled into a solid to make it easier to transport. At the same time, he knew that as nitroglycerin thawed, it became even more unstable.

In Jimmy's imagination, the piles of crates changed shape. Some of them even became transparent. In a flash, he could see exactly how this bomb was supposed to work.

Against his will, he felt a rush of pleasure. Something inside him was impressed by the artful construction of the bomb – even thrilled. It was built in such a way that only a single detonator was required. That would shoot a charge through the wires, setting off a chain reaction as it raised the temperature of each tube of nitroglycerin, melting them in a specific order. That intricately organised relay would multiply the size of the explosion a hundred times.

The beauty of it was that the bomb was virtually sabotage-proof. The detonator was nowhere to be seen – presumably hidden at the very centre of the pile of crates. Then Jimmy noticed tiny gold rings round the connections between the wires and the glass tubes. *A second trigger mechanism*, he realised. Any attempt to disconnect the wires or get to the detonator would set off the chain reaction early. That left no way of stopping it, and no way of predicting when it would explode. Even with the expertise of an assassin inside him, for all Jimmy knew this bomb could blow up at any moment.

About the author

Joe Craig studied Philosophy at Cambridge University, then became a songwriter. Within a year, however, his love of stories had taken over and he was writing the first novel in the *Jimmy Coates* series. It was published in 2005. He is now a full-time author and likes to keep in touch with his readers through his website www.joecraig.co.uk.

When he's not writing he's visiting schools, playing the piano, inventing snacks, playing football, coaching cricket, reading or watching a movie.

He lives in London.